ALL I WANTED WAS A GLASS OF VINO BUT AN ALIEN DUKE KIDNAPPED ME INSTEAD

BUBBLE BABES
BOOK 3

PETRA PALERNO

Copyright © 2023 by Petra Palerno

All rights reserved.

No part of this book may be reproduced in any form or by any electronic or mechanical means, including information storage and retrieval systems, without written permission from the author, except for the use of brief quotations in a book review.

Cover by Getcovers.com

To Bowie and all my introverted readers who might not mind being kidnapped by a sexy alien duke.

CONTENTS

☆ BEFORE OUR ADVENTURE BEGINS ☆

Whether this is your first trip to Sontafrul 6, or a return visit, I hope you enjoy your stay.

This book is intended to be read either as a standalone or as a continuation of the bubble babes series. Reading the two previous books isn't necessary, but will only enhance the story. Also, don't let the cute cover of the book fool you, this is a smutty adventure for adults only. These pages hold graphic content of all kinds. Use the link below to view this books trigger warnings and content warnings. Your mental health matters.

XOXO, Petra

Trigger/Content Warnings:
https://www.petrapalerno.com/trigger-warnings

CHAPTER 1
☆JUST A DOG☆

"LISTEN, Marta, I'm really gonna need you to tighten it up. Your father is gonna kill me, and I one hundred percent cannot bring you back to the brownstone this drunk. Do you understand? Tighten it the fuck up!" my cousin Nick complains loudly. His hands gesture quickly in my general direction.

Nick stands there in his linen suit and badly hidden side piece. He's as stereotypical a *soldato*[1] as ever. There's one too many buttons undone on his white dress shirt, and a gold cross hangs heavy and nestled in his chest hair. He's looking at me with a cross between anxiety and annoyance.

I think he's sick of me manically switching between euphoric, drunk, and so distraught I don't know how to breathe. But he can suck it the fuck up. This is his job, isn't it? He's supposed to take care of me because, apparently, my father thinks I can't take care of myself.

"Can you cut me some slack? I've had a fucking terrible week." I put a finger up for the bartender to bring me another Aperol spritz. I know this annoys my cousin as I can see his eyes roll, but I don't give a shit.

"I really didn't want to say this, because I know he meant a lot to you, but for Christ's sake, Marta, he was just a dog."

Just a dog?

"How dare you," I say almost too softly to hear over the upbeat pop music blasting out of the wine bar's PA system.

Nick immediately knows he's fucked up big time.

"Bruno wasn't just a fucking dog, he was my dog." I thump my hand over my heart. "He was part of my soul." I want to cry, but I don't think any tears are left. I've been sobbing nonstop since I had to put my sweet pit bull down.

Bruno wasn't just a dog, he was my confidant. Even though our brownstone was technically home, it was more of a gilded prison. Home was where my dog was, and now that he's gone…

Nick just wouldn't get it. After he clocks out, he gets to go live his life. Being my bodyguard is just a nice way to make a paycheck. Hell, I even convinced my dad to let him do it because he didn't creep me out compared to all of my other options. I'd much rather have him than one of my father's stoic mercenaries. He might be a pain in my ass, but he's still my cousin, and I know I can trust him.

I'm not allowed to do anything by myself. Someone in my father's position can't take the risk of leaving me alone. If I get into the hands of one pissed-off rival family, it's over for me. Being a kidnapping risk lends itself to a less-than-stellar social life. I can't even convince my Pops to let me get a day job.

Although Pops has a reputation for being ruthless. He'd give me anything, besides the only thing I truly want—freedom. He didn't know what to do when Bruno died. Even though neither of us is the hugging type, he squeezed me hard when I wouldn't stop crying. I think that's why he's even allowing me this small freedom. To have just Nick here tonight, even though the bar is in our family's territory, is a big deal.

"I know! Ugh, God, I'm sorry. I'm just a little on edge that your dad is going to break my fucking legs if I take you home right now. Can you at least switch to water?" His face softens, and I realize he's right. If I come home drunk off my ass, it's not gonna be me who feels my father's anger.

Honestly, that's fucked up, right? How is it his fault that I'm shitfaced? It's the consequences of my own actions after all. I mean, what would Nick even do? It's not like he could stop me. Just imagining him trying to wrangle the wine glass from my hands makes me crack a small smirk. Sure, he's a big bad *soldato* now, but I've got that miraculous older cousin strength. It's like some law of the universe that even though he's technically bigger than I am now, birthright gives me the advantage in family butt-kicking.

He's here to protect me, so that I can't be attacked, kidnapped, or killed because of some vendetta against my family. I wonder if it would have been easier for my father if he'd had a son. Someone he didn't have to protect as fiercely as he does me. I crave the kind of freedom it would have allowed me.

I'll cut Nick a break, just this once. It is getting late…

"Yeah, I can switch to water. I'm sorry I'm being such an ass" —I turn my head—"and water!" I shout at the barback.

When the bartender returns with my orange and bitter tasting cocktail, I hand it to Nick and gulp down my cup of water in record time.

"I am sorry your dog died." Nick awkwardly checks his piece at his hip. It's something I notice he does a lot. Maybe the gun makes him nervous? He's not exactly a made man yet, which is one of the reasons I had to beg Pops to let him protect me. "I never had a pet, so I guess I just don't really get it."

"You know what it's like for me." I look around the bar to make sure no one is in earshot. "That because Pops does what he does, I get to live half a life."

"He only wants what's best for you—"

"Does he? How could this be the best thing for me? Jesus, this life is a fucking lonely one." I set my drink down hard on the bar in frustration.

Nick bites the inside of his cheek, as if he's unsure of what to say. Normally, I would quip something teasing to my cousin to break the tension, but I can't help my mind from drifting back to my dear departed pup.

After Pops discovered that a rival family had started a dogfighting ring, he decided they needed to be taken down a notch. By the time the dust settled, there were fifteen pit bulls left. It may seem silly to have a crime boss give a shit about fighting dogs, but my father did.

One by one, the dogs were rehomed—until only Bruno was left.

He was unlucky enough to be the bait dog. His gentleness, the thing I loved most about him, was his downfall. Scars marred the whole left side of his face. The pink lines cut through his elegant gray fur.

No one wanted him, this puppy with the ruined mug.

No one but me.

"You should get a dog, Nick. They'd probably make you seem more like a normal dude and less like the absolute douchebag you are." I tease him as I pull myself back to reality, buttoning up his shirt as a smirk forms on my lips. "Hell, you might be able to convince a nice girl to have sex with you if you had a dog." My smirk turns into a full-blown drunk belly laugh.

He waves a hand at me. "Aw, shut up about it already, won't ya?" He quickly grabs my Aperol spritz off the bar and downs it.

At the last wheeze of my laugh, I move to whack him on the shoulder, but I realize I can't. I'm frozen in place, and a static charge is running through my muscles. I can't even breathe; everything in my body is held in some suspended state.

Nick has the cocktail glass to his lips, head thrown back, but the orange liquid no longer flows into his mouth. It spills down his cheeks. The Aperol stains his white linen shirt as it trails down his neck and onto his chest. The gold cross looks slick.

Everything inside my mind is screaming that this is wrong. I'm trying to shake my frozen arm, to flail my limbs. My body remains like a marble statue, frozen in time.

The music plays on, some saccharine pop blasting over the speakers. As the melodic voice of a teenage girl sweeps through the bar, the dread and the lack of air make my chest burn.

I feel as though I'm about to pass out, that I can't go without a breath. My chest frozen on some forever exhale.

A white light flashes through the room, brighter than any camera flash I've ever seen. It's so blinding that my eyes sting and I can actually feel my retina begin to burn. I want to cover my hands with my eyes, to snap my eyelids shut, but the pain continues.

Then, just as quickly as the light filled the bar, everything returns to normal, and I take a breath. The air hits me hard as my body moves again.

My grunt rumbles through the pop star's lyrics, and I nearly punch myself as my hands spring to my face and I barely dodge them.

I'm gasping for air, trying to understand what the fuck is happening when I barely feel the prick at my thigh before my knees buckle. I reach for where my skin was pinched. I drop quickly as soon as I move my arm, like a cartoon character hit with a tranquilizer dart.

My head slams onto the floor and a purple dripping claw brings what looks like an ear-piercing gun to my temple.

"What the fuck?!" I yell as I try to push it away from my head. My nails hit my attacker's flesh, and it's slick with slime. The light has blown out my vision. The world is overexposed and I can't make out my attacker.

There's a sharp pain above my temple, and the stinging winds its way behind my ear and deep into my skull. I can barely scream before the world falls to black.

---

1. A **soldato** or **soldier** is the first official level of the Italian-American Mafia

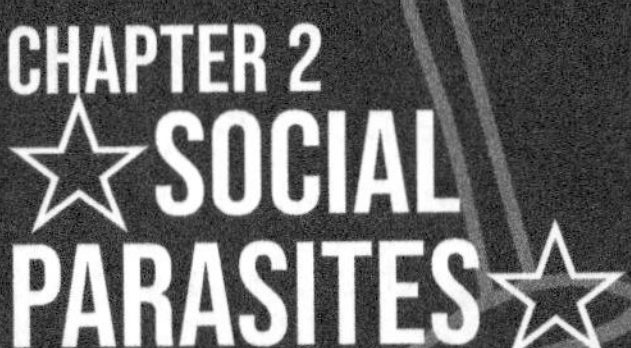

CHAPTER 2
☆SOCIAL PARASITES☆

☆RAF'ERE

THE ELEGANT FI'LEN females sitting in the parlor of my bedroom ooze pure sex. I know their every move is deliberate, an attempt to snag Sontafrul 6's most eligible royal bachelor—me.

Not because I'm good-looking or charming...but because of the title I hold.

His Grace Duke Raf'ere of the Liin'gan Reefs.

It's amazing how insufferable Kir'ron and her lackey Tri'ot are now. Their personalities and lack of any sense are something that annoys me to no end now that I can't bring myself to bed them any longer. It's been over for me since my discovery on the Deenz ship.

That's when I saw her.

That tiny, weak-looking human, asleep in her cryopod.

It felt like I was dying. The pain in my chest was so intense. I thought that maybe one of my hearts was finally giving out after a night of smoking too much nebula leaf. Two hearts, instead of most modern fi'len's one, is a biological quirk from my mother's line. The people of the Liin'gan Reefs have remained aquatic much longer than others and still have a fully formed gill heart to prove it.

But no, it wasn't partying that made my hearts ache. It was the f'teeing mating bond.

Just seeing her frozen face was enough to trigger my body's biological purpose, to activate some deep instinct in my DNA.

I thought I would feel some overwhelming euphoria when I found my fated mate—not this nagging and painful need in my chest. The bond pleaded with me to cradle that small human up in my arms that day. To feed her, woo her, and drive my cock deep into her until she's moaning my name.

But I can't have a human mate—they've caused quite the logistic nightmare for the Sontafrul 6 government since we discovered they're being brought here against their will. We're in an unwinnable war against the Deenz aliens that brought them here in the first place. That hive-minded piece of shit doesn't care how many of it's puppet bodies they lose in battle, they'll just make more.

All this for bubble dancing? The humans are shuffled around to all the high end clubs in the galaxy, stuffed into plastic security pods and forced to perform. The universe assumed the human species was just naturally more amorous and therefore suited for the task at hand. Only recently have we found out they're in fact drugged to be the vision of sexuality that the rest of the universe believes them to be.

"Raf', I'm sick of cocktails—let's fool around," Kir'ron lets the complaint fall from her pouty lips. She reaches her dainty hand out for my ass, but I grab her wrist and stop her in her tracks. Her eyes shoot up, startled.

"I'm not in the mood." I release her wrist and she rubs the joint like it burns. Kir'ron frowns, narrowing her eyes at me.

Tri'ot cocks her head as if my curt reaction to her friend amuses her. Maybe she believes she can finally get me to herself.

"If you're not interested in playing, can I have one of your toys to go? You've always got such good taste," she coos.

"Maybe the one that Kir'ron likes, the one with the spinning bit!"

At any other time, before the human, I'd love to take out my frustrations on these two. I've always found it calming that I can please females. Maybe their pleasure makes me feel better about the mess that my face has become. I have to stop myself from reaching up to my scars. It's like whenever I think of the sad state my visage has been left in, I can't help but run my fingers along the textured skin.

But the thought of even touching them makes my stomach churn with distaste now. I probably wouldn't even get hard. The bond only begs me for the tiny Earthling mate, asleep in her cyropod and stashed in my dressing room.

"Oh yeah, Duke Daddy, that one is fabulous!" Kir'ron recovers, letting her disappointment slide beneath the sultry mask I'm used to seeing. She even adds a giggle, a little flourish that might once have had the blood racing to my cock.

"If I give you the sex toy, do you promise to leave so I can get some sleep?" I ask exasperatedly. I pinch the bridge of my nose, sighing.

Sleep, I wish.

Instead of sleeping these past few days, I've sat with my nose pressed up against the window of the cryopod.

I hate her and what she's done to me.

"You're such a grump tonight, Raf'ere. What's gotten into you?" Kir'ron complains, obviously not pleased with this new indifference I hold for her. Her voice is cloying, and it grates on my nerves even further.

"Work," I tell her, pushing the hidden door to my closet open. I open it only enough to discourage them from following me.

Despite their cut throat attitudes towards climbing the social ladder, they still understand some of the royal protocol—they're lucky enough to be in my chambers. They wouldn't dare follow me into my private dressing room.

But as I edge into the closet, a scent that makes my hair stand on end hits me. The fear scent that fills my closet is intense and unique. It's something I've never smelled before. Although the scent's central note is acrid and desperate...there's something sweet and musky beneath it. A nectar I would give anything to taste on my lips.

I sense a figure to my right, and my army training instinctively has me pushing a hand out to block something heavy swinging toward me.

The cool glass shaft of a dildo hits my palm, its weight familiar in my practiced hands even in the dim lighting. The toy in question is one I only use for my more experienced lovers. Its impressive size makes it the perfect impromptu weapon. I trail my eyes from the phallic weapon to the tiny hand that holds it.

Tight black curls, the hair stopping right below her chin in a blunt cut, frame her round face. The woman's skin, once pale and blue in her cryopod, is now olive and tanned. A wild red flush is spreading over her cheeks and chest. The deep brown eyes that stare at me are wide, her mouth agape as she tilts her chin up slowly to gaze at my face.

"F'tee," I mutter, my body overwhelmed by her nearness. If I thought the mating bond between us was strong before, to breathe in my mate's scent, to be so close to touching her round body—my every cell burns for her.

"I, what?" the human, my mate, stutters. Her expression softens. "Bruno?"

"Who the f'tee is Bruno?" I ask bitterly. Jealousy boils inside me. Does she already belong to another?

I would kill him, wrench his heart from his ribcage, and spit on his corpse.

She is mine.

I grab the toy from her grip easily and place it on the nearby island. I take a deep breath, trying to calm all the emotions flooding my system. My brain feels as though it's short-circuiting, and I'm no longer in control.

"You weren't supposed to wake up," I whisper. As much as I want to know more about her, I don't want a mate—*especially a human female.*

"Why…did you think you killed me?" Her face blanches, and she slowly backs away.

She's frightened of me.

"What are you?" she mutters meekly as she slinks into the shadowy corner of my closet.

I'm annoyed that she's been woken from cryo, and I'm not as practiced in kindness as I am in pleasure. I don't try to comfort the shaking Earthling in front of me.

"Stay here," I say, quickly backing into the doorway and snapping the door closed in front of me. I must be alone to come up with a solution…I need to get rid of the social climbing parasites in my chamber. "Get the f'tee out," I say firmly, lifting the two females from their seats to standing.

"What in the goddess's name are you on about?" Kir'ron asks, her voice frantic.

"Get. The. F'tee. Out." I enunciate every word, so there's no misunderstanding. Each syllable stings like a poke'en barb.

Both fi'len females stand in front of me, shocked. I push past them, swinging open the double door of my chambers into the hallway. My personal butler, Jens'i, waits at the ready.

"The females are leaving now. Do not disturb me for the rest of the night." I push both females unceremoniously into the hallway by their backs. Their faces are still shocked and confused as I wait for them to be escorted out of the estate, happy to finally be rid of them.

Jens'i nods and signals to the guards stationed in the hallway. Their faces are still shocked and confused as I slam my chamber doors shut, happy to be rid of them finally. I head back to the dressing room door. I hear the females' grunts of displeasure as the house staff shows them out. I'm almost as happy to be rid of the overly ambitious duo as I am stressed about the angry human I've got locked in my room.

I face the closet, my hand twitching on the hidden handle until I can deliberately slow my breathing. I won't let this earthling get the better of me.

Pulling my shoulders back, I swing the closet door open.

As if spring loaded, it releases my mate, who flings herself at me. Her fist slams down hard onto my sternum. She is deceptively strong, given how tiny she is. The air rushes out of her chest as we collide.

My arms wrap around her by instinct alone. For the first time, I can feel her skin on mine. She's deliciously much warmer than I am. I can't stop myself before I tilt my head down and bury my nose in her hair, inhaling her musky sweetness, a scent that reminds me of temple incense and thru'ik liquor.

She stills for a moment and holds her breath, tensing her muscles. But quickly begins pushing against my chest, struggling.

"I will drag your ass down to hell with me!" she screams, her nails digging into my skin. "You should have killed me when you had the chance, fucker!"

My small mate is like a wild xor'ro, whipping around as my arms encircle her even tighter.

"If I wanted to kill you, you'd be long dead. You should feel honored I didn't let you rot on the Deenz ship." I grit through my teeth, twisting my chin up to avoid the worst of her thrashing.

"Honored? Fuck off, you monster!" Her voice seems too loud for the size of her body.

Monster, maybe she's right. I turn the scarred side of my face away from her.

"I saved you from the Deenz, from a life of sexual servitude, from *dying* in that f'teeing cryopod." I tell her some version of the truth I think she can handle right now. I don't mention the other humans or that she's here secretly. That I stole her away in the dead of night from the Deenz ship's wreckage. Not even

Jens'i, keeper of my secrets and my confidant, is aware of her existence.

She huffs, her chin wobbling as fat tears threaten to crest over her lower lashes. Her face is now angry and red. Despite her small size compared to my people, she has a fierce look in her eyes that suggests she won't back down easily.

"Why would you help me?"

"Because I didn't have a choice," I tell her, and it's not a lie. The bond wouldn't have let me leave her there.

She doesn't respond, but she stops her flailing. I set her down on the club chair, hoping she would mask the scent of Tri'ot's perfume still lingering in the air. She sits straight as a board and stares at me. I'm sure she's disgusted by my scars.

"If you can manage to control your post cryosleep mood swings, maybe I can introduce myself. My name is Raf'ere. I'm the Duke of the Liin'gan Reefs—the part of the universe where you now find yourself. Since you are here, in my domain, you are now my subject," I assure her. "I am bound by royal duty to ensure your safety..." I let my words hang in the air as I wait for her to tell me her name.

"Marta, my name is Marta." The snarl on her lips turns into a fierce expression as she lands a punch right under my rib cage.

CHAPTER 3
☆SINK OR SWIM☆

THE FUCKING monster doesn't even wince as my fist meets his thick and muscular ribcage. My knuckles thud dully against his solid core.

"Fuck!" I yelp, recoiling my hand.

Hitting his chest is like punching a brick wall, and my split bloody knuckle agrees with the sentiment. The big gray beast straightens to his full height over me. He must be over seven feet tall, his broad shoulders blocking any of the light from the room behind him.

I gulp as I realize I've just attacked this giant…and if he wanted to, he could snap me in half. He glowers down at me as I grip his bougie upholstery with my uninjured hand. Setting my jaw, I brace myself for his reaction, half expecting him to back-hand me.

Exhaling a burst of air through his nostrils, he frowns before scrubbing a palm over his face.

His arm shoots out, and I wince, squeezing my eyes tightly shut. When I feel his hand brush past me, I crack open one eye.

His four-fingered hand, larger than my head, pulls a piece of cloth from the table behind me.

"You don't have to like your current situation," he starts as he pulls my bleeding hand from my chest. "But I can only tolerate so much disrespect."

The duke of whatever he said he was the duke of seems annoyed. I should fight, I should run—but given how well my punch went over, I resign myself to hear him out, for now. Maybe I'll be able to learn something to help me escape. Perhaps if I show him a little respect, I can even get him to help me. *Respect is something I can understand.*

"I'd appreciate it if you didn't bleed all over my home." He wraps my hand in the cloth much more gently than I would have thought was possible for someone his size. His gray fingers gingerly tuck the fabric in on itself until it's tight enough to stay put on its own.

"I don't know you at all. That's the problem here." I look down at the origami of white fabric that's wrapped around my hand as it blooms with small pricks of blood. "I don't know what you even are…"

Raf'ere cocks his white brow and sits in an easy chair opposite me.

"I am fi'len. I suppose to you I'm an alien." He says the word "alien" with a grimace, as if the taste of it is bitter in his mouth.

"Alien…No fucking way." The corners of my mouth draw up in disgust. "You're telling me some fucking oak tree of an alien came down to Earth and kidnapped me?"

"Well, no, that's not what I'm saying. The first thing is we're not on Earth. I've never even been to Earth. I have no f'teeing desire to go to Earth. Also, I didn't kidnap you, that was the Deenz." He smiles smugly, as if he's deserving of some reward for not committing felony kidnapping.

"You rescued me and put me in a coffin in your closet?" The words falling from my mouth are full of venom.

"Well, it's not a coffin—"

"But you didn't want me to wake up?" I narrow my eyes.

"That's not exactly true…"

"I didn't expect you to wake up?" I parrot the first words he said to me, my hands making a talking motion.

"You're skewing my words! It's not that I wanted you to stay in cryosleep forever. It's that…"

"It's what?" I bark. The big gray alien in front of me does a double take. I can tell he's not used to anyone contradicting him…and I know for a fact he's never felt what it's like to have *una donna incazzata*[1] Italian woman yell at him.

"The beings who took you were trafficking you." He speaks slowly, as if trying to control his temper. "You were in a cryopod, in stasis, for transport. Did you really want to end up dancing in a security pod on an off-world station? To have some marauder scum leering at you?" He tightens his grip on the arm of the plush chair.

"Why do you care?" I gruff.

Raf'ere takes a deep breath, "Because you're my ma—"

"I just want to go home!" I cut him off, anxiety welling in my chest.

"Are you f'teeing dense? I already told you—you're my subject. The Deenz ship crashed in the reefs, so you fall under my jurisdiction." He releases his grip on the arm of the chair, his four fingers leaving deep imprints.

"Thanks for your help," I try to sound grateful, but I know it's coming off as insincere. "Can we skip to the part where you take me home? What spaceship do I hop on that's headed to Earth? My father is probably shaking down his entire territory looking for me right now." I stand, making my way to the door.

"Go back to Earth?" His voice trails before he breaks out into a full belly laugh.

"You take me home now!" I holler over my shoulder, placing my hand on the door handle. "Hop to it. I'm ready to go."

"Earth is not an option for you any longer," —His laughter stops as quickly as it started— "Not now or ever."

"What do you mean?" I frown tightly and draw my brows together, throwing him a death glare over my shoulder.

"Earth is off limits. Only the Deenz had the necessary permitting from the Universal Governing Senate. The Deenz decontamination tech, a crucial defense, was believed to be the sole safeguard against human viruses eradicating the entire universe. But now that it has been revealed that your kind is being kidnapped, any contact has been outlawed entirely." He touches my shoulder, tugging me away from the door.

"I don't accept that." I shake his palm off with a disgusted grimace.

"It doesn't matter if you don't accept that. It's the truth. Going home is not an option."

I turn away from him, clicking the emerald-green doorknob and pushing the door open. But when I see what's beyond the doorway, I quickly lose my momentum.

A huge convex window fills nearly my entire eyeline. The room I'm in is on the second floor and overlooks a large room below. It's the roof to what I can only assume is some grand alien ballroom. Blue and purple lighting hits some of the most ornate and jewel-encrusted appliqués I've ever seen inlaid in walls made of shiny black stone.

Looking up again, my mouth agape, I realize the window isn't made of glass. It ripples and undulates and is made of some jelly-like material. And beyond the window, an ocean scene. Rainbow-colored coral reefs provide a backdrop for creatures of all shapes, colors, and sizes that flip and swim through the currents.

"We're...underwater?" My voice catches.

"My name is His Grace, Duke Raf'ere, Ruler of the Liin'gan Reefs. The reefs in the Liin'gan sea have been my family's home for eons." He walks us toward the banister. "My species, the fi'len, embrace a less landlocked lifestyle than yours." He raises a finger to his neck, pulling down a ruffled collar. It's the first time I see the duke's gills.

Suddenly, despite everything I'd seen before, it hits me that the man standing next to me is actually an alien. His skin is gray, he's gotta be over seven feet tall, and he has fucking gills. Even if you ignore the pointed ears and four-fingered hands...Raf'ere is out of this world.

I turn my eyes back to the expanse of water beyond the gelatinous window. My breath catches in my throat, and my pulse quickens. I should fear the monster at my side, but the enormous block of water in front of me scares me more.

I never learned to swim. The fear of water is as constant as my father's seclusion of me from the rest of the world.

Although supposedly for safety, both of those reasons have still held me back.

When I look up at the undulating waves, I am struck by the immense power and vastness of the water just over my head.

Shuddering, I imagined the crushing weight of all that water and the feeling of being submerged, unable to reach the surface, if that delicate-looking jelly were to collapse.

My throat tightens, and I can't stop myself from saying, "I can't swim."

I feel stupid as soon as I do, giving information that could hurt me to my captor. It's like I'm letting him see all the ways he'll be able to control me.

Stupid. Stupid. Stupid.

As the panic washes over me, my breaths come in short gasps. My breathing becomes shallow and rapid.

Imprisoned beneath the ocean's depths, I am at the mercy of an alien stranger.

---

1. Italian: (vulgar) a pissed off woman

CHAPTER 4
☆YOU GOT A FUCKING PROBLEM WITH THAT?
☆

☆RAF'ERE

THE WEAK HUMAN can't even swim.

I wish I could be embarrassed, but I'm worried instead. This silly girl could get hurt and put me into a world of trouble.

Marta, a name I've only just learned, and it's like a melody that plays on repeat in my mind. I will have to teach this ill-equipped human how to survive on my planet.

Before I can stress about our future much more, I realize something is wrong with her.

She can't tear her eyes away from the biofilm bubble that covers the ballroom, her gaze distant and unfocused. I can feel the moisture on her palm as her fingers lace tightly between my own.

I hate that I enjoy the feeling of her, but I allow myself this momentary contact. When I scent her fear, though, my urge to protect her spins into overdrive.

"What's wrong?"

She inhales shallow and frantic breaths, her chest rising and falling in erratic patterns.

When I tug on her hand, her feet are stuck to the floor. She's panicking, of course she is—she just admitted to me she can't swim and here I am presenting the entire ocean over her head.

"Marta, biofilm is safe…just calm down," I try to explain, but now she's hyperventilating.

I'm responsible for thousands of subjects in the Liin'gan reefs —but I've never been responsible for just one person. I'm sure there's some better way to go about this, to calm her down, but I don't know any.

Without warning, my body takes charge and pulls her toward me, leaving her even more startled than before, I'm sure. As I hug her, I realize I'm holding her too tightly and end up lifting her from the ground. Her tiny feet dangle in the air, and she goes rigid.

I walk us back into my room, only to see that the curtains have opened on schedule. They reveal the biofilm windows in my own chambers. I move to the only place I can think of that isn't exposed to the sea around us and push open the door to my dressing room.

Once we're within its windowless walls, her breathing slows. The mate bond relishes the intimacy as I hold her in my arms, but suddenly, I see recognition of our close contact flicker in her eyes. Marta gasps, her eyes becoming wide.

"You're strong," she says, as if it's a surprise.

I take that as my cue to set her down. She braces herself against the large island and clutches her fist between her breasts as she tries to get her breathing under control.

"The biofilm is structurally sound, I can assure you of that," I tell her before grabbing a bottle of thirty-cycle thru'ik reserve and pouring it into a glass. When I reach the cup out to her, she grabs the bottle instead and swigs it back. The blue liquid drips from the corners of her mouth, and when she comes up for air, her eyes seem clearer.

"Got anything stronger?" She doesn't hand me back the

bottle and grabs one of my dressing gowns off a nearby rack, wrapping herself up in it.

"Than thru'ik? Not unless you're looking to smoke some nebula leaf…which would melt your tiny human brain." I scoff. "I can get you some more suitable clothing tomorrow…to get you out of that?" I run a finger up and down, gesturing to her obscene ensemble.

The light blue compression garments she wears mold to the dips and curves of her body like a second skin. She's so different than a fi'len female. She's so f'teeing short. I towered over her, with the top of her head barely reaching my chest. It's as though the goddess compensated for her small size by accentuating her curves in ways I never knew could be so alluring.

The line of her sharp chin and graceful neck descend to a pair of soft and enticing breasts. Their size is smaller compared to most humans I've seen, but significantly larger than that of a fi'len female. Further down, the strap of the blue body suit tightens around her waist, leaving a faint red impression on her supple tummy. The leg openings of the suit are cut high, showcasing the most stunning set of hips and ass I have ever laid eyes upon. Their expanse seeming so innately of some divine feminine that I have to look away for fear that my cock will harden even more.

I said her outfit was obscene, but I never said I didn't like it.

"Anything is better than this blue ACE bandage I'm wearing now." She frowns, walking over to the cryopod. As she runs a finger down the edge of the open door, she asks, "So I was frozen in this thing, and you rescued me?"

"Well, not frozen. You can't just freeze a living organism and expect its cells not to explode—but yes, you were in cryosleep. Your ship crashed close to here, and I was able to extricate you before the Deenz could take off again." Extricate sounds so much better than kidnap. I don't sugarcoat things normally, so why am I doing it now?

"And they want human girls to be space strippers?"

"Yes, that and for the off-world brothels."

Marta's face switches from curiosity to disgust as she wrinkles her nose.

"So, out of everything in the universe, somehow human women are the best piece of ass you can nab?" Her tone is incredulous.

"Humans are very desirable to many species. Until recently, we weren't aware you were kidnapped and drugged to perform. We just assumed human women were naturally more...amorous."

I'm trying to be polite in my descriptions of her people. Until I saw her, I found human beings to be nothing more than a tax burden. They had never been my taste sexually, save for a few of their more fi'len proportioned women.

"So, do you have the hots for humans, then?" Marta's voice isn't playful, and her shoulders are drawn up. She fears how I might answer.

"Humans aren't my type." It's not a lie. Because it's not humans that are my type, it's f'teeing Marta. The mating bond balks inside me, trying to stop me from saying what I'm about to. "You aren't my type." I swear I feel like I've swallowed hot coals when I lie to her face.

Marta breathes a sigh of relief, her posture relaxing. "Good, because I want you to know right now that I'm thankful you rescued me—but don't expect any thanks beyond the gratitude I just expressed. No matter how amorous you think humans are, I'm not putting out, got it?"

"Putting out?" My translator chip struggles with her phrasing.

"I'm not fucking you, point blank, ever." The venomous words fall from her lips but are quickly replaced by another swig of thru'ik.

My body recoils at her statement and each fiber of my musculature tenses. I want to scream as the perverse feeling of wrongness lingering between us—to put my arms out and shake her.

She is my mate.

"Noted," I say as smoothly as I can muster, my nostrils twitching as my jaw sets.

She flops down onto the floor next to the cryopod and leans back against the wall. Her knees are pulled up close to her chest, and my robe's excess material pools between her thighs.

"So, when you say there's no going back to Earth, is that like a hard no? Like there's no amount of money or ill-advised plan that could get me there?" She looks up at me, her eyes sad and misty. "Or a soft no, where if I had enough resources, I could negotiate a trip back to my family…because my father would pay anything to get me home."

I step closer, reaching my hand out to comfort her before pulling it back. She doesn't see the gesture, thank goddess.

"How many times do I have to tell you the same thing before you believe me?" I worry that maybe her brain's been damaged in cryo.

"I don't know. Fuck, I don't know. This isn't fucking fair!"

Her sadness turns to anger, and she swigs from the bottle and slams her other fist against the cryopod—harder than I thought she could. It must hurt because she pulls her hand in and rubs it against her thigh. Dropping her chin against her chest, she closes her eyes and takes deep, angry breaths.

I reach my hand out again, but this time, I grab the bottle from her.

"Hey!" she yelps, standing and trying to grab it back. I easily hold her away with my much longer arm, flail as she might. My palm is pressed against her forehead, as it seems like the safest option to touch.

"You have the willpower of a child. Pull yourself together."

She drops her arms to her sides and leans against my hand, holding her up. "Fine."

She stays pressed against my palm for a moment longer, as if

I'm supporting the weight of her anxiety. The moment is broken, though, as her stomach gurgles loudly. She stands up straight.

"You're hungry?" I ask, annoyed again that I must care for someone so incredibly helpless.

"I'm Italian. Of course I'm fucking hungry." She frowns and puffs a short burst of air through her nose.

My translator chip displays pictures of noodle dishes, arguing old men wearing gold chains, singing captains in unique boats, and beautiful landscapes with green fruit trees.

"Italian," I say, as if I understand at all what that means.

"Yeah, you got a fucking problem with that?" My angry mate scowls.

"No, of course not." I am afraid of admitting I don't understand what that means. Maybe Italians are some different species of human…I could call my cousin the king and ask him to ask his human mate, Opal. That would require me admitting to kidnapping her in the first place. Which is something I'm not keen on doing yet, or at all if I can help it. Especially after the tongue lashing given to me by the human Jessy for refusing to wake all the women in cryosleep on the crashed ship.

"Stay here," I tell her.

I exit the dressing room and click the button on the wall data pad. The austere voice of my butler breaks through the static.

"Can I be of any assistance, Your Grace?"

"Food, several plates in many varieties, quickly."

"As a reminder, dinner is due to be served at its normal time shortly." He sounds as annoyed with me as his station could allow him to be.

"I will dine alone in my chambers for the foreseeable future. Adjust my schedule accordingly."

I swear I hear a sigh before he says, "As you wish, Your Grace."

I turn back to the dressing room to find Marta clinging to the door frame, mouth agape. Her eyes are turned to the two stories of biofilm windows directly behind my bed.

"I thought I told you to say put. I take it back, you're worse than a child!" I rush toward her, blocking her view and pushing her back into the closet.

"I…I… forgot about the water." She pushes her back against the wall.

I'm frustrated that my mate is not only a human, but incredibly f'teeing helpless. "Who the f'tee doesn't know how to swim?"

She narrows her eyes. "You don't get to tell me what to do just because you're some alien duke! I still have free will. If I want to leave this room, you bet your ass I'm going to!" Her hands fly into wild gestures as she yells. It's bizarre looking, almost like she's performing some angry interpretive dance.

"Then do it." I step to the side and gesture out the door.

She blinks rapidly, as if not parsing what I've offered.

"If you want to leave so bad, be my guest!" I let my voice boom, her absolute f'teeing insolence firing me up.

"I will!" She stomps into the bedroom, never turning her eyes to the windows. She flings the door open with gusto—but she is unable to avoid the view of the ocean from the ballroom's ceiling. Her escape attempts are seemingly dashed as she grips the frame of the door, and her knees begin to buckle.

My anger at her stubbornness changes so quickly to protectiveness that I don't even feel my feet as they move. I reach her in record time, putting my hand neatly in the small of her back before she crumples any further to the ground.

Just then, my butler steps in front of the door, a floating cart overflowing with food in front of him.

The elderly fi'len male's eyebrow raises, giving me a simultaneously judgmental yet confused look.

"Dinner, Your Grace, as requested."

Marta clings to me, as if by sheer necessity. Her fingers leave blue marks on my forearms.

I pull us from the doorway and deposit my mate back into the dressing room, closing the door behind me.

"I wasn't aware you were *entertaining*..." Jens'i side-eyes me as he moves the abundance of food to the table in the parlor area of my room.

"I'm not."

"Ah, well, what are we doing with the human woman in one of your best dressing gowns, currently locked in the closet?" He lifts one hand elegantly toward the room I've shut Marta in.

"I...I'm helping a human refugee." I stumble over my words.

"Ah." His tone is condescending, but only in a way my practiced ear would hear.

"I'd appreciate it, Jens'i, if you could keep *her* presence a secret for the time being." I keep my voice low on the off chance she can hear me through the door.

"Is this situation something I need to contact the royal attorney for?" He inclines his head to me.

"Gra'eth? Absolutely not!" That's the last person I need knowing about my "guest."

"Well, do promise me you'll let me know should anything here escalate to the point we'll need to address the optics?"

"I don't like what you're implying," I growl as I lift the lid off of a steaming tray of sq'aurks. The pastel puff balls wriggle around as they're eaten alive. The steam coming from their body temperature is akin to their volcanic homes.

"I think it's best that you don't bring up the human unless I do going forward." I can't tell if it's some protective part of my mating bond or not wanting to get caught with Marta—maybe it's some combination of the two that's putting me on edge.

Jens'i nods in acknowledgment as he bows. He walks backward to the doorway before turning as a sign of respect for my position.

"Jens'i?"

"Yes, Your Grace?"

"I'm serious, not a word."

My butler raises a brow but nods. When he leaves, I rush to the dressing room doors to check on Marta.

She's back to sitting on the ground, nursing the thru'ik. She looks up at me, tears threatening to spill over her lashes.

"How am I going to have a life here if I can't even leave this fucking closet? I want to go home!"

CHAPTER 5
☆A TASTE SENSATION☆

☆MARTA

"WHAT PART OF 'NO' are you not picking up?" I don't stop Raf'ere when he snatches the bottle of alien booze out of my palm. I can already feel myself getting sloppy, sad-girl drunk. The alcohol doesn't have the telltale burn that the high-proof stuff has on Earth—I fear that I may have slipped past sober with little warning.

"Ugh, on Earth," I sob, letting my anger stay firmly in the territory of self-pity. "When I said I wanted freedom, this isn't what I fucking meant!" My hands lifted toward the sky, bargaining with some unlistening god.

The alien duke's attention wavers as he fumbles with the bottle, stealing occasional glances of me from the corner of his eye. He looks like he's embarrassed of my display. I know I'm a mess but it doesn't mean I have to like the looks ole Judgy McJudgerson is throwing my way.

"If you're that hungry, there's food in the bedroom. Eat it or not, I don't care," he tells me, placing the bottle back into the closet bar.

I sniffle and frown, grabbing his extended hand and pulling myself out of the pity puddle I've created. My stomach is entirely empty for probably the first time in my life. I am a snacker, a meal eater, a person who enjoys a taste sensation. The padding around my hips is proof of that point. I don't dislike my body, though—I'd rather be happy and eat delicious carb-filled pasta than thin and bitter eating bland salad. Not that I begrudge anyone thin, just genetically, that's not my body's happy place.

I angle my head to avoid looking through the window at the water. I thankfully don't panic if I can't actually see the water—even though I know it's there.

Raf'ere guides me to sit on one of the plush sofas by the low ebony coffee table filled to the brim with plates of food. Everything smells strange but incredibly enticing for being as hungry as I am. He sits next to me, grabbing a silver plate and two-pronged utensil.

"I don't know what any of this is." I am suddenly overwhelmed by the spread of alien food before me.

"Does it matter? It's food." He slides the prongs into steaming pastel dumplings, which wiggle and make a high-pitched noise once he does.

"I mean it might. What the hell is that?"

"Sq'aurks. I should specify that although they have no nervous system, they are technically eaten raw. I'm not sure if that's considered cruel in your culture." He waits for my answer, hovering the pink dumpling-looking creature over my plate.

"Oh, no, that's fine." I think about a veal…which seems worse than an insentient puffball. These steaming blobs must be like space oysters in that regard.

He drops the sq'aurk onto the plate, followed by little heaps of all kinds of food in colors I'm not used to consuming. Blues and purples seem to be the most common hues.

He hands me the plate and the two-pronged fork. I should probably wait until he serves himself to dig in, but I'm starved.

I take a big bite of something akin to purple noodles. They're cold, and the flavor reminds me of a spicy lemon. While it's a taste profile uncommon to me, the bite is incredibly satisfying.

"Oh wait, that's spicy—" He holds his hands up, attempting to halt me.

"I like spicy, no worries," I garbled out with my mouth full. I want a hunk of crusty bread. Besides the noodles, the table seems woefully lacking in carbs.

I move onto what I think is meat, but its color is cerulean. I slide my fork into it and the flesh flakes apart similar to salmon.

"Fish?"

He waits, eyes growing distant, before answering. "Scal'pin… it's a similar aquatic creature to your Earth fish, from what I can tell."

I move to take a bite. Just as I do, an image flashes in front of my eyes. A creature, long and blue, winds its way through teal waters. Four fangs hang from its open maw—it darts, viciously snapping a pink ball of tentacles into its mouth.

As quickly as the image arrives, it leaves. I drop the fork, and it clangs against the side of the coffee table.

"I'm sorry, but did I just stroke out?"

He eyes me, cocking his in confusion.

"The fucking snake monster? Didn't you see it?" There's no way I made up that nightmare creature on my own.

"Oh…your translator chip." The realization dawns on him.

"My what?"

"The Deenz would have installed a translation chip for you. I think it's silly to assume we both speak whatever human dialect you do. A translation chip makes it easy for us to communicate. The words you speak to me are fi'len, and the words I speak to you are your own language. The chip allows our brains to translate automatically. If there is no direct translation, images are shown from the chip's database." He picks up the fork off the ground and offers me his own. "So that *fucking snake monster* was more than likely just a scal'pin." He grabs a new utensil and puts another piece of the blue meat on my plate.

"Oh." I get itchy thinking about what other things might have been done to me while I was unconscious. "Do you think that's all they did?"

"What do you mean?"

"Did to me, did to my body?"

The duke's jaw sets, his face growing serious.

"I'm not sure if they would have modified you after the decontamination process." He looks directly at me. "If you can't remember, maybe it's for the best."

"Maybe you're right." I shiver, thinking of having a stranger do something that sounds so invasive.

I try to distract myself with a bite of the scary snake fish. It tastes amazing, like sautéed mushrooms drizzled in balsamic.

"Yuuummm," I moan, eyes closing as I shovel another bite into my mouth. I sway my head back and forth, so fucking happy with how good this food tastes that I momentarily forget my current situation.

I only snap to as the duke clears his throat. When I open my eyes, he's shifting away from me uncomfortably.

What a stuck-up ass. He can't even handle me savoring something this tasty? Seems rude since he's my host, but whatever. I adjust the robe, which has fallen off my shoulder during my happy food dance.

"I have some…things…that need my attention." He's curt as he addresses me, avoiding eye contact.

"Whatever ya gotta do," I say, leaning over him to grab another hunk of the scal'pin filet.

He stands quickly, then walks awkwardly to the door while I continue my taste buds' adventure. Everything right now kind of fucking blows, but I'm glad I didn't end up on a planet where everything tastes like oatmeal or some shit.

My stomach is making so much noise that I can't even think

about a game plan yet. Until then, I'll savor every bite of this miraculous spread.

I'll get home, one way or another. There's no point in doing it on an empty stomach, though.

CHAPTER 6
☆FOR NOW AND ETERNITY, MARTA☆

☆RAF'ERE

MY PACE IS ONLY HINDERED by my attempt to hide my raging erection as I rush down the hall to one of the guest rooms.

I try not to think of the way the robe slipped from Marta's shoulder, revealing the soft curve of her chest as she swayed. As she savored the food, the sounds she made were almost indecent. I can only imagine the moans and sighs that would escape her lips with my face buried between her legs.

I enter the room with such urgency that I nearly rip the door off its hinges, the impact causing chips of tre'al stone to hit my back.

I have my hands already on my waistband's auto fastener when I see a member of the house staff.

She smirks, glancing down at the tented crotch of my trousers. Her white structured uniform sways as she moves to touch me, the white plaited hair standing out against her gray fi'len skin. Her name is Far'ep, and she is *known* to me.

Far'ep is from some closed chapter in my life now, a time before Marta. One where I would have happily had Far'ep help me work through my frustrations. My current timeline, for now and eternity, is after Marta.

My mate, a human stranger whose rejection I refuse to face, has ruined any other female for me.

"Out," I say through a clenched jaw, trying my best to regain any small shred of dignity I have left. She pauses her hand, hovering it over my hip.

"You look like you need my assistance, Your Grace," she says smoothly. Her hand quickly activates the auto fastener of my waistband, letting my cock spring free. The air feels cool and uncomfortable. It knows I need something soft and warm to rut, and the mate bond screams for Marta.

"Out!" I yell, pushing her to the side before she can reach for my shaft. She stumbles, tripping over her own feet, and crumbles to the floor.

"Your Grace?" she says my title again as if it's a question. Her eyes are wide, and her brow is knit in confusion. Turning away from her, I shove my cock back into my pants. The brush of fabric is painful on its engorged deep blue length.

"Far'ep," I say, slowly facing her, "leave. Do not assume we are familiar in that way ever again." I want to make sure my point is clear.

She scrambles to her feet, straightening her skirts and smoothing her hands over their crumpled fabric. Far'ep's eyes flash briefly with hurt before she drops them to the floor.

"Yes, Your Grace, it must be my mistake. Please accept my apologies." She raises her cupped open palms to me as is customary when apologizing in the Liin'gan reefs. I know my next move should be to push her hands down with my own, but I don't want to touch her.

I don't want to touch any female but f'teeing Marta ever again.

But when her hands shake, I push them quickly down with the pads of my fingertips. She lets out a quick burst of air before backing up and opening the cracked door frame. It creaks on its ruined hinges, and she tries to close it as delicately as she can once she's entered the hallway.

As soon as she's out of sight, I run to the ensuite bathroom and wash my hands—trying desperately to erase any trace of the maid's scent. My fingertips are raw from the friction of how aggressively I rub soap on my skin.

I know I won't be able to do anything until I stop the pounding of the head between my legs. Unless my cock finds some relief, I won't be able to form a plan.

As I slide my blue and throbbing cock from my pants fly, I spit on my length and roughly begin to work my shaft.

The vivid recollection of Marta savoring that single bite fills my mind, and I can still hear her sighing blissfully as her eyes rolled back in ecstasy. The thought of being able to make her feel that good sends shivers down my spine. I could use my toys on her drenched cunt and bring her to the brink of orgasm. I could wring every ounce of pleasure that existed in that lush body.

I imagine how she would preen for me on the bed, how I would hold her hands over her head and hold the vibrator against her most sensitive spots. The weight of her body would push back against me as she arched with pleasure. I would extend her orgasm as long as possible, even if it meant she would eventually beg me to stop.

Her screaming my name would be like music to my ears.

I come, my semen spilling into the sink basin, all the while still imagining Marta's face.

If I don't want this, if I don't want her, why does this feel so good?

As I run the faucet and watch the pale liquid swirl, mixing with the water and eventually down the drain, I want to tell her the truth.

But to what end?

I am the ruler of the Liin'gan Reefs and I champion a return to a more aquatic way of life for my people.

Marta can't even swim.

I turn to the shower unit and shrug off the rest of my clothing. Once inside, I close the door and activate the warm water from the jets on the walls. I rub my skin harshly, trying to wash away how badly my body screams for Marta.

I won't let her get the better of me, not after it's taken so long to craft the mask I wear now.

CHAPTER 7

☆LITTLE HUMAN, BIG PROBLEM☆

"YOU CHANGED?" I ask the duke.

I tilt my head to the side and look at the disheveled alien standing in the doorway. His clothing is completely different, more formal than his previous robes—incredibly pompous and over the top.

He ignores my question, tugging the lapels of his jacket and straightening its hem. He pulls his shoulders back, letting his head cock to the side, and reveals a slow smile.

It's as if he's changed into a different person, or alien, *or whatever*. The mask his face has become is a clear sign that he's hiding something from me.

"Never mind that," he says, eyeing the remains of all the food I just inhaled. "Did you enjoy dinner, little human?"

Little human.

The phrase makes my hair stand on end, a reminder that humans aren't the top of the food chain anymore. Standing on the other side of the empty plates, he's acting so strangely.

Plates that only I ate from.

"Did you drug me? Poison my food?" I sit up straighter,

pushing the balls of my feet against the cool floor, readying myself to run.

"What?" He reaches for me, rolling his eyes, annoyed. "Why would I do that?"

I feint to the right, dodging his touch.

My body, restored by the food I pray to God isn't drugged, is finally seeing my current situation more clearly.

I'm in danger.

"I want to go home, I want to leave." I garble my words, my mouth going dry.

"It's the same answer as earlier. No, not an option." Panic flashes behind his eyes as he grabs for me again. His palm brushes the side of my face before I flinch away.

"Don't touch me." I set my jaw as I slide over the arm of the chair. The robes catch on the ornate carving along the furniture's edge and are ripped from my shoulders, exposing my body in the skimpy blue outfit I woke up in.

My near nakedness catches his attention, and his eyes darken. The duke's gaze slowly drags over my bare skin, making me feel as if I'm being stripped of what little clothing I'm wearing.

"I told you, there's no f'teeing going home." His eyes betray his cool tone. He looks like he wants to eat me alive.

"Anywhere but here, then. Give me supplies, get me to the surface and I'll be someone else's problem." I try to negotiate. I can't believe I let my stomach win over my common sense.

"Goddess help me, no!" He lets his arms go slack to his sides, setting his jaw.

"I'm not safe here, I'm not safe with you," I hiss.

"No." The single syllable almost echoes in the room. His voice is low and loud.

"No? Fuck you! I'm leaving, capisce? I can't stay here with a monster!" I'm trembling with an emotion that I can't quite identify, whether it be anger or fear. As if feeling trapped on Earth wasn't enough, the idea of being trapped with an alien is unbearable. I'm not even sure if he has any plans to keep me alive. I can't believe I was naïve enough to put my trust in a stranger.

The alien's expression is one of dejection that quickly shifts into stubborn resolve. I realize I can't wait for his help. The only option left is to risk drowning and hope for the best. I grab a plate teetering on the edge of the table and chuck it at his head. With a swift movement, he sidesteps the object and glares at me as it shatters against the wall.

Run!

I decide to swing wide around him, feeling the wind rush past my face as I sprint to his right. The open door is within reach, but Raf'ere's hands around my waist stop me in my tracks. My limbs windmill forward as my body freezes under his efforts.

Spinning me around, he pins me against the door frame, my arms above my head. Raf'ere settles between my legs, his hips pressing firmly against mine. As much as I struggle, I won't get out of this hold.

"Stop struggling," he grits through his teeth. The duke's stare is too direct, my position is too compromising—for one of the first times in my life I'm at a loss for words.

The weight of his gaze makes me uneasy as I close my eyes and turn my head away from him. Our breaths are synchronized, and I find myself lost in the sound.

I'm only pulled out of my daze by the thick bulge growing in his pants, which makes me acutely aware of our proximity. Raf'ere's lips brush against the column of my throat and I stop breathing.

"No," I tell him, my voice shaking. It's like my words snap him from his own trance, and he stiffens. He allows some tiny space between us, quickly glancing toward the open door and checking if anyone is watching us.

When he looks back at me, he tilts his head down, tucking his jaw against his thick neck. His nostrils twitch, and it's the only warning I have before he picks me up.

He circles his huge hands around my waist—lifting me high over his shoulder. I kick and thrash against the brick wall of an alien. I pull at his hair and bite at his shoulder, but it's useless.

He drops me on the ground, turns out the light, and slams the door shut.

In the darkness, it takes a moment to realize where I am. But as my eyes acclimate to the lack of light, I can make out the coffin-shaped pod I fell out of earlier.

I'm back in the closet.

Scrambling to my feet, I rush to the door. But like before, there's no handle to speak of. I can barely make out the outline of the hidden panel.

Slamming my fist against the cold, unfeeling wall. As I do, the events of the past few hours hit me like a ton of bricks.

I'm stranded, kidnapped by aliens in space. The person who should help me, who rescued me from the bad aliens, is now holding me captive in his closet. No one is going to save me.

I'm going to have to help myself. He won't leave me in here forever, not if that look in his eyes was any sign of what he'd like to do to me.

When he comes back, I'll be ready. I look at the racks of clothing, the open drawer of alien sex toys, and the bottle of liquor.

I can only hope that years of watching *MacGyver* reruns have prepared me for the level of ingenuity I'm going to need.

I funnel all the sadness, fear, and panic into a blind rage, propelling me to get the fuck out of Dodge.

I'm about to be everyone's fucking problem. I grab a dark green shirt from its hanger, sliding it over my nearly naked body. It's huge, of course, and fits me more like a tunic. I'd kill for a pair of yoga pants, but we're working with what we've got.

I grab the half-empty bottle of liquor and shove a silk-like cravat into its narrow neck.

I rummage through the first drawer, frantically searching for anything that looks electronic. While trying to find an ignitor for the Molotov cocktail, I find my situation so absurd that I nearly chuckle. Will a tiny spark be enough to ignite the gaudy wick? I know it's strong enough stuff to burn, as I'm still fighting off the lingering buzz from earlier.

I throw every imaginable size and shape of sexy toys out from the duke's drawers. I can hear as some of the more fragile ones smash against the wall behind me.

Fuck him, I think as I wrench something that looks like a vibrator apart, smashing it on the hard island countertop.

Eventually, wires spring out as the cover snaps, and the smile that splits my face must be manic as I pull the wires apart. I laugh when I hit the button and watch a tiny spark arc between the frayed metal.

It's not a lighter, but it'll do.

CHAPTER 8
☆A LITTLE KINDNESS☆

THE DOOR MUFFLES the sound of her fists pounding, but I can feel the vibrations. Settling onto the smooth panel, I let myself slide down and rest with my elbows on my knees.

This is going to be a f'teeing problem…*Marta is going to be a problem.*

I pinned her against the doorframe, frustrated by her actions. But when I was that close, I could feel my mouth watering in my eagerness to taste her lips. With every breath, her scent filled my nostrils, intoxicating me like a dangerous drug. I lost myself for a moment, something that hasn't happened to me since Yar'oh.

Yar'oh is the reason I have such a grip now, the reason I can function outside of emotions. Marta, being my f'teeing mate, is throwing a wrench in any progress I've made, and the bond is making me feel weaker than I have in my entire life. I hate it.

With my eyes shut and a deep breath, I focus on the thumping of Marta's fists on the door. Maybe I'm sick, but I'm oddly comforted by their rhythm. She's here, and she's safe—the fact she probably wants to murder me doesn't really play into the equation.

I run my hand down the scarred side of my face, feeling the ridges of my old injuries. I curse the iridescent scales on my cheekbones, a genetic variation that only highlights the most damaged parts of me.

Every time I feel my face, I'm assaulted by the memory of the Andjin soldier's studded tentacle thrashing against me on the Korlyan Moon. Close combat was supposed to have been a thing of the past, I remember thinking as he shredded the delicate muscles covering my cheek.

What the Andjin wasn't expecting was the searing pain in his chest after my blaster blindsided him. I held a sick satisfaction in knowing I hurt him maybe more than he had me. That was my last thought before I passed out from the pain.

My scars? They barely hurt anymore, just the occasional twinge of twisted tissue when I shift my mouth too quickly.

Her words echoed in my head, and I couldn't help but wonder if she was right—am I a monster? She cast me as the villain in her story, but I'll play that role if it means I can take back control over the mess my life has become since she entered into it.

"Ahem." Jens'i breaks my destructive thinking.

"Yes?" I say, not opening my eyes, my hand still rubbing my jaw.

"Is there anything I might assist you with, sir?" He crosses his arms over his starched white uniform.

"No."

"Not even our guest, currently locked in the closet?" He gestures to the door I'm blocking.

"Not unless you can convince her not to run away."

My butler pauses, throwing me a glance that's almost thoughtful. Pulling up a chair near me, he sits, leaning forward onto his knees over me.

"Is there a reason we want this *guest* to stay—when there are so many willing females who would happily take her place?" He looks down at me, as if expecting me to reveal my secret.

"No."

"Are you sure? I could easily place her elsewhere in the territory. One quick call to Ke'ain, His Grace the King of Sontafrul 6, and I'm sure she could be on her way to the Earth Two dormitories at the palace."

"Don't you f'teeing dare call my cousin," I seethe.

Gra'eth, Hand of the King and also his best friend, and his human mate Jessy would crucify me for what I'm doing to Marta right now. They would take her away in a heartbeat. The thought of her leaving the reef's estate…no, just her leaving my bedroom, makes me ill with rage.

Mine. Mine. Mine. The bond screams.

He puts his hands up, dropping the subject.

"So, she stays…in the closet?" The butler cocks his head to the hidden door behind us. My jaw sets, a sign of my annoyance. "Okay, so she stays in the closet."

Jens'i taps his foot.

"Can I attempt to make her more comfortable? Maybe some kindness in that regard would go a long way in convincing this person of absolutely no importance to *want* to stay here."

Kindness. I can be kind, mostly in the bedroom.

"If you think it will help, I'll allow it." I try to say nonchalantly, rising to my feet. There is no middle between my rational mind and the mating bond. The thought of her leaving the estate makes me as physically ill as the thought of having to deal with a human for the rest of my life.

Our life, the mate bond corrects.

"Of course, Your Grace."

"And Jens'i?" The butler turns to me. "She doesn't leave my chambers, not without my permission. She doesn't speak to anyone but you."

"You are entirely understood." He turns back to the door before pausing and asking, "Your Grace, do we know the human's name?"

"Marta," I say, letting the syllables linger in the air like a melody. "Her name is Marta."

CHAPTER 9
☆WHY RISK IT?☆

THE DOOR CRACKS OPEN, and a beam of light floods one corner of the closet. I stand behind the door, frantically attempting to light the fabric stuffed into the bottle.

No matter how long I depress the button of the vibrator, the arc of electricity refuses to catch fire to the silky cravat. I give up entirely, dropping the former sex toy turned lighter to the ground, and prepare myself to just chuck the heavy glass bottle at the duke's dumb gray head.

But he's not who peeks around the corner, instead a much smaller alien does. His white hair is thin around the crown of his head, and fine lines extend from the corner of his eyes and his mouth. I assume his age is much more advanced than Raf'ere's.

"Hello, Marta," he says calmly.

I know he's still an alien, and alien equals enemy, but I can't bring myself to give an old man a head injury, regardless of the species. There's something about him that reminds me of Pops. Maybe it's the male-pattern baldness or the way he holds himself? I can't quite place it. It's probably another example of me being fucking stupid, but I'm exhausted. I don't know how my situation could get much worse, anyway.

"You know my name." It's a statement, not a question.

His blue eyes scan the scene before him. A broken vibrator on the ground, a silk cravat stuffed into a bottle of liquor, and a human woman in an oversized green tee shirt somewhere on the verge of screaming or crying.

"I do. His Grace, Duke Raf'ere, asked me to come help you. To see if you needed anything." He leans over and picks up the vibrator from the ground. "Can I ask what you're doing?"

"I'm…I'm making a Molotov cocktail," I whisper as he gently takes the bottle out of my hand.

His eyes get some far-off look, and I remember when my translator chip showed me the scal'pin. It must be doing the same for him now. I doubt there's an alien translation for Molotov.

"Well, I hate to break it to you, my dear." He pulls the cravat from the bottle and dangles it in front of me. "The fabric here is aqua-phobic, it doesn't absorb liquids. The same properties that allow it to be resistant to wetness also allow it to be flame retardant. So, as *industrious* as your plan was, I think it was always doomed to fail."

Doomed to fail. That's how I feel right now.

"Oh," is the only reply I can eek out.

"Now, you've just come out of cryosleep, and your emotions will be varied at best. Beyond maiming the duke, is there anything I can get or do for you, anything that might make you more comfortable while you stay at the estate?"

"I just want to go home; can you help me?" The words bubble up from my throat. God, a minute ago I was ready to murder Raf'ere, and now I'm about to beg a stranger for help. I can already feel the fat tears brimming behind my eyelids. "Varied emotions" is an understatement.

"That, I'm afraid, is truly impossible," he says kindly.

I swallow a sob, not wanting to break down here with this stranger, no matter how unusually comfortable he makes me.

"What I can do is get you some new clothes—and maybe some time to shower and refresh yourself? I can't imagine cryosleep is particularly kind to your body." He grabs one of the duke's ornate robes and places it over my shoulders like a cape. "Maybe once you're clean and dressed, you'll be able to figure out the best use of your time here."

"As if I have a say in that? That sick fuck wants to keep me as his...as his... I don't know, his sex slave or something," I say, pulling the robe tighter around myself.

The butler raises his four fingered hand to his mouth, stifling a laugh, like what I've just said is the most hilarious thing he's ever heard.

"What's so funny?" I demand, as my current predicament doesn't really lend itself to humor. Maybe I just don't understand alien humor very well.

"His Grace, the duke, has so many willing bedfellows. I highly doubt that he'd ever force you to attend to him in that way. His Grace is many things, incredibly forward being one of them… but rapist he decidedly is not." He regains his composure and continues picking up bits of the broken sex toys from the ground.

"So if he's got so many willing suitors, why won't he let me leave? Why the hell did he look like he wanted to eat me just now?" It doesn't make sense. If he's such a playboy, why is he holding me captive? I felt the bulge in his pants, I know what his body wants.

"That is peculiar, and I won't pretend to know his motives, but I do trust him. Maybe it's for the best you stay here with us, take this time to relax and learn about your new world." The butler deposits the pieces of trash into a nearby bin and straightens to his full height.

"Stay here with him? He's a monster! I can't—" I feel a tear roll down my cheek as I yell.

"His grace is a hero." The old alien's face grows serious as he cuts me off. "He fought for our planet during the Korlyan Moon wars, and he sacrificed so much to keep Sontafrul 6 safe. He's one of the only people on this entire planet in a position of power that fights for our people's natural way of life, under the water." His tone is curt.

"Convince this hero to let me go, then. I don't belong here under the waves." I panic, thinking of the water that surrounds me here. "It doesn't have to be Earth, but anywhere else…"

"I can provide some small comforts, Marta. Take advantage of them." He puts the liquor back into the bar of weirdly shaped bottles. "Raf'ere isn't as bad as his first impression comes across. I promise that."

I don't even have the energy to tell him I don't fucking care. I slump back onto the ground, like I have a hundred times this past hour, and start to sob.

"I'll have some clothing brought to the duke's shower unit. When you're ready, please let me know. Just knock and the duke will summon me—my name is Jens'i."

"Like Gen-Z?" I ask between sniffles, not able to stop crying.

"I don't think so," he says, closing the door, his face confused. He must not want to deal with an inconsolable human woman.

What he does do, that the duke didn't, is hit something on the panel near the door which turns on soft yellow lighting that's integrated into the cabinetry of the wood.

At least he didn't leave me in the dark.

I pull the robe tightly around myself, my fingers brushing the intricate beading along the shoulders of the garment. In the glow of the new lights, the metallic beads glint, and I catch the detail in their shape for the first time.

Each bead, long and tapered, is sewn into the garment in the style of fringed epaulets. I finger one and it's featherlight in my hands. As I inspect the bead closer, its shape becomes familiar.

The slight twist, the tapered end…it's a cornicello. How in

the world am I wearing an alien garment covered in hundreds of tiny Italian horns? I stop crying immediately and tug one of the beads free, ripping the thread securing it to the garment.

Most Italian Americans don't believe in coincidences, myself included. The amulet in my hand is supposed to protect you from the evil eye, and holy fuck, is that something I need right now.

It's also supposed to make you more virile, but that's beside the point. I'll take any good luck that the universe will hand me.

Using my forefinger and thumb, I pluck the plasticky thread that once secured the bead. As I do, more beads fall to the floor, but I eventually work a length long enough to tie the horn around my neck. It might be superstitious, but seeing as I didn't believe in aliens until just a few hours ago, why risk it?

Is it stupid that something so small could make me feel so much better?

I still don't believe Jens'i. I don't think the duke is anything but the monster I've seen...but maybe he doesn't want to hurt me.

I've been combative, not that my aggression isn't warranted. Maybe if I don't try to assault him every chance I get, convincing him to let me go would be easier.

I sigh, realizing what a steep hill that will be to climb. The duke's stubbornness seems only akin to my own.

I decide I do need that shower I was promised. Maybe the warm water can help wash away my anxiety. A clear head would do me good.

Wrapping my fingers around the cornicello, I clutch it at my chest. *Please let luck be on my side.*

CHAPTER 10
☆HE KNOWS☆

JENS'I CLOSES the door softly behind him. There's no yelling or pounding of fists as he does. I've moved to sitting on the sofa and raise my eyebrows to him.

"I fear you've made quite a terrible first impression, Your Grace," he says, setting the half empty bottle of thru'ik and silky cravat onto the sitting table in front of me.

"Well, that's f'teeing obvious," I sigh. "How is she?"

"Afraid, anxious, angry—your pick." Although he rarely sits while on the clock, the older fi'len male takes a seat in the chair next to the one where Marta sat. "You should let her go." His voice is filled with pity. For me or for Marta's situation, I'm unsure.

"Not an option."

"Why is that, Your Grace?" He seems tired of my non answers. I've never truly confided in anyone but Jens'i—it must feel strange for me to keep secrets from him. "Is it possible that you suffer the same affliction as his royal highness, Ke'ain, and his hand, Gra'eth? I mean you yourself support our human queen—do you not?"

He knows. The fact that he knows leaves me feeling like a helpless child. If I can't even keep this situation under control at home, how can I ever keep it together anywhere else?

"The goddess wouldn't curse me with a human mate," I sigh. "What kind of life could a terrestrial race have under the waves? It would undermine everything I've fought for, for our people's right to exist in their natural habitats."

He pulls his mouth into a tight line. I don't think I've convinced him of the lie I keep saying aloud. I know the truth, I know what Marta really is.

"Well, seeing as she's just left cryosleep, I offered her use of your shower unit. Coming out of cryosleep can be incredibly taxing on the nervous system…she still seems to be experiencing mood swings. I think it's best if we allow her some time to relax. Do you have any issues with this?"

"It won't hurt anything to allow her time to clean herself up," I nod.

"A step in the right direction for Marta to see how hospitable the reefs can be, perchance? Something to improve her spirits and give you a chance to convince her it's not so terrible here."

"I haven't harmed her—I could have left her on that ship."

"Yes, you could have. But you didn't, and now we have a crying human female locked in your closet." His tone is on the edge of condescension.

"Wait, she's crying? I thought she was angry." The shift in her emotions is unsettling.

"She can be both at once, and yes, she's crying."

My fingers dig into the arm of the sofa. I'm angry, at myself, at how I've handled this, and most of all at the goddess for choosing her.

The mate bond tugs at my mind. It tells me I can't keep her captive forever. That no matter how strong she thinks she is, a life with me, her monster, might be worse than the Deenz.

But I push those feelings down into the box inside my chest. I lock it away with the memories of Yar'oh and of my life before the war. If I don't accept her as my mate, or worse yet, if she refuses me, I'll truly be alone. I won't be able to find any joy in pleasuring females…I won't have my control. I'll be a broken hull of a male.

It's all her fault.

Yet when she knocks at the door, a soft and steady rhythm—nothing like the frantic pounding of before—I can't help but hold my breath.

Her curly black hair is wild, strands clinging to the wetness on her cheeks. Her eyes are tired, swollen and red from crying. When she steps from the closet, she's wearing my ceremonial robe and its matching undershirt. The beaded robe trails behind her, as if she's walking through the temple's cavern. Both pieces of clothing are the deep green that signals the royalty of my breeding, the beading on the shoulders made from precious alloys derived from the walls of our sacred caverns.

Marta looks stunning in green—something out of a dream.

I don't breathe as Jens'i guides her over to the double doors that hold my bathing chambers. She doesn't acknowledge me, but I don't expect her to, either. Our last interaction was…tense.

My butler points out how to turn on the shower and tells her he'll bring some clothing up while she bathes—something more suited to her frame is what he says.

She looks behind at me only for a second, as if to check that I'm still there. Her ample curves fill the robe so uniquely. She truly is the alien here, her body so strange and alluring.

She doesn't wait for Jens'i to shut the doors entirely before dropping the family heirloom of a robe onto the ground. I only hope the beading isn't damaged.

CHAPTER 11
☆YOU SHOULD HAVE KNOCKED☆

☆MARTA

THE BATHROOM IS HUGE, bigger than one person would ever need. The same black stone and ornate gold, teal, and green details from the rest of the estate are repeated here.

Jens'i showed me how to activate the shower inside of the large glass enclosure. The beads clink as I sigh in relief and let the heavy robe drop to the stone floors.

As I shuck off the duke's green shirt, I peel away the stretchy blue bandage style bodysuit that covers me. My skin feels clammy and sticky, and my cheeks are on fire from the salt of my tears. I slip off the faux cornicello around my neck and set it on the sink's counter. Lifting my arm, I am hit with a pungent odor of stress-induced sweat.

Maybe a shower isn't such a bad idea after all.

I look at the door, trying to figure out if it locks, but get flustered at the combination of the handle and locking mechanism on the door. The object's design is a blend of rococo and futuristic elements, but the locking mechanism is so advanced that I can't even figure out the first step.

That's kind of what this whole place feels like, new but old. It makes me think of the first few lines of the old *Star Wars* crawl. I feel lost in the past, far from home. Memories of my family's faces race through my mind. *Memories.* I guess that's all they'll be now.

I step into the glass enclosure, clicking the door shut behind me, and hit the button Jens'i instructed me to press. I look up, searching for some faucet head, but there is none.

Instead, I jump in surprise as rows and rows of jets emerge from a hidden panel in the wall. With little warning, strongly pressurized water hits my body from all directions.

Although shocking, it's far from unpleasant. The water is warm, almost as hot as I like it, and the strength of the jets leaves my skin feeling clean and tingly.

My legs are tired, though. I mean, I'm tired—*no, I'm exhausted. Does being frozen alive cause any damage to your body?* I turn to the wall and close my eyes, savoring the relief of the cool stone against my forehead. With my arm above my head, I take in a deep breath, feeling the humid air of the shower around me.

If convincing the duke is not possible, I'll make the best of the situation and try to find some good in it. Perhaps Jens'i isn't an outlier, and the other aliens are more level-headed and agreeable than the duke.

I try to enjoy the relief of the shower, knowing that all my gumption to plan an escape is gone for the moment.

I shift my hips, feeling the jets of warm water soothe the tension in my lower back. The stream of water from the opposing jets hits me in just the right spot, and I can't help but moan softly.

I quickly jerk away, surprised by the sudden touch that made my clit throb with pleasure.

What in the actual fuck is wrong with you, Marta? Now is not the fucking time or place to be getting your rocks off. But I let the jet spray my pussy again.

It feels good, too good for me to stop. As the water pulses against me, my hips buck reflexively.

You've always found comfort in getting yourself off. If you can't use it during the most stressful experience of your life, what's the point?

My hand finds its way to my breast, and I run my thumb over the nipple, feeling it harden. It's probably a dangerous move because it makes me spread my legs a little wider.

The sensation of the water hitting my clit is so intense that I bite my arm to keep from moaning.

Just a brief release—that's all I need to take the edge off, to feel better, to—

"Fuck," I whimper, clenching my ass together as I can feel my orgasm build. The constriction of the muscles in my pussy make me feel hollow inside. As good as this feels, I need penetration. With two fingers I position myself to soothe the insistent urge inside me.

Despite the water, I can feel how fucking wet I am. There's no turning back now, even if I wanted to stop. With the finish line in sight, I let the water pulse directly against my clit and plunge two fingers deep inside myself.

The sensation of fullness is so intense that my moans echo through the room. I'm sure Duke Fuckface can hear me, but I don't care.

My clit throbs hard as I approach the edge of climax, and every nerve ending in my body come alive. The blissful and tingling tightness fills my lower belly.

Just as ecstasy is in reach, the door crashes open behind me.

As I jerk my head toward the opening, my legs twist awkwardly and I stumble.

I close my eyes tightly as my foot slips too far forward, and I prepare for the inevitable impact of my back with the hard stone floor.

Suddenly, something smooth and warm is pressed against my shoulder, followed by the same sensation under my knees. It's as if the laws of gravity have been turned upside down—I am floating up instead of falling down.

When I open my eyes, I realize the duke is holding me. The spray of water hits his skin and makes his gills pulse. His brows are furrowed in confusion as he looks at me with unfocused eyes.

I want to stop, but I know I'm too far gone. I shouldn't arc my fingers against my g-spot or flex the muscles of my thighs, and I most certainly shouldn't look him directly in the eyes as I come.

But I do.

In his embrace, waves of pleasure rack through me, leaving me boneless. My fingers dig into his bicep as I try to anchor myself in reality.

It doesn't work. My entire body is consumed by a cloud of pleasure, and I feel like I'm floating on air. The duke's voice is the only thing that tugs me back to the real world.

At first, his speech muffled, like the hum of a stereo after a bomb blows in a movie, but as he keeps speaking, it grows clearer.

"Are you...what...did you just f'teeing come?" His face flushes a bright blue, and he looks like he's stopped breathing.

Whether he is shocked or uncomfortable, it doesn't matter to me. I don't give a damn about his fucking feelings.

Will I be embarrassed later? For fucking sure. But for now?

"You should have knocked!"

CHAPTER 12
☆COME ON ME☆

☆RAF'ERE

Her hands are…oh f'teeing goddess, she's finger fucking herself in my arms. Marta's pointer and middle fingers are buried deep inside her cunt, its soft mound covered in curly black hair. It's a mane in a place I wasn't expecting.

I thought that maybe she had slipped, or scalded herself on the water when I heard the noises she was making through the door. I even buzzed Jens'i to have him deal with *her*.

When he didn't answer and I heard her nearly scream, the protective nature of the mate bond took over. I kicked the door open when, in retrospect, I'm sure that the knob was perfectly functional.

Even though I noticed the water sluicing off her ample curves, I saw her feet begin to fumble.

I wrenched the door open just in time to catch the clumsy Earthling before she smacked her head violently against the floor. I enjoyed about all of three seconds of my heroic gesture before the scent of her arousal hit me.

Now our eyes are locked, and hers narrow at the same time I realize she's pushing her fingers deeper inside herself. She is obstinate in her actions as her hips buck skyward and the muscles of her legs clench.

Marta shudders as she comes apart in my arms. The soft moan that escapes her lips is almost like a melody, one that my body begs to harmonize with.

"Are you...what...did you just f'teeing come?" My face heats, and I'm short of breath.

Her lip curls, not into a smile, but a look of defiance.

"You should have knocked!" she barks, unfazed by our current predicament.

I'm dumbfounded for a minute. I don't bother telling her I thought she was hurt, seeing as she wasn't impressed with my already having rescued her.

"But...why?" I think I'm asking the obvious question. What would possess her to touch herself in my shower?

Could it be that she's as affected by the mate bond as I am? From the shitty little look on her face, I can tell some part of her despises me. But maybe there's some conflict inside her as well.

I scent the musky aroma of her cunt that fills the small shower enclosure, waiting for her answer.

"I don't have to explain myself to you." She releases my arm. "Put me down! You can't just barge into the bathroom and pick up a naked woman." She bristles, using her arms to cover her breasts and mound.

So, I drop her.

Not in a way that would hurt her, but enough to knock the wind out of her lungs. She fell only a few inches to the ground.

"Excuse me? What the fuck was that?" she yelps from the shower floor.

She's flushed red with swollen lips, a side effect of either her orgasm or her anger—either way, I like it. I run my eyes down her body. She is nothing like a fi'len female.

The shock of the fall has her bracing her arms against the floor, and her body is laid bare before me. Marta is luscious and covered with curves. Her breasts, lined with faint pink striations, fall toward her arms as she lies on her back. Her nipples are still hard, and I find my fingers twitching to grab them. My gaze travels down her soft tummy, which I know from our brief contact feels like a cloud. I get one more look at the curious dark curls above her sex before she's covering her body again.

"Yo, get the fuck out of here!" She curls to a sitting position.

"Next time, keep it down." I turn heel and walk back to the sitting room. I don't close the door behind me but hear her scramble to stand and slam it not long after I leave the bathroom.

Both sides of me, my rational one and the part controlled by the mating bond, like toying with Marta.

I won't pretend as though I expected her to be touching herself when I opened the door—I was sure she was crying again. I think it was the bond that drew me in. Before she slipped, the other side of me wanted to tell her to knock it off. Crying wasn't going to help her situation any.

I didn't even think when I saw her footing fumble. I was there in less than a second, and she was in my arms.

It felt f'teeing good, the bond rewarding my close contact with a rush of endorphins.

But the bond wants more…*and it will always want more.*

I enjoyed watching the little human squirm, and I loved watching her come in my arms—but then, where does that leave me?

I cannot mate a human.

It just won't work, not with my life, not with the mask I've crafted for myself, and not with my goals for the Liin'gan Reefs.

I can't.

I slump back into my armchair and let my head fall back to view the windows behind me.

The Ocean is my home, the Reefs are where my people belong. I've worked so hard to bring fi'len back into the water.

Marta is terrified of the very ocean I call home.

I should send her to the palace, to let her be with her kind, and maybe she can become someone else's problem.

My stomach riles at the thought, and I have to push the bile back down my throat.If I let her leave the bond will always remind me that I'm one half of a whole. It would be torture to be without her. So for now she stays.

Before I spiral much deeper, Jens'i opens the double doors to the hall, his hands full of a variety of palace uniforms. I arch a brow in his direction.

"Your Grace, it's clothing for *our guest,*" he tells me with the most lackluster bow I've ever seen. I am but an afterthought as he walks quickly to my bathing chamber. He knocks, and when Marta opens the door enough to peek her head out, my hearts begin to thump wildly.

"I wasn't sure if the sizing would be right, but I grabbed a few things at hand." He passes them through the narrow opening.

"Thank you," Marta whispers before shooting me a death glare.

"My pleasure. If those don't work, please have His Grace notify me. We can have someone come in for some custom-sized garments shortly."

She clicks the door shut, and my butler turns back to me.

"*Custom clothing?* Jens'i, that seems a bit extravagant," I complain.

Jens'i, my distinguished butler, who is often regarded as one of the most levelheaded and wise members of the estate staff, rolls his eyes at me.

"Your Grace, with all due respect, your clothing budget exceeds that of the King's. I think it's only fitting that we offer *her* something that actually fits her alien body."

"A budget that is afforded to me due to my station, lest we not forget. The human is—"

"No less deserving. I can keep your situation private, but do not assume I don't understand the circumstance you find your-self in now. Keep in mind that although I am your butler, and proud to be so, first I am a mate to Hi'lar. As a mated male, I can see exactly what's going on—"

"Enough."

"You won't be able to deny the truth much longer, and you shouldn't have to. Humans are being integrated into our society. It might even be a good thing from a diplomatic standpoint—"

"Enough!" I growl. He doesn't understand.

"Your Grace." He bows deeply but lets his eyes show their disappointment. It's not often he has an outburst like that. His feelings must truly be strong to tell me so plainly.

But he knows. My mask is down, and I am laid bare.

"I'm arranging a bed to be brought up for Marta, among other comforts. Shall I tell them to furnish it in the dressing room?" He moves on to the business at hand, as if to recover from my slight against him.

"Yes, I think that's the best place for her at the moment. We can figure out specifics about her stay here in the morning." I soften my tone. I don't often snap at the person I consider my one confidant. He nods.

"Unless anything further is needed, Your Grace, I will be retiring for the evening."

"Of course, please give my regards to Hi'lar. I'll see you in the morning."

He gives one last look at the bathing chamber doors.

"Patience and understanding will go a long way, even if it's what you grant yourself. It's okay to put your needs first, Raf'ere." The lack of formal title is bristling at first, but I know it's done with sincerity.

I don't have the heart to tell him Marta will never work, she'll never fit into my life like he thinks she will.

"Thank you."

CHAPTER 13
☆ESTABLISHING DOMINANCE☆

☆MARTA

THE WHITE UNIFORM doesn't fit me well, but it's the best of the pile. I'm short even on Earth at a cool five two, but in space I'm tiny. I know these garments are probably cut for alien proportions, but swimming in the oversized dress doesn't make me feel any less dowdy.

The fabric feels unnatural, but still somehow breathable. It has the texture of plastic but doesn't make me sweat like a polyester does. There's a teal belt that is held up by loops, but the waistline of the dress is at my hips. It creates a strange silhouette. My hips are wide and while in my youth I hated them, now at twenty-eight I look at them with much kinder eyes.. They're still not my favorite part of my body, so I likely wouldn't have chosen to emphasize them like they are now. That, in combination with sleeves about six inches too long, makes me look like a chunky toddler wearing her mother's business casual attire.

Who gives a fuck about fashion right now? Oh, maybe the girl who thought it'd be a great time to rub one out? I'm a hot mess all around.

But the dress is the only thing in the stack of clothing that doesn't absolutely tent over me. I roll the long sleeves up until they reach my mid forearms, for easier use of my hands. I take the belt out from the loops that rest on my mid-thigh and just tie it a bit higher where my natural waist falls.

I allow myself a quick glance in the mirror once I've fixed the outfit as best I can—and honestly, I've looked worse. I tuck my makeshift Italian horn necklace into the high neckline of the shirt.

My hair is still damp from the shower, but I don't see any towels or blow dryers around. I guess that makes sense given that Raf'ere's skin and hair never truly seemed to get wet, even in the direct spray of water.

Leaning over the sink, I try to wring the water from my hair. The curls bounce as I release my grip and it seems to have helped my drowned rat chic look a bit.

Knowing Duke Fuckface won't lift a finger, I take the time to fold the clothes that didn't work. I don't want the kind Jens'i to have to deal with my mess, amidst Raf'ere's terrible attitude.

As I do, I find my mind wandering back to earlier, when I came in his arms. Why in the fuck didn't I stop? I could have played it off, pretending like I had just slipped.

I sure as shit could have taken my fingers out of my pussy.

Was it a power move? I don't know.

I didn't hate it.

What if I let things go further? If his heated gaze was any indication, he would have been more than willing to help.

I shake my hands, trying to rid myself of any confusing feelings stirring in my belly.

With a deep breath, I open the door. It must have been a power move. I was establishing dominance, just like when Bruno wouldn't stop humping my bodyguard. That's it, nothing more. And despite the fact that I was masturbating…it was nothing sexual.

As the doors open, a large bed is carried quickly across the room and toward the closet door. A set of burly alien men hold either end. They're big but not as tall as the duke. The aliens moving the furniture don't see me as I gawk at them, but Raf'ere does.

The duke hurries up to me, I expect to tell me yet again how weak and useless humans are, but instead he closes the door right in my face.

"Yes, the bed will go into the dressing chambers. Excellent, thank you."

I hear his muffled speech through the door. Wiggling the handle, I attempt to reopen it. But it doesn't budge. That asshole must be holding the doorknob on the other side.

I know he's stronger than me, so I don't waste the energy trying to force it open. I sit cross-legged on the floor and wait for him to decide when I'm allowed out—tired of fighting with him for now.

When he swings the black stone door open, he stares in the space he expects me to be and opens his mouth as if he's got something to say.

"I'm down here. Am *I allowed out yet?*" I ask sarcastically.

"Yes." He chuffs, the corner of his lip ticking up. "There's a bed in the dressing room if you'd like to get some sleep." He gestures indifferently to the door across the room.

"Every girl's dream, to be kidnapped and get her very own bed in some alien's closet." I roll my eyes.

"I assumed you didn't want to stay out here." He narrows his gaze and points to the spot where I know the ocean looms through the jelly window.

I scoff without looking in that direction but move toward the closet.

"You know, a lot of fi'len females would die to be this close to me," he says bitterly. He turns his back to me, as if I'm no better than the scum on his shoe. "You should be grateful I feel *obligated* to help you."

I clench my jaw. "I'm just so grateful," I mock. "Do me a

favor, at least leave the door unlocked so I don't have to pee in a corner tonight?"

"You are truly the spirit of graciousness." He sits, pulling some kind of tablet from his jacket pocket. He doesn't acknowledge me again, so I take it as my cue to leave.

When I step into the closet, I have to put my hand over my mouth. I can't have the duke hear the awe I feel right now. The dark and utilitarian space has been transformed during my short shower.

A cool glow is coming from a glass sphere filled with glittering and swirling teal liquid—*is it like an alien lava lamp?*

It casts a comfortable light around the space. A bed is tucked against a wall that once held racks of gray suit jackets. The bedding looks incredibly cozy, with it's arrangement of inviting soft textiles.

In fact, many things are missing from the closet. My cryopod is gone, as is the evidence of my manic destruction of sex toys.

At the bar that once contained only liquor, there are trays of food covered by glass domes. A carafe of water sits on a purple glowing disc, and there's frost accumulating from where the bottom of the container rests on the soft light. I touch the side, my fingers tips chill instantly.

Is it weird that the idea of constantly cold bedside water has me giddy?

A side chair has been moved into the closet as well, a small dressing gown thrown over its arm, something smaller than the duke would wear.

No pajamas to speak of, but I've always been a naked sleeper, anyway. I guess I don't have to worry about the duke catching a glimpse of the goods, not since our little encounter earlier.

Maybe I can just stop giving a shit in general here. No one knows me and there's no family reputation to uphold.

I guess others' perception of me only applies if the duke lets me leave the bedroom again.

It doesn't matter now, and I suppose I should take advantage of the situation and get some sleep.

Even though I just put it on, I shuck off my ill-fitting dress, folding it neatly and placing it on the chair. I pull back the soft orange covering on the bed and slide my freshly cleaned body between the alien sheets.

Taking one of the pillows off the pile behind my head, I clutch it tightly against my chest. *I wish Bruno was here.*

I might sound like a crazy dog mom, but even despite the shit show that my life is shaping up to be, Bruno would make it better. He would lay his pittie head on my chest, stare up at me with his pale blue eyes and calm my anxiety.

And hell, maybe he'd even hump Duke Fuckface and put him in his place.

For as insufferable as the duke is, I don't think he'll kill me. He seems to hold himself to some level of royal duty. I guess that's a step in the right direction.

Wiping a reluctant tear for my late pup off my face, I turn away from the open door. Maybe my mood swings are calming down, or maybe the exhaustion is just setting in, but sleep comes easy. I let myself be taken away to the world of dreams.

CHAPTER 14
☆NOCTURNAL SATELLITE EMISSIONS☆

☆RAF'ERE

IF I THOUGHT my sleep was suffering when Marta was in the cryopod, having her breathing feet away from me all night is making me an insomniac.

The mate bond heightens my senses when she's near, our heartbeats are even synced. How do I know that? Because I can hear hers, even though she's tucked away in the closest. I hear her pulse and the slow pace of her breathing while she sleeps. Her smoky scent is overpowering any other smell in my chambers. If I closed my eyes, it would seem as though she was lying in bed next to me.

It's pure unadulterated torture, and I know sleep won't be within my reach tonight.

I roll onto my side, trying to find some corner of my room unsaturated with Marta's scent. When it doesn't work, I groan, sliding my data pad off the nightstand.

Bright blue alerts flash, and I bring the screen up to my face. My calendar for the upcoming few days is stacked deep with meetings for the upcoming Andjin treaty talks. I have six missed calls and messages from Tri'ot, which I delete without reading.

Before Marta, I would use this sleepless night to prepare for those meetings. Peace between the Korlyan Moon and Sontafrul 6 is tense at best.

But I can't focus, and every time I close my eyes, all I can see is her face twisted in pleasure as she came apart in my arms.

I swipe to a new screen and click the search bar of the satellite transmissions database. The cursor in the search bar blinks, waiting for my input.

I type

HUMAN

and hit send.

My screen fills with tiny video thumbnails, my search returning billions of recordings of human entertainment. Wars, historical events of Earth, game shows, and news broadcasters fill my screen.

The database doesn't understand subtlety, and I am afraid to type what I really want. So, I split the difference.

HUMAN "ITALIAN"

There are just as many clips, but I pull up the first one, hoping to understand better what she said earlier.

The clip plays, and three human males in a wheeled vehicle drive out into a field. One of them pulls a weapon and kills another human in close contact.

"Leave the gun, take the cannoli," the portly male tells the other after the brutal murder.

Although my translator chip shows me this "cannoli," I don't understand what the white-filled tube is. I also still don't understand what in the goddess's name an Italian is.

Given this clip, I'm going to assume that the humans who call themselves Italians are some kind of warriors on Earth.

I turn my head to the open closet door, the soft glow of the lamp casting strange shadows across the room. It's filled with the waters of I'loh, from the springs and ancestral tunnels of our temples.

The lamps are often given to fi'len children, as they are thought to have a supernatural ability to calm and restore—the waters being a gift from the goddess.

Marta, as a warrior, doesn't seem far off the mark. She's not built like a fi'len warrior, but she has the attitude of one. Maybe human men are the smaller and weaker of the species?

I realize how little I actually know about Marta's kind.

I finally type what I wanted to search to begin with.

HUMAN FEMALE ORGASM

As the thumbnails fill my screen, I can feel my cock hardening. There are so many photos that are just up close shots of human female cunts. The shapes and varieties are astounding.

From pale pinks to deep browns, each one unique—I am almost positive, and disappointed, that none of them are Marta's.

I flick through the thumbnails until I find something that *feels right*. Dark and dewy curls frame a tight shot of a swollen and pink cunt. The crotch mane, so similar to Marta's, it has me clicking to play the footage.

The camera is static, and the tight framing of the shot remains. Slowly, a hand with long red fingernails crests over the top of the mound. She slides a finger in between the petals of her cunt, gathering the slickness.

Without warning, a moan escapes from the speaker of my data pad, and I clutch it to my chest to muffle the sound. I've never shared a room before, but I feel stupid not to have muted my device before searching for filth on the satellite database.

I wait a few moments, holding my breath, praying to the goddess that I haven't woken my wild human mate.

Luckily, I don't hear any stirring from my dressing chambers.

I pull the screen away from my chest and continue the movie.

The female has picked up her pace, and she now furiously rubs a small gem of flesh at the apex of her sex. One hand pulls the lips wide, while two fingers stroke against the curious little nub.

She bucks her hips, and I slide my hand under the sheet, grasping my cock.

The camera is so zoomed in, I can see her empty but spasming cunt, greedy for a cock. I spit in my palm then fist my hand over the head. I'm much bigger than Marta's fingers, and I wonder if she could take all of me.

The video female pumps her hips, sliding an excessive number of fingers—*I only have four*—down her cunt. I can tell from the video alone, I would hear how slick the human is—her hand rubbing the entirety of her swollen mound from side to side with flat fingers.

Would Marta like that? Does it ache with an insatiable craving like my cock does as I caress it now? My fingers tightly wrap around the tip of my shaft, exerting pressure all the way to its root.

The outside of my thumb hits the edge of my sucker, and it grasps on, confused that I'm not a female ready to breed. The fi'len females possess a protrusion it can grab onto to help keep mating partners together underwater. It pulls the skin of my knuckle and with a pop, releases as I slide up my hand back up to my head, squeezing the sensitive tip of my cock.

My sac tightens, and I know my release is near.

With Marta here, I'm sure just her breathe against my neck could undo me and have me spilling in my trousers.

The female in the video is clenching her ass. With a final stroke of her hand over her cunt's gem, she unravels. Clasping both her hands on her crotch, her hips lift into the air, and she rides out her orgasm. My pace nearly as frantic as hers was, I am on the brink.

The transmission cuts out, the screen on my data pad going black.

F'tee.

I toss the data pad to the ground, my cock still in my hand, and stand. Turning to the closet, I take a few steps in its direction before I stop myself.

I go in there and do what?

Instead, I waddle awkwardly, but quickly, into the bathroom. I flick a switch and the room floods with light. I wince slightly as my eyes adjust. The mirror above the sink reveals a sad truth. I'm alone, with my cock in my hand, too scared to confront a puny human female.

What have I become, what has she made me into?

I'm too close to care. I grab her discarded blue thermal bandages. Balling them up in my fist, I slide them down my length.

Two more rough jerks are all it takes, and I come into Marta's clothing.

With a frustrated grunt, I throw the garment into the corner of the room.

I feel no relief. If anything, the smell of my cum on her clothing, mixing our scents together, makes me hard again.

I lean against the wall, slowly stroking. My cock is oversensitive, but I can't help myself. I stomp over to the dirty clothing and hold it just under my nose. Imagining filling Marta with my seed and having it drip from her swollen cunt, has me coming again in record time.

I will get no sleep tonight.

CHAPTER 15
☆MOURNING WOOD☆

☆MARTA

I AM SMALL AGAIN, *sitting on the shore and playing on the beach.. Frustration overwhelms me as I kick at a castle. The chunky shell-filled sand doesn't form the neat towers seen in movies.*

I look into the waves, expecting to see my mother swimming in the water.

"The ocean makes me feel free, the vastness of it, the life teeming just under the surface—it's like another world, something far away from the troubles on land," she would tell me when I asked why we spent every summer at the beach.

My eyes scan the horizon, but I still can't find her.

I blink.

I'm an adult, laying in my bedroom. Bruno's gray and scarred head rests gently on my chest. Soft puppy snores puff from his lips.

I'm happy and safe—I am home.

I blink.

I sit by my father's side, his lip trembles and he tries to keep the burgeoning tears at bay.

Mom's right in front of us, in her favorite white dress. Her chest is unmoving—her skin is unnatural and waxy. The makeup she's wearing isn't right either. She always wore a red lip.

She's in a light blue coffin, with her dark curls arranged on a silky white pillow, her lips are painted a pink that's not a color she wore. Everything in this church feels wrong, the lights are too bright and organ music is too loud.

A hand tugs my own.

"Marta," my father says, "Marta, wake up."

I open my eyes. My hand is twisted up in a blanket and I'm covered in sweat. I shake it from my grip and shoot up.

I haven't dreamed about Mom in a long time, but I'm grateful my subconscious didn't sprinkle in bad memories of Bruno.

As terrible as it is to think, her death hurts less than Bruno's right now. The wound of having to euthanize my sweet pup is just too fresh.

I grab the robe from the nearby chair and stand, tying the belt. Thankful to have this weird icy alien water so close at hand, I grab the frosted pitcher from its lighted pad and pour it into a tall, thin glass.

When the water hits my mouth, I am instantly restored. I gulp it down quickly, not realizing how dehydrated I must have been yesterday. I pour another glass and drink half of it before my thirst is quenched.

But after chugging all that water, I face a new problem. I have to pee.

Setting the glass back on the table, I suddenly become nervous. The feeling of having to walk into the duke's bedroom to get to the bathroom reminds me of the anxiety of being the first kid awake at a sleepover.

Maybe I would have eventually gotten over that fear, but after Mom died, Dad stopped letting me spend the night anywhere—not even my cousin's home was deemed safe enough.

The adrenaline of yesterday seems to have worn off. I'm

feeling a bit more like myself now, and despite this bizarre situation I find myself in, I'm glad for it.

I pull my shoulders back, take a deep breath, and take my first step into the duke's dark chambers. The curtains are pulled, thankfully, and I tiptoe across the room.

It's not so much that I care if the duke hears me, or that I'm worried about his sleep—but I just don't want to deal with that asshole right now. I want to pee and slide back under the covers again.

Halfway across the room, when I'm at the foot of his bed, I pause. I look at his massive body, twisted in his sheets much like my hand was this morning.

Just like me, Raf'ere sleeps in the nude.

His skin is a patchwork of light grays, the mottled coloring lighter on his chest. He's on his back, one of his muscular arms flexed behind his head.

The glow of the lantern in my room flows into the duke's chambers. As the light moves, it catches iridescent scales that dot the duke's high cheekbones. They look like glittering freckles, and I hate to admit that the duke is a strange kind of handsome.

Even the scarring on his face that twists down his shoulder and onto his chest is beautiful. Like the roots of some ancient tree. The injury he sustained must have been a serious one, though, to have left marks that deep.

I can't help but let my eyes trail lower to his cock. I don't know much about alien dick, but it's safe to say he's hard. The huge shaft stands proudly, engorged and blue. His hand cups his sac protectively as he sleeps—men are men no matter the planet, I guess.

The frills and webbing pattern on its head resemble the delicate design on his ears—his cock kind of reminds me of an umbrella. Maybe aliens also have morning wood, considering it has to be close to sunrise.

Sure, he's got a weird dick—but can I blame Stockholm syndrome for the tingling feeling between my legs? Or is it just that my orgasm, no matter how embarrassing, felt really fucking good yesterday?

I wonder what he'd feel like inside of me—

"Are you going to stare at my cock all morning then, human?" the duke says at full volume without opening his eyes.

"I...uh." My feet start moving, knowing I won't be able to come up with a lie. "I had to pee, I was just making sure you were asleep!"

The bed groans as he shifts behind me. "I'm sure, and the fact that your arousal scent is choking out any other smell in the room isn't any indication of what you were actually doing."

Fuck, he can smell that?

I'm closing the bathroom door when I hear him laugh. "Make sure to keep it down if you're going to touch yourself again. I know the view was motivating enough." His deep voice booms through the door.

He's such an asshole, I think as I sit on the alien-sized commode.

After finishing my business, I sulk back to my closet-slash-bedroom and get all the way under the blankets. I hide my face because I'm still incredibly fucking embarrassed that he can smell me get turned on.

Girl, be for fucking real, you literally jerked off in his arms—how can you be embarrassed that he can smell your arousal?

That was my choice, but having no control over him knowing every time I get the tiniest bit turned on? It makes me want to never show my face again.

Light floods through the weave of my blanket and I pop my head out. The duke turned on the main lights in his bedroom, and I assume he's getting ready to start his day.

I pray he leaves quickly, to let me stew in my embarrassment alone.

My hopes are dashed when his figure looms in the doorway, blocking every bit of light beyond the glow emitted by my alien lava lamp.

"What did you do?" he seethes.

I pull my chin over the edge of the blanket, narrowing my brows.

"What are you talking about? I got up to pee, you yelled at me, I peed and came back to bed."

His fist juts out, clenching the intricate robe I wore yesterday. He points to the beading on the shoulders.

"How did you manage to destroy the beading?" He's actually mad about some stupid robe?

"Listen," I say, clutching my hand over the blanket where my makeshift cornicello sits on my chest. "There's this thing, Italians have it, it's kind of like a good luck charm. Those beads look just like it…"

"You destroyed a four-hundred-cycle-old ceremonial garment for a good luck charm?" A vein pops on his forehead, as if he can't believe what he's hearing.

"I didn't know it was some ancient artifact—I was scared!" I sit up to yell better. "Why would you let me wear some priceless heirloom?"

He doesn't answer me but storms out of the room and leaves his anger in his wake.

Angry? He's not allowed to be angry at me! I didn't know. Christ, I was barely functioning when I fell out of my cryopod.

I stand, ready to give him a piece of my mind. To yell at him to let me go if I'm such an annoyance.

But when I step into his bedroom, I barely catch the door closing behind him to the hallway.

The towering wall of water to my right has me frozen. I don't know how long he'll be gone. I turn my back to the ocean and shuffle over to the door that leads out of this room.

My hand touches the handle, and hope swells in my chest as I jiggle it.

The latch doesn't click, and I feel stupid for thinking my kidnapper wouldn't have locked the door behind him.

My back stiffens as the handle moves and I hear the locking mechanism engage.

I take a few steps backwards, my heel hitting the edge of the rug, and fall flat on my ass.

The door opens, and it's not the duke who stands in the doorway at all. It's a woman. She's wearing the same white dress I am—although the dress fits her alien proportions like a glove.

Her hair is long, a white braid swinging against her back, and her elegant, elongated fingers hold a keycard of some sort.

She has the key.

The alien woman's eyes widen in surprise, and her gaze locks onto me, as if trying to decipher my presence.—her mouth opening and closing a few times before any words escape it.

"Are you a placement from the palace?" she asks, still incredibly confused.

"What palace? This one? Is this a palace?" I scramble to my feet. I want to get more information out of this woman. Maybe she'll even help me escape.

"Um, well yes…but it's normally referred to as the Liin'gan Reef estate. I'm sorry, are you new to the staff? I don't think I was notified of a new employee, and certainly not a human one…" She trails off, looking at my white dress, which I now assume is some kind of uniform.

"I don't work here."

"Then what are you doing in the duke's chambers? Why are you wearing the uniform?" Her tone is suspicious.

I take a deep breath and drop what I assume is going to be a bomb. "I'm from Earth," I tell her, maybe a little dramatically.

"Yeah, I didn't know there were other options for humans. I don't care where you came from—if you don't tell me exactly what you're doing here, I'll call security." The alien woman gives me an incredulous look, puts her hand on her hip, and pulls a small tablet device from her pocket.

"No! You don't have to do that. In fact, maybe you can help me get out of here?" I know I'm coming off a little manic, but she's my first shot at escape since my failed Molotov cocktail.

"Help you…escape?" she asks slowly, her eyes wide and her brows raised. "Escape from what?"

I can already tell this is going to go badly.

"From the duke. He's holding me captive."

CHAPTER 16
☆YOU CAN'T ALWAYS GET WHAT YOU WANT☆

☆RAF'ERE

THE ANDJIN MALE in front of me won't stop shifting the color of his skin, and it's putting me on edge. His natural hide, yellow with blue rings, flashes and then suddenly he's the dark black of the tr'ael stone wall and then to the cool teal of the ocean biofilm window.

I know it's something he can't control, but I'm annoyed all the same. I hope my scars make them as uncomfortable as I am right now.

The fi'len male on my side glares at me. Gra'eth hates me because I made a pass at his now mate—but is it my fault if he had not yet staked a claim? I might be too weak to admit that Marta is my mate, but I'll be damned if I allow her near another unmated male—or anyone, for that matter. She is mine, and mine alone.

Humans, like Gra'eth's mate Jessy, don't seem to appreciate the bluntness that fi'len females do sexually. I've found that my confidence can blur the severity of these scars within my own species.

"King Ke'ain, Duke Raf'ere, and Hand Gra'eth." The Andjin

Emperor acknowledges us but doesn't follow fi'len royal protocol. Although I assume he considers us peers and feels as though no respect is due.

"Emperor Sutokal," Ke'ain says, matching his energy. My king turns to the emperor's attendant, nodding his acknowledgement.

"King Ke'ain, we appreciate you meeting us on such short notice," the attendant says, gesturing for us to sit.

"Of course. The fi'len want to uphold our peace treaty, we never wish to war with the Andjin people again. What can we do for you?" Ke'ain asks coolly.

Being the king suits him. He's much more levelheaded than his late and greedy father. Ke'ain is thankfully here without his wife. He wed and mated a human woman named Opal, who is now my queen.She is abrasive at the best of times, although I'd never tell Ke'ain that.

Her belly is swollen with the heir to the throne. Despite her protesting, Ke'ain had convinced her to commit to the fi'len nesting period. She's not to leave the palace until she gives birth but is waited on hand and foot. I know it must pain him to be away from her, but he's playing it cool.

I know because I have a mate and every time I close my eyes, all I see is her face.

Despite the fact she destroyed a priceless heirloom, I still can't bring myself to stay angry with her.

"We wish to discuss the human women," the emperor says plainly.

"What have we to discuss about my wife's people?" Ke'ain is already feeling defensive about his question.

I admit that I am too. What do the Andjin need with the humans? The Andjin are a very insular community. We assumed that it would be a matter of great importance if they were even leaving the Korlyan Moon to begin with.

"A Deenz ship dumped cyropods and security bubbles into our seas not long ago—"

"We'd be happy to let them come to Sontafrul 6 as refugees," Ke'ain interrupts.

"Yes, we're structuring many programs to help acclimate the women to how the rest of the universe operates. It's not an easy task, but we're building the framework to facilitate former bubble dancer's introduction into our society," Gra'eth adds.

"You misunderstand me," the emperor continues. "We don't wish to bring the humans to your planet—we want you to send them to ours." He crosses his arms.

"Why would we send humans to the Korlyan Moon?" I ask.

"Like I said, we already have a few human women that have been integrated into our society."

"What do you mean, integrated?" The corner of Gra'eth's mouth ticks upward.

"I mean, human women have been mated to Andjin citizens. Our gender disparity threatens the continuation of our species. Our mating rite, the great proving, grows smaller each year as fewer and fewer females are born," he says matter-of-factly.

"Did you…force them?" Ke'ain asks, his jaw clenched.

"Of course not." The emperor pulls back his lips in a sneer. "Might I remind you that 'The Fi'len Butcher' sits to your right? We are not the monsters here. We pride ourselves on a peaceful existence and would never harm a female." The emperor inclines his head to me.

It's me, I'm their butcher. The Andjin have twisted the fight for my life into propaganda—I want to laugh and tell him how wrong he is. But if they want to see me as their butcher, then let them.

"No human women will be sent to the Korlyan Moon, I can assure you of that." I cross my arms and lean further back into my chair.

"For the first time, I think I'm going to agree with Duke Raf'ere," Gra'eth says incredulously. "Did you think we would traffic women to your planet as mates?"

The emperor slides a hand over his face, obviously frustrated at the direction of the conversation.

"We won't force anyone to go, but we can make the women at the Earth Two dormitories aware of their options," Ke'ain, ever the mediator, finally weighs in. "If the women want to go to the Korlyan Moon, it is their own decision."

"No," I say simply.

"No?" Ke'ain raises his brows. "I remind you of your station, dear cousin—*I am the King.*"

His words are final, leaving no room for further discussion. What if Marta had been given the option to leave Sontafrul 6? She surely would have gone off world, to try to find a way back to Earth—she would have left me.

I close my eyes for a moment, a vision of Marta floats behind my lids. Her faces of anger, stubbornness, sadness, and pleasure infiltrating my every thought.

Am I as ungrateful to the goddess for my human mate as I keep telling myself? It's only day two of even having her awake in my world…but I can't imagine her leaving. Not even after she destroyed the ceremonial robes.

Even if I am grateful, it doesn't mean she makes me any less frustrated.

"Last I heard, you wanted to ship the entirety of the crashed Deenz ship's cyropods off world. You said humans are nothing but a tax burden." He imitates my voice in a less than flattering light. "What's changed?"

Just the human I've kidnapped and am keeping hostage in my bedroom—Marta has changed everything.

I can't tell them that. They would force me to let her go if that's what she wanted.

I'm not ready to do that.

"Send them to the planet that did this to me?" I point to my face, and Gra'eth visibly winces. "If I had any power to forbid it, I would. Humans might be a stress on our system, but none are deserving of this level of mutilation."

The Andjin emperor slams a fist on the table. "We would never harm potential mates! War is war, but those women would be a treasured part of Andjin society, and you know it!" He stares me down. The two longer tentacles on his head, what they call the fore tentacles, twitch violently.

I stand, unafraid of the consequences of decking the emperor of a planet across the jaw.

Somehow, his request for human women feels like a direct threat. As though he'll come and steal Marta from me in the middle of the night.

As the emperor stands, I roll my suit sleeve up, not wanting to bloody the bespoke cuff embroidery.

"Enough!" Ke'ain waves both the emperor and me off. "As king of this planet, my word should be final. Raf'ere, sit down and behave, or I'll have you removed. I've said I will let the human women know your planet is an option. The rest is up to them. We will contact you should we have anyone take us up on your generous offer. Can we agree to that?"

"I agree to the terms, if you allow me to have a pair of Andjin dignitaries at the palace to speak to the women. I don't trust the fi'len to paint Korlyan Moon's citizens in a kind light."

"Deal. We'll set up a space for your dignitaries. I'll have Gra'eth draw up the necessary plans."

Ke'ain extends a hand, which the emperor takes. On their shake, the deal is sealed.

There are no customary exchanges of goodbyes when the Andjin leave, neither party wanting to prolong the meeting.

The meeting breaks, and as soon as the Andjin pair are out of sight, Gra'eth leans in closely to King Ke'ain's ear.

"You do know Opal is going to kill you now, don't you?" he whispers.

"She'll understand eventually. The human women didn't have control of their fates when they were abducted. It's just as unjust to force them to stay with us if they want to go to the

Korlyan Moon. They all have to make that choice as individuals," Ke'ain reassures his friend.

"A little force is needed at times, cousin," I say.

He turns to me, putting a hand on my shoulder.

"Raf'ere, one day when you have a mate, you'll understand that subtlety is just as important. I, for one, can't wait until that day." My face must drop, because Ke'ain tilts his head to the side. "She will be worth the wait."

I shrug his hand off my shoulder.

If he only f'teeing knew.

CHAPTER 17

☆A FRIEND OF MY ENEMY☆

☆MARTA

THE ALIEN WOMAN just stares at me, mouth agape, as I tell her everything I can about my situation.

Well, almost everything. I leave out about how I came in his arms, and I got caught looking at his dick—we'll blame cryosleep mood swings and stress, right?

"His Royal Highness, Duke Raf'ere of the Liin'gan Reefs, has kidnapped you?" She raises a brow.

"Yep, you got it!" I force a smile.

"And he won't let you leave…but you don't know why?"

"Well, he said it's not safe out there for humans, and that he's protecting me by keeping me here…but that's bullshit, right?" I want to catch him in his little lie.

"Well, I mean, he's not 100 percent wrong—but why wouldn't he just send you to the palace?" She crosses her arms, looking up, as if she's trying to figure out why he wouldn't do something so obvious.

"Aren't we in the palace?" I need more information.

"No, the king's palace. You're at the Liin'gan Reefs estate," she says, as if I have any idea on the lay of the land here.

There's a king? My head is swimming.

"Take me there, please!" I beg, hoping he'll help me.

I look into the open hall, making sure the coast is clear in case we need to run. As I approach the alien woman, she puts her hands up in the air, halting my movements.

"Woah, the palace is all the way on the other side of Sontafrul 6. It's not like I can just covertly call a cruiser and shuttle you there like that." She puts her hand on her hip and changes her tone to one more challenging. "Why should I believe you over the duke…maybe you're not who you say you are? I mean, what does a small thing like you have that the duke even wants?" She glares at me.

What does the duke want? I know what he wants, I know he can smell it, I know he pretends not to watch me. Why else would you keep someone in your bedroom? My only confusion is why he's been waiting to take what he wants. I no longer think he'd hurt me, at least not physically. But I won't pretend I can't tell he's *interested* in me.

Maybe it's part of his game? His butler didn't seem surprised to see me, to say the least.

Can I tell the alien in front of me what I think? That the duke has kidnapped me and the only thing I can think that he could possibly want…is my body?

Would I let him have it? I shake the thought from my mind.

I open my mouth but close it quickly. In the end I don't have to tell her—women, no matter the species, can sense that kind of distress. Her eyebrows shoot up.

"Oh goddess." A flash of recognition sweeps her face. "It can't be, there's no f'teeing way that both the king and the duke…" Her face screws up in disappointment.

"The king and the duke what?" I ask, still confused. Did the king take a human woman hostage too?

The alien woman jerks her head to the side as we both hear footsteps in the hallway.

"I can't help you, I'm sorry." She goes to close the door, but I put my arm out, halting its closure.

"Please," I beg as her eyes dart from the hall to me.

"Far'ep?" I can hear the butler's voice carry from down the hall. "Far'ep...what are you doing? You were given explicit orders to stay clear of the duke's chambers. This is unacceptable —" Jen'si's voice trails off as he sees me.

I give him the same puppy dog eyes. *Please, just let me go.*

"Far'ep, pack your belongings. I'll have a cruiser escort you off premises shortly," the old alien tells her.

"What? I didn't do anything," she blusters.

"You violated a direct order from His Grace, the Duke. You're being terminated." He keeps his eyes on me as he dismisses Far'ep.

She huffs, balling her fists to her side. Giving me one last glare, she stomps away. Jens'i's eyes soften as he takes my hand and guides me back into the room. He deposits me into the duke's easy chair.

"I was coming by to see if there's anything I can get for you?"

"Help me escape?" I say softly, with a grimace.

"I can do many things for you, Marta, but that's not one of them. Perhaps some dinner? The duke sent word he'll be back much later than expected, so unfortunately, you'll be dining alone." The butler clasps his hands as he waits for my response.

"Dinner would be good, but Jens'i?"

"Yes? I'm happy to be of service however I can." He beams in my direction.

"Will you, can you just sit with me for a while?"

Jens'i's face grows pensive, but his smile quickly returns.

"If you'll allow me a break in etiquette, I'd be happy to have my dinner with you."

I'm not sure if I would call Jens'i a friend, but given my circumstances, he's certainly not an enemy...that might be as close to a friend as I get here.

CHAPTER 18
☆STILL A MONSTER☆

☆RAF'ERE

I STILL THINK it's ridiculous that we must humor sending the humans to the Korlyan Moon. Just the thought that Marta might have chosen to go off world, that I would have never met her, has an ache building in my chest.

That sharp pain reminds me that despite how hard I try to rationalize what I'm doing with her, my motives for keeping her locked up. That no matter how altruistic I convince myself Marta's captivity is, I keep her locked in my room for selfish reasons.

And the longer I'm around her, the more I want exactly what the bond wants.

As I approach the doors to my bedroom, my body reacts to the faintest whiff of her scent. My pulse quickens as I'm sure my chest is flushing blue. I try to control the biological response with measured breathing as I hold my data pad up to unlock the door.

I hesitate for a moment, realizing that she'll likely be angry with me. After all, the last time we interacted, my frustrated mating bond amplified my justified anger over the destruction of my heirloom robe.

Will I attempt to smooth her ruffled feathers, or will I meet her anger with more of my own? There's no way to know which direction the scales will tilt while standing in the hallway.

Pushing open the door, I peek my head around the corner. The main chamber is dark, save for the soft moonlit ocean beyond my window and the small glow of the lantern in Marta's room.

It's late, maybe she's already asleep? I can feel my stomach drop slightly at the idea I'll get no contact with her tonight. Even in her anger, I find some pull.

But that's when I hear it—something I'm sure wouldn't be audible to human ears. My hearing is much more refined, though, and I catch a soft whimpering and sniffing coming from behind the cracked closet door.

Marta is crying, and it's the only sound I can focus on. The nerves of my gills prickle, and there's a pressure in my chest. Because of the bond, her pain is my pain.

I use one finger to gently push the cracked door wider. Marta is curled on her bed, wrapped in a sheet, and clinging to a pillow. Her face is buried into its down as her back heaves.

"Are you alright?" I inquire, already knowing that her sadness isn't a physical pain.

She freezes, maybe unaware I had even returned, and turns her head to me. My mate's face is puffy and red, her cheeks tear streaked, and the pillow damp from where her face had just been.

"Of course I'm not, what part of any of this is okay?" She swipes her fingers under her eyes and sits, pulling the sheet up and tucking it under her armpits for modesty. "And why the hell do you care? You're the one holding me hostage."

I look away from her, the pit of my stomach tightening at the word hostage. She's not wrong, though. I won't let her leave, I can't.

But I don't know what to do if she stays. I'll never convince her to love me. Why should she? I'm disfigured, I am an alien to her, and she just wants to go home.

"I won't hurt you. You are safe here with me, I wasn't lying before. I won't go back on my word." I don't bother disputing the fact that I am holding her hostage.

"How can I believe you? I've seen your eyes when we get close…if that's what you want, what's stopping you, huh?" She scowls, and her tone is a bitter one.

What I want? I cock my head at her, confused. But as I stare, she pulls the sheet around her even tighter.

Oh goddess…she thinks that I would force her to…

"No fi'len would ever do such a thing, ever, not even to our worst enemy. Mat—Females are treasured in our society…I could never do that to you, ever. The thought makes me f'teeing sick I—" I ramble, my head hurting that she thinks I could ever do such a thing.

"Then why are you keeping me, why can't I leave? Why am I a secret?" Her eyes narrow, the frustration visible on her face.

Because I can't let you go, because my body burns for you every second—I want to scream. But I can't, I can't face her rejection.

If Marta was only a fi'len, if she could feel the bond too, it would be easier.

But she can't, and she never will, and I won't let her go.

"Because it's not safe for humans off Earth, you're under my jurisdiction here and—"

"It's just the same shit, different planet. I was trapped on Earth, I'm trapped here. I don't even have Bruno to make it tolerable. Am I doomed to be trapped forever? Will I never have my own freedom?" Marta isn't speaking to me anymore. Her hands fly as she speaks, looking down at her lap.

Trapped on Earth? I'm confused, but I gesture to the chair near her bed.

"May I sit?"

Marta shrugs. "Like I could stop you?"

I don't want to fight with her, so I leave that statement floating between us.

"What do you mean, you were trapped on Earth?" I sit near her, and every cell in my body urges me to touch her. Instead, I clasp my hands tightly on the tops of my thighs.

"I mean trapped, that's what I mean." She doesn't want to elaborate. Marta sniffs, wiping her hand under her nose.

"I don't understand, Marta…did someone keep you and— were you forced to…" I want to vomit at the thought of anyone putting their hands on her—but something inside me needs to know.

"No, god, not that—My father is, well he's, he's important."

"Important, how so? How would that trap you?"

Marta looks up, her mouth pulled into a thin line.

"God, I guess it doesn't matter anymore, does it? What's the point in keeping the secret—it's not like the spacefeds are gonna go get him, right? My father is the leader of an organized crime racket. He's good at it, too. Our branch of la familia is a strong one." She takes a deep breath and leans back against the head-board. "But it doesn't mean there weren't challengers or vendettas that needed to be fulfilled. I was always at risk. Our area of orbit was limited to certain spots in the city, and always under guard. There are men ruthless enough to kill the children of their enemies as a power move." She's talking fast, and I don't understand every word, but I get the gist. Her father holds his power with fear, like a warlord.

"Why would he do it, why would he risk his family?" The thought of doing something to put your mate or your children at risk in my culture is unfathomable. What good is power if you lose everything that's actually important?

"You can't just leave once you're a made man, it's not an option…I have never lived a normal life. I've always been held back by the decision of men who tell me they want to protect me." She sets her jaw, a look of defeat on her face.

Silence hangs between us for what feels like a beat too long.

"I understand not being in control of your life, of your destiny," I whisper. If I was a stronger male, I would put my hand over hers. I would comfort her.

"You're a duke, you seem like you do whatever the fuck you want here."

She doesn't believe me.

I suck in a deep breath, not sure why I'm going to tell her about how wrong she is. Maybe I just need to tell someone, anyone. Will it feel better just to say it aloud?

"I thought I was in love once, before the war." It wasn't love, but in my youthful foolishness, I didn't know any better.

Marta turns to look me in the eyes, and she seems surprised at my admission.

"What does that have to do with anything?"

"Yar'oh promised she loved me back, and that we didn't need to wait for the mate bond. That if we loved each other enough, it wouldn't matter. I believed her." I haven't said her name in over fifteen cycles, but it doesn't sting as much as it did before Marta.

"Mate bond?"

"The fi'len have a biological mechanism. Our body chemistry works to attach us to each other. It's supposed to only trigger when the perfect partner is present…but I'm not sure I believe in that." I simplify it, unable to look at her as I talk. I want to believe in the bond, in Marta, in the goddess.

"So, what happened?" Marta's voice is cautious, but her interest is piqued.

"The war…this," I gesture to my mutilated face. "I didn't want to go, but I had lost my parents, the former duke and duchess, in the first round of the plague. I was the only representative from the Reefs who could lead our troops. They are my responsibility alone. I couldn't just leave them, I love my people." *Yar'oh begged me to stay. To send someone else in my stead.* "I was trapped by my duty."

"Oh," she whispers, finally understanding what I meant.

"When I came home, Yar'oh didn't want me. I guess no amount of money could make her look past what I'd become."

"What do you mean by what you've become?" Marta's brown eyes search my visage as if she can't see the deep grooves on the side of my face.

"My scars…"

"Oh those, they aren't that bad—she seems like a bitch, bullet dodged." Marta says the statement so nonchalantly that I don't know what to do.

It's not that bad? It's bad enough for a beautiful, young fi'len woman to cancel our wedding. I leave out the part where her mother and father, who were prominent dignitaries from the Ram'bola Steppes, brought her back to the estate and begged her to reconsider.

"You can look past his face, darling, can't you? Look, look at all this splendor. Surely His Grace the Duke will treasure a beauty such as you. Think of your future…think of your family!" her mother begged.

If I had been stronger, I wouldn't have let them in. But Yar'oh held my hearts captive. I could stomach bribing her to marry me—but it wasn't enough. My injury was still fresh as I tried as hard as I could to smile. I moved the muscles of my face until they seared with pain.

"He's ruined, Mother, my beautiful Raf'ere is gone. Just let me leave!"

She didn't address me once, casting her eyes down to the ground. All the while, her mother gripped her wrist, trying to drag her to me. Yar'oh twisted and flailed, trying desperately not to approach me.

"It's not so bad, my dear, and in time they'll fade."

When her mother wrenched her chin up, she winced.

"I can't marry a monster like him! What will everyone think? I'll be the laughingstock of Sontafrul 6…"

I shake my head, willing the painful memory to stop.

"You know, she's not the only one who called me a monster." I call her bluff—*not that bad,* my ass.

"Oh god, I didn't mean it like that," Marta says, rolling her eyes. "It's like you've forgotten that humans don't know aliens actually exist. Ugh, I've never seen anything like you." She gestures at me aggressively with her hand.

"Still a monster, though," I chide.

"Dude, you have gills. Your skin is gray, and you're damn near like seven and half feet tall...I panicked. I take it back, happy?" She seems angry that I'm harping on this point. "I'm sorry she did that to you though," she adds a little more kindly, maybe sensing my discomfort.

At the same time, I don't understand why she's trying to downplay my scars. She has no reason to be nice to me.

I don't want to think about it anymore.

"Who is Bruno? Was he your mate on Earth?"

Marta's brows furrow and her mouth screws to the side.

"Mate? No, Bruno *was* my dog...he was my best friend," Marta's voice cracks when she says his name.

Dog. A four-legged animal covered in hair, a wagging tail, neck encircled in a collar.

Bruno was an animal companion. I internally sigh in relief.

"We don't have many pets here. We have a few, but they've always seemed somewhat superfluous to me."

"But that lace cravat isn't? For someone who dresses like you do, you don't have much room to call anything superfluous." She chortles before telling me sadly, "He was more than a pet, I miss him so fucking much."

There's a moment of silence between us. Maybe we're both still grieving something we can't have. Me for my life before my injury, her for a pet on Earth.

"So, why did you call me Bruno? Do I look like a dog to you, then?" I am curious about her first reaction to me.

"No...well, yes, kind of?" She seems confused. "You and Bruno are the same gray color. He had scars too—people had done terrible things to him." She gulps. "But he still loved me right away, that's how great dogs are. They don't need you to prove your worthiness. They love unconditionally, no matter how horrible their past is. Even if you don't deserve it." Her eyes get glassy and red again. I hate seeing her like this. I'd rather she be angry than this.

"I'm sure he'll be alright without you. We don't have dogs here, but from what my translator chip showed me, they seem like decent predators. I have no doubt Bruno was able to fend for himself," I say, hoping it will smooth over her burgeoning sadness.

"Bruno is dead. As much as I miss him, I won't have to worry about if he's being cared for on Earth," she whispers.

"What happened?"

"He got sick, too sick to get better." Her voice warbles as she continues. "So I just loved him until the day came where I couldn't keep him comfortable anymore. Once the cancer had progressed too far, I euthanized him. I just didn't want him to suffer." Her whimpering returns and quickly turns into choking sobs.

As her body shutters, my defenses drop, and I wrap my arms around her.

Marta stills, her back straightening as she holds her breath.

I should release her from my grip, I should keep up the facade of disinterest—but her broken heart is breaking mine. I am not stronger than the bond.

I turn my face to hers, our lips hovering a hairsbreadth away from each other.

I want to grab her face, to press my lips into hers, to probe the depths of her mouth with my tongue.

But this isn't the right time.

"You must have been very strong to let someone you loved go," I say to the top of her head. "Bruno knew he was loved, I'm sure of it."

As if that statement breaks the last bit of her resistance, she wiggles her arms under mine and squeezes me like a vise. Her crying gets worse, but I don't think she's holding anything back now.

She sobs against my chest with no restraint. I stroke my hand down her hair and pull her harder against me.

We stay like that for a long time. Eventually Marta cries herself to sleep, slumping against me in exhaustion.

Cradling the back of her head, I lay her against the pillow and pull the blanket high under her chin.

Standing, my mind wanders as I take in the sight of her snuggled into bed.

Could I let Marta go? If it would truly make her happy? Would I be strong enough?

CHAPTER 19
☆CURTAIN CALL☆

MY EYES ARE dry and angry at how hard I cried last night, like there's no way I've got any tears left to spare.

I let my fingers linger, my hands touching the parts of my biceps where Raf'ere wrapped his arms around me.

What even was that? Did he feel bad for yelling at me about the stupid robe earlier? I find it funny that a big scary alien would feel bad for me. But should I? I feel bad about myself and my current predicament. I felt like shit about Bruno.

Bruno knew he was loved. How can something be so gut punching while simultaneously comforting?

There's a shuffling from the main bedroom through the still cracked door to the closet. I wonder if he's getting ready to leave again. I was embarrassed before, and even though I don't think I have any control over it, I'm embarrassed for crying on him.

Even if it felt good. Of course, I'd cried about Bruno before, but no one had ever let me grieve so openly with them until last night. Not without some backhanded comment about a pet not being worthy of my level of sadness. It was incredibly kind of the duke.

That, in combination with his strange admission of feeling trapped, was frustrating. If he sympathized with me, why can't he let me go? Is it really that dangerous in the world outside these walls?

Would the risk of freedom even be worth it?

Even though I want to hide from all these strange lingering feelings, I feel like I have to face them—I have to face the duke. If I stand any chance at all for having a life in space, I can't keep hiding.

After throwing on my white dress, I open the door, hoping that the kind duke from last night is the one still here today. I tuck the makeshift horn necklace under its high neck.

When I swing the door fully open, I catch sight of Raf'ere admiring himself in the mirror as Jens'i fusses over some gaudy shoulder epaulets.

And when I say gaudy, as an Italian American I mean it with my whole chest. They have gold bases and are absolutely encrusted with some of the biggest emeralds I've ever seen. The gems are rough cut and stand at attention. They nearly poke Raf'ere's strange pointed ears as they sit on his shoulders. When the duke turns his head to inspect the suit, he catches me in the background.

"Marta," he says in a formal tone. Jens'i stands with a quick nod to me before leaning over again to smooth the duke's suit.

So not the vulnerable duke of last night, then. We're back to Duke Fuckface's old ways.

"Hey," I say nonchalantly.

As I appraise the rest of his ensemble, I notice things beyond the ridiculousness of the epaulettes. The suit jacket is the same dark green as most of his clothing. I wonder absentmindedly if it's his favorite color?

Cruising over to the array of plates on the coffee table, I try my hardest to avoid eye contact with his ocean window. The best part of my day here is when the butler comes in and draws the curtains shut and I can relax just a bit.

Well, that and the food. I pop a blue piece of fruit between my lips and savor its sweet taste.

"So, are you planning to be gone all day again?" I ask, with my mouth full, playing at indifference.

"I have a meeting this morning with my infrastructure chancellor, but I should be back before dinner," he says, and I think I hear what must be the final smoothing of his hands over the suit.

"Raf'ere?" I question, still with my back to him and the massive windows of water.

"Hmm?"

"Do you think maybe you could show me some other parts of the estate?" Maybe I can find an escape route if I know where I'm going—could there even be a spot shallow enough I could just float to the surface? Maybe an island?

"Well, it's customary to look someone in the eyes when making a request." His voice sounds slightly annoyed.

"Well, I would, but you know there's a terrifying ocean on display," I tell him simply, keeping my back turned, and munching on another strange yet delicious fruit.

He doesn't respond, but I can hear the whoosh of the curtains as I assume Jens'i closes them. When I turn, the curtains are closed, but it's the duke standing next to them. The duke has hidden my source of anxiety behind thick, dark green drapes. I must look surprised, because Raf'ere gives me a questioning look.

"If you wanted them closed, all you had to do was ask," he says as if it was obvious.

"Well, seeing as I keep asking to go home, I assumed no was your favorite word, *leccanculo*." I sneer and whisper the last insult under my breath.

The duke winces as I assume his translator chip shows him images of an ass licker. His hearing is better than I give him credit for.

"Closing the curtains is something within my control, letting you go is far too unsafe—I wish humans were a more reasonable species," Raf'ere says the last part to Jens'i alone. Who, to his credit, says nothing and shows no approval for the duke's remark. "But to answer your second question, yes. I had planned to take you to the estate chapel, so tonight is as good a night as any to do so."

I nearly fall out of my chair with the force at which I roll my eyes when he puts on another accessory. Honestly, this alien gives my great-aunt Teresa a run for her money on tackiest in the room. And she thinks it's alright to mix animal prints because "they're neutrals."

I bite my tongue, and I hate to admit it, but I'm anxious to see more of this new world after days of being stuck in this room. It's just my luck that I travel to space and the only thing I've seen is the inside of a closet.

"What's the chapel like? Is it far?" I feel like a kid ready to go on her first field trip.

With her alien kidnapper.

But I'm still excited.

"We'll talk details when I return. I'm already late." There's a beat where we both look at each other, like he's expecting me to say *see you later, babe,* or something.

But he clears his throat when I don't say a word and leaves the room quickly, his little alien iPhone in hand. Jens'i follows him but turns to me right before he clicks the door shut.

"There are some new garments for you folded by the duke's bed. I'll be by with luncheon later, Marta."

The door clicks shut after that, and I'm left alone again. I eye the pile of folded clothing on the duke's nightstand and head over to get a closer look at my new wardrobe.

It's as gaudy as the duke's.

Don't get me wrong, I enjoy a statement piece as much as the next gal, but there isn't an article that isn't dripping in accouterments. Beading, gilt threads, honest-to-god emeralds stitched into intricate designs.

It's beautiful, but it's too fucking much.

After sorting through the heavy and uncomfortable looking fabrics, I'm able to find a dark green slip under one of the gowns. I pair it with a simpler sheer brown wrap meant to go over a shorter dress that's so heavy with beads that I can barely lift it up.

Standing in front of the duke's enormous dressing mirror, I shuck off my ill-fitting white dress.

As I slide on the green slip, the fabric feels incredibly smooth on the inside. When I pull it gently over my hips, I realize it fits me better than anything I've ever worn. There's none of the usual tugging to get things over my ample butt.

It's like the garments are custom made for me, which they have to have been given how small I am in comparison to the maid I met yesterday.

The thin straps don't fall off my shoulders and when I place the sheer topper over the slip, I'm just a little impressed at the silhouette it creates.

A little editing goes a long way. I think of the duke's own ridiculous wardrobe.

"All dressed up and nowhere to go," I say to my reflection, admiring how nice I look.

I collect the dress I wore this morning from the floor and pick up the remaining new clothes from beside Raf'ere's bed.

As I lift the heavy stack, one of the beaded appliqués catches the knob of Raf'ere's nightstand drawer, and it slides open as I walk backward.

If I wasn't so nosy, I would shut it and be polite.

God, is my Stockholm syndrome really that bad? Why would I ever need to give my actual kidnapper that courtesy? If anything, maybe there will be a keycard or some alien phone I can steal.

So, I set the clothes back down and snoop.

The black drawer is lined with a green felted material. Placed neatly in rows are devices of all shapes and sizes. By some of the ones with more phallic shapes, these must be sex toys.

After copping a peek at Raf'ere's cock, I can say they're

modestly sized for an alien…but still really big if you're a human. I never got into sex toys much on Earth. I was always a "use the shower head" to get the job done kind of gal.

But as I look over the second stash of sex toys Raf'ere keeps in his room, I'm curious. *Hell, what else is there to do?* Everything in the drawer is immaculately clean and shining—thank god.

There's a metal collar and placed in its center is a remote. I pick them both up, holding one in each hand. I can't read the alien's written language, so I have no idea what the buttons do.

Does that stop me from pressing one? Sure the fuck it doesn't.

When I click one of the buttons, my hand instantly is cold. The fine hairs on my arm rise followed by a swath of goosebumps.

"Woah," I say aloud, not expecting the collar to give me the chills.

When I depress the button next to it, heat floods through me. I drop the collar when I feel the warmth spread to my pussy.

A necklace that makes you horny at the touch of a button was not on my abducted-by-aliens bingo card. But neither was any alien sex toy.

Outer space is weird.

I place the collar back quickly, but take a moment to admire the rest of the items near it.

So many things that I have no idea what their intended purpose would be.

I can't decide if the number of sex toys this alien keeps at hand is a red flag or a green one. Could these devices really be all that much better than a shower head?

I palm a clear ball from the drawer next, wondering how this little orb was going to get me off.

I'm sure I could convince Raf'ere to show me, if it came to that.

How much can I blame these feelings on the stupid idea that I'm asserting my dominance?

I tap at the crystal sphere, trying to distract myself from the thought of Duke Fuckface using his toys on me. As soon as my finger touches the ball with any force, it sends out a purple electric shock.

"Shit!" I yelp before tossing the clear ball into the drawer and slamming it shut.

Maybe I need another shower.

CHAPTER 20
☆THE LITTLE BEAST☆

☆RAF'ERE

I STAND LOOKING at the hideous little creature as it swims behind the tank glass. Its whip-like tail pivots its body in tight little circles.

"This is the most popular companion? Are you sure?" I ask the salesperson, a young fi'len women.

"It is indeed, Your Grace. In fact, we have a waitlist for any new kahne'ah that arrive. It is considerably long." She looks at me as though she's slightly starstruck. I guess I've never frequented the companion parlor. "But for you, Your Grace, there is no waitlist," she tacks on.

I lean in close to the glass, as the small blue creature pulls itself clumsily onto the fake outcropping of rocks resting just above the surface of the water. It spies me and presses its flat snout against the glass in an attempt to smell me, which splays the two antennas coming from his wide forehead.

Would Marta like something this ugly? Its flat face is accented by huge black orbs for eyes. His short snout mostly consisted of an underbite. I worry about those predatory teeth that poke out of his bottom lip. In the water, he looked to have skin similar to my own, but blue. Now on dry land I can see that it's actually short, thick fur. It puffs up along his back as he investigates me.

"Would you like to hold him? To see if maybe this kahne'ah is a good fit for you?" She's already unlocking the top of its enclosure.

"He won't bite, will he?" I ask, dubious of those teeth.

"I mean, not if you're true of heart." She smiles like she's joking, but when I don't respond she course corrects. "No, they aren't usually aggressive unless their owner is threatened."

Well, that's a pro. At least it could protect Marta if need be.

She reaches in and the thing scrambles for her hand, almost crawling to her bicep before she even has her arm out of the enclosure.

"Who's a handsome boy?" she coos in its face as it licks her chin. "Such a pretty thing, be nice and meet His Grace, the duke."

It's still licking her neck as she pulls it free and faces it to me. Her hands are under his armpits as his back legs dangle in the air.

"Hello," I tell the blue lump, holding out my hand. He sniffs my knuckles, and I'm taken aback as the tips of his antennas light up. The blue light casts strange shadows on the creature's face.

"Oh! I think he likes you!" the shop attendant says enthusiastically. The little beast reaches for me, and she presses him into my hand until I'm forced to pick him up. He scrambles up my suit jacket and plants a wet kiss on my cheek.

"He doesn't need to like *me*," I say, pulling him just far enough back to be out of the reach of his tongue. "I'd like to purchase him for someone." He gets free of my grip and jumps on my shoulder. I'm left holding him like a youngling that needs burped.

Maybe I'm not an animal companion person, but I wince as it snorts in my ear.

"Of course! I have no doubt that Your Grace will find the

perfect owner for this sweetie. Shall I ring you out?" she asks, eager to make a sale.

"Yes, and please include any of its necessaries with the bill as well."

Her grin broadens as she grabs the kahne'ah off me. She slips him into a blue plastic crate and heads to the register.

"And who shall I register as the owner?" Her hands hover over the data pad expectantly.

"Just…Just put me as the owner."

The sales attendant tilts her head. "But aren't you giving the companion as a gift?"

"It will remain in the palace. My name is fine."

She raises her brows as she types, but I assume she enters all the pertinent information as when she's done typing, she passes me the data pad to transfer the credits.

"There must be a mistake, there's no way that little thing costs this much?" Surely, she's added a few too many zeros to the bill.

She arches an eyebrow. "It's an incredibly long waiting list, as I said, Your Grace."

I wince as I flick my finger on her screen to authorize the payment.

"Excellent! I'll have my staff deliver all his supplies to your estate." Her smile is broad as she hands me the crate. The little beast scurries around in a circle inside.

I let out a sigh as the attendant shows me to my cruiser.

Maybe it'll help Marta adjust, I find myself hoping as the kahne'ah whines and snorts insistently in my arms.

CHAPTER 21
☆NUBBINS☆

I'VE BEEN LYING on the duke's bed for the past few hours, counting the number of swirls in the ornately carved ceiling— *I'm already up to 142.*

I don't want to admit that I'm excited to hear the door lock activate. I don't even care that it's Raf'ere. Even if he makes me angry, I'll have some relief from the all-encompassing boredom that this room holds.

His hulking form backs in through the door, quickly latching and locking it behind him. He's struggling with something large and blue under his arm.

He faces me, his eyebrows shooting up before I realize I'm still on his bed. I jump to my feet, smoothing the wrinkled bedspread.

"What's that?" I ask, gesturing to the box.

His eyes rake over me. I almost forgot about my new clothing.

"You look…nice," he manages to choke out.

There's something behind his eyes, but I don't know if it's the hunger from our last meeting.

"What's in the box?" I ignore him and ask again.

"Oh this, it's a gift from one of my subjects. I'm not sure I'm going to keep it." He places the box on the floor with a disinterested sigh. "Seems like more work than it's worth, honestly."

The box moves, jiggling slightly as though something alive is inside. No, something is definitely in the box, I realize as soft grunts emanate from the slits in the blue plastic container.

"Do you want to see it?" He asks over his shoulder as he drops his data pad on the table. I kneel in front of the crate, curious.

"Is it dangerous?" I have no idea what kind of things aliens keep in crates.

"Probably not...I think," he says before unlatching the door.

My breath catches in my throat as one of the most adorable things I've ever seen waddles out of the crate.

"Oh my fucking god," I squeak out as I instinctively hold my hands out to the chunky blue creature in front of me. He's slow to approach at first, sniffing my fingertips cautiously.

He waggles closer before a purple tongue darts out of his flat snout and he licks my knuckles. He smacks his lips as if trying to decipher my motives by taste alone.

He blinks his eyes rapidly, the black dewy orbs shining, before the two antennas on his head light up. The blue light is so bright I squint my eyes a bit as they adjust.

Without much warning, he shoots toward me, his legs almost spring loaded.

"Marta!" Raf'ere shouts as he does.

But I can't bother with him, when this sweet little bean is kissing my face with wild abandonment.

"With my eyes closed, I would think this thing is part pug!" I laugh, pulling the cutie off my face and sitting to cradle him to my chest. He's covered in short, thick fur that reminds me so much of Bruno's coat. I stroke my hand down his back, and he wiggles his shoulders in pleasure.

When I open my eyes, Raf'ere is standing over me. His brows are furrowed in concern, and he pulls the little creature off me.

"He's so cute. Someone gave *you* a pet? You don't strike me as the pet type…no offense." I eye the duke, holding the creature under its armpits with straight arms.

"None taken, I'm not."

"You're not really going to get rid of it, are you? Also, what is it?"

"*He's* a very desirable animal companion, apparently, a kahne'ah."

"Aw, what a good boy!" I baby talk to the little blue lump.

"I certainly have no use for a pet—"

"Yeah, you've already got me, don't you?" I can't stop the words from escaping my lips before I realized that I just called myself *the duke's pet…* We both feel the weight of the implication of that title for a minute before he clears his throat and brings us back to the matter at hand.

"Would you want him?" the duke asks.

Do I want this absolutely adorable little alien pug to love?

"I mean sure, if you're just going to get rid of him." I try to play it cool, but I am already in love. The little guy is just so ugly, he's cute. "I don't know how to take care of him though…there's nothing weird about alien pets, is there? I don't have to feed him drops of my blood like in *Little Shop of Horrors*, do I?"

I guess Audrey II is the closest thing I know to an alien pet.

"Goddess, no. Would you feed that thing your blood?" Raf'ere's concern is only deepening at this point.

"I mean, probably not." I pause, taking in the teeth sticking out of the little alien's underbite. He squeals again when I reach to pet him. "I mean, not unless he *really* needs it."

My humor might be lost on Raf'ere, though.

"Are all humans as concerning as you are?"

"I think I'm just special," I let the sarcasm drip off my tongue.

"I don't think he's especially hard to take care of. The occasional swim and regular feeding was all I was told. His belongings are being delivered later."

"The occasional swim, huh?" I gulp.

"Oh, don't let your human emotions get the better of you." He passes me the kahne'ah. "In fact, we don't even have to see the ocean to let him swim."

"Oh really? How's that going to work?"

"The chapel, I'll show you shortly—just let me have a drink first," Raf'ere drops into his favorite easy chair and hits a button on his data pad.

"So, he's really mine?" I ask, waiting for my hopes to be crushed at any moment.

I could have a friend again. I don't have to do this alone.

"I said you could, didn't I?" His annoyance is palpable as he gives a curt reply to my repetitive questioning.

"Thank you Raf'ere!" Rushing to him in excitement, I move the water dog thing to my hip, like he's some fat toddler. I kiss the side of the duke's cheek.

"I think I'll call you Nubbins!" I say, nuzzling my nose against the space puppy's.

"Nubbins?" Raf'ere asks incredulously, his hand on his face where I kissed him as he throws back a gulp of liquor. "He's already an ugly little thing, can't you give him a dignified name?"

"He's not ugly! He's just a lil bean, huh Nubbins?" My baby talk inspires another round of wet kisses from my new pet.

"Do I have to call him *Nubbins*?"

I ignore the duke and hold the kahne'ah like a baby in my arms.

"He's always this grumpy, you know," I whisper into the pet's floppy ear.

The duke rolls his eyes and swigs the rest of the drink down.

"Well, let's take Nubbins to the chapel for a swim, shall we?"

I expect the duke to open the door to the terrifying ballroom with its glass ceiling, but he heads to the far wall and presses his palm against the molding.

A hidden door, much like the one to my room, springs out of the wall.

"How many hidden doors do you have in this place?" I ask, dumbfounded.

"That, Marta, is really none of your business, is it?" Raf'ere smirks. "After you."

He gestures into the doorway as purple lights flash on in the dark corridor. It illuminates a spiral staircase made of the same black stone as is present in most of this palace.

I approach the opening and tilt my head down. The steps seem to go on forever.

"I'm not sure Raf'ere…"

The duke groans, snatching Nubbins out of my arms.

"Hey, be careful with him!" I protest before he grabs me with his other hand and swings me over his shoulder like a sack of potatoes.

"Be careful with me, asshole!" I beat a fist against his broad muscular back.

CHAPTER 22
☆CHURCH NUDITY REQUIRED☆

☆RAF'ERE

"PUT ME DOWN!" Marta screams in my ear, all while Nubbins wiggles to kiss my face.

"Sure thing," I tell her as I drop her flat on her ass as we reach the bottom of the stairs.

"Geez Raf'ere, I can walk myself, you didn't have to—" Marta begins to complain, but she is cut short as her gaze rises to the chapel in front of her.

"What is this place?" Her eyes go wide, and her pupils dilate in the dim cavern.

I try to view the chapel with new eyes. The cavern is carved from emeralds, their jagged edges decorating the ceiling and walls. The floor is stepped with shallow pools. They're filled with the waters of I'loh, glowing and warm.

"The chapel. The waters of I'loh are fed into the pools here."

"The waters of what?" She screws her face up, not even angry with me anymore. Just in awe of her surroundings.

"The waters of I'loh…the life source of our planet. It gives us a direct connection with both the goddess and our ancestors." I kneel next to one of the shallower pools and place Nubbins into the warm waters.

Like all creatures of Sontafrul 6, including the fi'len, the kahne'ah find the waters restorative and incredibly calming. Nubbins flips onto his back and floats–his normal scurrying stopped for the moment.

"Like holy water then?" Marta moves her hand from her head to her chest then from shoulder to shoulder. It's a strange gesture, but she's always so wild with her hands that I ignore it.

"Are they deep?" Marta asks tentatively as she approaches the edge of the pool. She places a hand on my back as she leans over me to get a better look.

When she touches me, the nerves in my skin fire on overload, I want to pull her into my arms so badly. I bite the inside of my cheek to stop from grabbing her and pulling her against me.

"No," I finally say. "All except the furthest from us in the chamber. That one alone connects to the ceremonial tunnel system. The tunnels were either discovered or created by our ancestors. They are sacred and only used for the highest of ceremonies."

"What kind of ceremonies do you need an underwater tunnel for?" she asks without a hint of malice. I remind myself once again that everything is new for her, and I try to grant her the patience she deserves.

"Weddings, offerings in time of war and hunger, and to pay tribute to the goddess during our solar eclipse—just the big stuff." I try my best to summarize thousands of years of religion.

"I'm imagining a first communion underwater, and while I don't think that's quite it, I get the gist," She laughs as she sits next to me, on her knees with her feet tucked under her perfect ass. "Where does the tunnel lead?"

"To a shrine at the surface," I keep it brief. I don't really want to give her a fi'len religion lesson.

Nubbins hops back out and heads to another nearby pool. He

practically falls in but recovers quickly. The kahne'ah are much more graceful in the water than they are on land.

"Aren't you afraid of the water?" I'm surprised she's gotten this close to me. I can feel the fine hairs of her arm as our skin reacts together, creating a tiny amount of static electricity.

"Well, not this water. This is small and contained. A hot tub is very different from the entire ocean, you know?"

I guess that makes sense, but it's never something I will truly understand. The ocean is my home.

"Can I ask, is the fear of water common among your people?"

"Well, maybe? Humans are scared of lots of things…for a lot of different reasons. It's not unheard of, if that's what you mean."

"Why are you specifically afraid of the water, then?" I keep my voice soft as I reach out to her with my words. She tilts her head at me, like she's surprised I asked.

"I…well, my mother—" She looks down at her lap, running her hands over the silky slip she's taken to wearing as a dress. "My mother drowned in the ocean when I was very young." She drops any emotion and just lets the words race out. As if she's stating a simple fact.

We're both motherless children.

My mate turns her head to me, the glow of the pool casting beautiful, diffused light over her skin. Her pupils dilate.

"You're beautiful in this light, the spots on your cheekbones sparkle down here." Marta's voice is soft.

Is it possible we're feeling the same thing for each other in this moment?

Protect her, keep her.

I shuck off my jacket and shirt to the ground. Activating the auto fastener of my trousers. I slide my legs free, and ease myself into the water, letting the goddess do her best to calm me.

Marta's hands fly up to cover her eyes, as if she hasn't already admired my body while I slept.

"What are you doing?" Marta speaks through her hands, rambling uncomfortably. "You can't just skinny dip in a church!"

"Skinny dip?" I laugh at the flood of naked swimming humans that my translator chip shows me.

"Whatever you wanna call it! Naked swimming, skinny dipping, or in my case, chunky dunking." Her eyes are still covered, but she laughs nervously at her own joke.

"You know there's nothing wrong with your body, right?" In fact, it's the most perfect shape I've ever seen.

"I'm allowed to acknowledge that my body has fat without it being self-deprecating… you know that, right?" She mocks my serious tone. "Whatever you want to call it, I don't think I should be swimming in the nude at your sacred religious site, you big weirdo."

"Well, that's where our religions are different, Marta. Most of our ceremonies are done without clothing, just as the goddess made us. So get over it. I'm going to teach you to swim—you won't have to be afraid of the water anymore." I'm confident in my ability to do so.

"Oh god, you don't have to—I mean I'm not getting naked! This is stupid…" She's flustered, *and I like it.*

"You know, for someone who wasn't afraid to come in my arms, I'm surprised you're being so modest now." I raise my brows.

Even through her hands, I can see her flush that strange red color. It creeps from her cheeks down to her cleavage.

"I don't want to talk about it," she whispers.

"It seems like talking about it would be less trouble than actually doing it, but maybe that's the human condition?"

Marta groans like she's ashamed.

"How about this? You let me teach you to swim or you tell me why I caught you pleasuring yourself in my shower." I know I'm pushing it, but there's something so intoxicating about her embarrassment. Her flushed body, her fidgeting, even her little groans. I never realized how close embarrassment is to arousal on a physical level before.

"Quit making it weird. I'll do the stupid swimming lesson!" She stands, removing the sheer wrap. The hunger in my gaze must betray me, though.

"Cover your eyes, pervert," she says before removing the dress.

I obey, and I'm not sure why. The Raf'ere of old would have found a way to convince her to let me watch. He would have had some clever line—but then again, the old Raf'ere would have already had Marta in his bed.

The f'teeing mate bond drives me to protect her as much as it does to breed her.

But there's a connection between us, beyond that bond, that wasn't there before. The mate bond wouldn't have bought Marta a pet, it wouldn't have closed the f'teeing curtains.

It wouldn't have held her as she sobbed.

Whatever it is, chemical or emotional, I keep my eyes shut tight—even when the soft waves hit my chest as she enters the pool.

How has it only been a few days since she woke up in my closet?

"Okay, you can look." Her voice wavers slightly.

My lids snap open, and every fiber of my being focuses on not letting my eyes wander. The water hits Marta right at the edge of her shoulder. Even as I look at her face, I can see the swell of her breasts bobbing gently. And floating up from her cleavage is one of the beads from my ceremonial robe…a bead that she surely ripped from its design.

"A human good luck charm, eh?" I think I let the sexual frustration turn to anger when I yelled at her about the f'teeing robe.

"I don't know if it works in space," she says coolly.

"Why's that?"

"Well, I'm still here, aren't I?" She lets out a sad chuckle.

"There are worse places you could be in the universe."

She rolls her eyes and dunks her head under the surface of

the water. When she crests back up, her nipples flash briefly as she flips her soaking wet hair slick to her skull.

I'm simultaneously wondering how annoying it must be for a human's hair to hold so much water and in awe of the water sluicing down her curves. My breath catches at how her palms slide her tresses back.

I wonder what her hands would feel like on me.

She sees me looking at her. Marta gestures with two fingers to her face.

"Eyes up here, dukey," she orders.

Even though the water is glowing and clear, I hope it's enough to obscure the fast swelling of my malehood. The intense ache in my shaft longs for the touch it so desperately craves.

"I'll do my best," I say with a forced grin.

"So, how do we start?"

"Let's try treading water. I guess just start by lifting your feet and feeling how your body floats. You might be different from me, but we can adjust." I pull my heels up off the floor and sink a bit deeper into the water.

Marta sets her jaw in a look of determination before bringing her feet up off the bottom of the pool. Her head immediately sinks under the water, her arms shooting up as she panics.

I grab her hand and pull. She chokes out big gulps of the glowing water and clings to my forearm, pressing my elbow hard into the spot between her breasts.

"Why didn't you just stand up?" I scold, a little more impatiently than I should.

"Because I panicked!" Her eyes are wide, and the soles of her feet are still pulled up against her butt.

"Why aren't you standing up now?" I ask.

Marta's brows knit and she shifts her eyes quickly from side to side. She releases me before dropping her heels to the pool's bottom.

"Sorry." Her response is curt.

"Okay, so step one, if you get scared, just stand back up. Sound good?"

"Sure," she sniffles. "How the hell do you just float there?" She's frustrated already, my little human is so quick to anger.

"Like I said, our biology is likely different. We'll adjust."

Could we adjust…in all things? Could I, ruler of the Liin'gan Reefs, adjust to a human mate?

"Maybe we should switch tactics." I take her hand and guide her to the pool's edge. "Use your hands to hold on, get good use of that extra finger of yours, and kick. Feel the water pushing your body up and forward as you do."

"Just kick?" she asks apprehensively.

"Like you're trying to kick the side of the wall, the pressure of your movements against the water will push you up," I say, hoping she's not as helpless as she seems.

She takes a deep breath, gripping the edge of the pool so hard her knuckles turn white. With a little hop, she slams her foot against the wall.

"Shit!" she yelps, releasing one of her hands to grab what I'm sure is a throbbing toe.

"F'tee, human, don't actually *kick* the wall. A kicking *motion*…" I scrub my hand over my face.

"Listen, I don't know what I'm doing here!" She pouts and crosses her arms. "This isn't going to work, so we can stop."

"Do you always give up this easy?" I hit a chord somewhere inside her.

"Only when I have shitty teachers," she snipes under her breath.

"One more, human. Surely you can muster a second attempt before giving up completely."

She gives me a look of annoyance but puts her hands back on the wall.

CHAPTER 23
☆THE GEM☆

THERE'S no way I'm letting Duke Fuckface get the better of me. It's just stupid swimming—the water here is even safe and shallow.

Come on Marta, even babies can swim.

"So a kicking motion? Show me," I demand of Raf'ere.

"Point your toes down, let the water catch the top side of your foot." He demonstrates with his own legs. He's so graceful in the water that I almost miss his huge and at attention cock.

Almost. Is it weird to think a penis is pretty?

Task at hand, Marta, Jesus.

I try not to think about it and do my best to replicate his motions. Slowly but surely, I can feel my body's resistance against the water. Before I know it, I'm floating up.

"Oh my god!" I say, almost surprised it's working.

"That's it, kick harder!" Raf'ere almost sounds giddy.

I get a little overeager and feel my body begin to tilt. It threatens to sink back down.

Before I can give up, I feel a huge hand brace itself dangerously low on my belly. I want to freeze, and my legs halt their motions. Raf'ere's hand still supports me, causing my hips to float up, and my ass to break the surface of the water. I don't let go of the wall, but I do look back at him over my shoulder.

"Good girl," Raf'ere breathes as we lock eyes.

I should tell him to let me go, I should put my clothes on.

Instead, I start word vomiting things to avoid the feeling of heat pooling between my legs.

"I, I did what I did in the shower to self soothe. It's how I calm myself down," I blurt out.

Why the hell is that the first thing that came out of my mouth? Oh, who knows, maybe it's the lack of blood currently flowing to my brain?

"But why didn't you stop when I caught you?" His voice is deep as he stares into my soul.

"Because…because I didn't want to. I wanted you to see, but I don't know exactly why."

Oh god, please, please, please, let me stop telling the truth.

"I liked it. I liked seeing you lost in pleasure." Raf'ere's eyes darken, and his fingers curl against my belly as his gaze rakes over my exposed ass.

Raf'ere's other hand roams up my backside. The fact that it's out of the warm water in combination with his smooth hand sliding over my skin makes me buck involuntarily.

"Did that feel good, Marta?" He asks, even though he already knows it does. *Is he toying with me?* He slides the hand on my stomach lower, tracing his fingers just above my mound.

I whimper into the crook of my arm.

"Do you need a release, human? Are you so frustrated with me it makes you want to come?" His fingers are now gently tracing the curls of my pubic hair, and I involuntarily am pressing my thighs together. It feels so fucking good.

Marta, don't let him get the better of you. You're not some simpering little horn dog! My mind is full-out yelling.

"I can do it myself, thank you very much." I try to press my hips back, hoping he'll slide his hand back up.

"You silly little human. I could make you come harder than

you ever have. You don't even know what a good orgasm is, Marta…" His mouth is so close that I can feel the warmth of his breath on my hip. "I'd milk that cunt for every bit of pleasure it could handle—and then when you thought you couldn't take anymore, I'd push you past bliss." He growls as his finger slides just over my clit before he pauses. "Do you want that? Do you want me to make you feel good, like you wanted me to see you come?"

I am nothing better than a weak woman begging for an alien to touch her pussy.

"Yes," I whisper.

At my consent, his hand slides deftly over my clit. Using the large pads of his two fingers, he strokes up and down over the sensitive flesh.

I'm too far gone to think about anything but instant gratification, and I press my hips into his hand.

"So, this little gem is as good as the videos would have me think, then? Does it make your human cunt ache with need?" The muscles of my pussy contract sharply as he bites the flesh of my hip.

"Ugh, fuck," I moan, holding onto the edge of the pool for dear life.

"I like it, almost as much as I like the wealth of softness here," he purrs, grabbing the meat of my ass and digging his four fingers into my flesh. "What's it called?"

"My h-hips?" I stutter as I grind onto his hand.

"No, *the gem.*"

He pulls at my ass, spreading me to get a better view. His hand traces the bottom of my lips while the underwater hand swirls slow circles over my clit.

"It's, oh god—" The finger presses against my lips, inching higher as he teases the sensitive nerves at my entrance. "My…my…"

I can't form a fucking thought beyond getting off.

"Use your words, Marta." He plunges his thick finger into

my channel. My walls clench over him greedily, wanting him to be rougher, to fuck me with his hand.

"Clit," I sigh, "it's called a clit."

"Interesting," he hums.

Removing his hand from inside of me, he shifts, pushing open my legs and spreading me wide.

"I wonder what it tastes like?" he says before slipping beneath the water's surface and grabs me. His hands, holding my stomach, pull my ass back against his face. He moves low, and tilts my hips back so that my legs settle over his shoulders.

His hold on me is tight as he licks my slit from clit to ass. His pace is torturously slow, and I buck against his mouth in retaliation. I need more.

He nips at my inner thigh as if to scold me, and I'm almost annoyed at the pain before he works his finger into my pussy. But when his tongue picks up the pace, any pain only heightens the pleasure.

I release one of my hands from the wall to pluck at my nipple. When I look down, the bottom of my chin dipping below the water. I can only see a watery blur of his gray jaw working open and closed over my sex.

Stupidly, I wonder when Raf'ere will come up for air.

I almost forgot about the gills, I realize as I make a sharp cry of pleasure when he sucks my clit between his lips.

The slow, delicious start of a well-earned orgasm builds in my core. Sparks and electricity signal to my body that I need a little more to crest over the edge.

But just as I'm ready to give way to my release, his mouth leaves me. He surfaces, wrapping his arms around me.

"I want to watch your expression when you come on my face," he says, his tone no longer suave. There's a needy edge to his voice, as though he's desperate for me.

And holy shit, do I want to watch him work me.

He pulls me up and sits me right on the edge of the pool. As he sinks to his knees, I can't help but thread my fingers into his shoulder length white hair. When I touch him, there's a flash of something strange behind his eyes—but he quickly switches back to the mask I know before placing a hand on my breast, massaging it deeply.

With hooded eyes he descends, and my legs snap open. I pull him closer, but he resists, taking his time.

"Tell me you want to come…tell me you want me to make you feel good."

"Please," I beg him, so close to the edge.

"Say it."

"Please, Raf'ere, make me come," I breathe.

On command, he closes his mouth over my clit, sucking and thrumming it with his tongue.

We lock eyes while he works, some unspoken pact that we won't look away from each other has formed. Even as my back arches, even as the pulses of pleasure beg me to close my eyes, *I look at him.*

Only when the taut thread inside me finally snaps do I shut my eyes. He slides me back into the warm waters of I'loh, wrapping his arms around me. We float together for a while before I slump against him, letting the weightlessness drift me into some post bliss meditative state.

I don't fully come to when he pulls me out of the water or wraps me in something dry and warm. I vaguely feel Nubbins rustling beside me as we scale the stairs.

When I open my eyes, I'm in Raf'ere's bed and he's attempting to wring the water from my hair.

"So strange that your hair holds so much water," I hear him say as if to himself. When he sees that my eyes are open, he smiles.

"Raf'ere," I say, not sure of what I want to tell him.

Thanks for the mind-blowing orgasm? Does this mean I'm

upgraded from hostage to fuck buddy?

Instead, all I get out is, "I should get dressed." I'm suddenly hyper aware of my nakedness.

He shakes his head slowly.

"But we aren't done yet." His voice is as smooth as silk.

"We aren't? I mean…I'm done—do you need help being, um…done?" I say, unsure of if I'm ready to "help" the duke in that department. It's not that I'm unwilling, I just don't know the first thing about getting an alien off. And after the performance Raf'ere just gave, I'd have to give it my all.

"Marta, when the time comes you'll be begging for the chance to please me…but this is about you. No reciprocation needed." The cockiness drips off his words.

"I'll beg you? I doubt it…" I say, a little unsure of myself. "But if that's not it, what do you mean we're not done?" Maybe it's some post-coital haze, but I'm still confused.

"You still haven't begged me to stop, so I say we aren't done yet." He stands. My cheeks heat as I realize that he's still naked.

Although the lighting is dim, I can make his cock out more clearly than before.

It's huge, bigger than any human's I've ever seen. It bobs, standing out proudly as his balls hang heavy below. It's incredibly textured and looks more vascular than a human's. The head has the same soft flexible spines, just like his ear frills.

Then, right above his shaft, where you might expect there to be hair on a human, is a strange little cupped bit of flesh. I wonder what that does—

"Eyes up here, Marta." He mimes the same motion I did in the chapel. Raf'ere slides open his bedside drawer and chuckles. "You've already been playing with my toys?" he asks, surveying the mess I made of his nightstand earlier.

"I was just being nosy…" I breathe, the anticipation that I might get to learn what all these weird alien sex toys are for makes my pulse quicken.

"Do you know what this is?" he asks, holding up the silver collar. A slow smile spreads across his face.

"You got a deal on chokers at the mall?" I raise my brows.

"No. It's a nerve stimulation collar." He leans over me, his broad body blacking out any of the light from above and his eyes light up with excitement. "Can I show you?"

"Sure," I say under my breath, trying to ignore his hard cock as it presses against my leg.

"You can tell me to stop at any time, and I will," he says more seriously. "Do you understand?"

I nod and lift my head as he unlatches the clasp on the back, giving him room to secure it around my neck. As the metal clicks, it sends a shiver down my spine and my chest arches up. Raf'ere traces a finger down my neck, like he doesn't want to stop touching me.

"I haven't even turned it on yet. Behave." He shushes me and backs up, the small remote in his hand. "But don't hold back once I hit start, there's no fun in that."

He grins as he clicks the button. Every nerve in my body fires at once. A tingling sensation almost like electricity spreads through me, and my nipples and clit feel like the only available exit points for the charge. The vibration sensation amplifies in my erogenous zones. My arms and legs shoot straight, and I grip the sheets with everything I've got. I make mewling noises as they're the only sound my overloaded nervous system can produce.

But just as suddenly as it starts, it stops, and I'm left breathless.

"Maybe you'd like to warm up a bit?" I hear his voice, and he clicks the remote again.

The collar's former tingling sensation is replaced by ebbing waves of heat. My tense muscles relax as some neural heating pad is applied to my body.

Raf'ere grabs something else from the drawer and hovers over me again.

"Just a small pinch," he says, clipping something onto one of my nipples and then the other. He's right, there's a slight pinch—but the constant pressure on my already sensitive nipples feels amazing.

So that's what that weird chain was for.

"That feels really good," I coo.

"You'll love this," he says confidently, nudging my knees apart with his hand. When I look down, he's got something long, green and glowing notched at my entrance.

"Wait...what...what is that?" I sit up on my elbows, watching as he works.

"This is an amorphous robotic pleasure tentacle from the Diiyom system. They're built in small batches and very hard to obtain. They're designed to find the pleasure points of any species."

He pushes the warm toy inside me slowly, and it adjusts to fill me entirely. I let out a sigh as it molds to my pussy, and it's not just fitting itself to the inside. Part of the glowing green tentacle slides up over my clit and strokes it.

The texture is bizarre, a cross between silly putty and silicone. Bizarre, but amazing.

"Oh fuck!" I arch into the motion of the tentacle. As I do, I hear another click and the warmth from the collar is replaced by a creeping chill. My nipples harden and inside the nipple clamps, the feeling slides from pleasure more toward pain.

Click.

Back to the warmth as my body relaxes again. I'm panting as one end of the tentacle slides up and down my throbbing clit. The other end pulses inside me, filling me so completely that every nerve inside my pussy is activated. When I feel a tapping at my G-spot, it all becomes too much.

"Raf'ere, it's too intense," I mewl, trying to push the toy away.

"You can handle it. I'm not stopping until you tell me you don't want this anymore."

Click. Oh fuck.

The collar's effect changes, this time it makes my head shoot back, the waves of pleasure that flow over my body is a delicious sensation. It's like the feeling you get the moment before orgasm, where your muscles are so tight and ready that they flutter before you're pushed into heaven.

But instead of just a second of fluttering, it's a non-stop pulsing. My pussy, my nipples, my ass, Jesus, even the column of my throat are all having tiny almost-orgasms.

When Raf'ere pulls the nipple clamps' chain down, my pussy finally gives way. My muscles' fluttering changes to spasms, and my eyes roll in the back of my head.

"Come for me, Marta," he growls.

And I do. I squirm and throb until I fear I might lose consciousness. The collar and tentacle never relent. I think I'm close to a second orgasm as the tentacle presses deeply onto my G-spot.

I pinch my shoulder blades together as I arch off the bed. Reaching for the tentacle, I try in vain to give my clit some barrier. The tentacle undulates over my G-spot relentlessly. There's a strange tightness in my belly, and I feel like I might have to pee. I clench my muscles, not wanting to wet myself.

Raf'ere leans over me, licking up the column of my throat, nibbling my ear lobe before whispering in my ear.

"Come for me, my pet."

"Oh god, Raf'ere, ugh, fuck!" I can't hold back anymore. All my muscles release and I'm lost to the intense throbs of satisfaction that rack over my body.

"Stop!" I scream, unable to take any more.

And all at once, everything goes quiet. The tentacle shrinks, and as it does, a rush of wetness coats my thighs. The collar powers down and the nipple clamps are gently removed.

"I told you," is all Raf'ere whispers in my ear as he unlatches the collar.

"Uuuggghhh," is my only response.

When I feel his tongue on my inner thigh, lapping at the wetness there, I don't even have the energy to tell him to stop. I give some weak attempt at closing my legs, but he just puts a strong hand out and holds them open.

"Don't worry, little human, I'll let you get some rest...but let me clean up first. It would be a shame to waste this—it tastes too good."

He laps gently through my lips, but thankfully avoids my over sensitive clit.

Sliding up over me, he puts his mouth over my sore nipples. He sucks any small pain away.

Finally, he rolls to his side, pulls me into his arms, and spoons me. He tucks his hand over my mound and presses his palm against my still throbbing sex.

"Mine," I think I hear him whisper.

"What was that?" I question weakly.

"Nothing, go to sleep," he tells me, holding me all the tighter.

CHAPTER 24

☆I LIKED SEEING YOU LICK MY PUSSY, ASSHOLE☆

☆RAF'ERE

I SLEEP with Marta pulled tightly into my arms. When I wake from the dream that was last night, anxiety sits in the pit of my stomach. It's as if the cold light of day is illuminating my new reality.

What happens next?

I'm doubtful that the only thing that will change between us is the number of orgasms she's having. Can I tell her the true depths of my feelings—would she even accept the mate bond as a reality?

Should she? Could she be happy with me, some ruined old thing?

I slide my arm carefully out from under her, as I want to let her sleep. For as beautiful as she is, Marta snores louder than any grizzled fi'len solider I've ever bunked with. Not that I mind, the vibration of her airway is almost like a soothing white noise.

There's a whining and shuffling from the bottom of the bed, and Nubbins pulls his thick short body onto my mattress.

"Shh, you little beast, let her sleep!" I whisper yell at him. But he's about as trained as any wild little thing. The kahne'ah immediately pounces on Marta's chest and a whoosh of air leaves her lungs, her eyes snapping open.

She's kinder than I am, her gaze softening as soon as she sees the kahne'ah.

"Aww, who's awake before Mommy?" Her lids are heavy, but she clasps Nubbins's fat little cheeks and accepts all the sloppy kisses he gives her.

Once he's finally settled, she turns her eyes to me.

She smiles. Marta's f'teeing face lights up when she looks at mine.

"Hey there." Her voice still sounds groggy.

"Hello, Marta," I respond. My chest is full of a something I haven't felt in a long time.

Completeness.

"So, what's next?" she asks.

"What do you mean?"

"I mean, are you planning on keeping me locked up in this room for the rest of my life? If I trust you...*with my body*...can you trust me with more freedom?"

"Our experience last night wasn't a transactional one, Marta. I wasn't keeping you here until you let me touch you..."

And just like that, the feeling fades. What replaces it is something familiar. It's the feeling I first felt when my parents died. It haunted me when I first looked at my reflection after the war... and the cold crept even deeper into me when Yar'oh's true motives were known.

"You think that just because you're some hotshot alien duke that I slept with you to get more privileges? God, you're such an asshole, you know that?!" Marta's demeanor turns cold.

"Then why did you?" The spread of darkness inside my hearts halts for a moment.

"Because I wanted to, you fucking jerk! Because you were beautiful last night...because I liked seeing you lick my pussy.

Mother of God, don't twist this into something it's not." Her face is flushed with anger.

She liked seeing me lick her pussy. It's not a declaration of love… but I'll take it.

"You know what, let's pretend like it never happened." She swings her feet over her side of the bed and clutches one of the sheets tight around her body.

"I'm sorry," I say, and she freezes. "I…I'm not used to people not having ulterior motives. If you can be patient with me, I can try harder to trust you."

She turns to me, a tight frown on her lips.

"If you can respect me, like I deserve, I will try to be more patient with you."

I nod, feeling like a small boy being scolded by a schoolmarm. "I promise."

"Samesies," she huffs.

"So, more freedom?"

"It would be appreciated," Marta says curtly.

"Dinner, in the dining hall?" I feel like I'm negotiating some off-world treaty. But Marta's frustration is still palpable.

"I would like that." She pauses. "But how are we going to avoid the giant dome of water that will send me into a panic attack?"

"Oh, um…If we take the stairs down to the chapel, there's a service hallway we could use. It has back entrances to the kitchen and dining hall."

"How many secret tunnels are in this place?" Her eyebrows arch.

"A lot. Would you like that?"

"Yes, it's a start."

Nubbins whines, breaking the tension between us.

"I think this wittle guy is hungy." She speaks to the little beast like it's a baby. "What does a kahne'ah eat?"

"I'll have Jens'i bring his belongings up today. I believe his nutrient kibble is among them. Why don't you go get dressed, and then you can take him to swim down in the chapel—I'll inform the staff of your new freedom."

"I can go there by myself?"

"Isn't that what we just agreed on?" There's an edge to my tone I can't control. Doesn't she see it's already hard for me to let her out of my sight?

"Okay, okay, don't get testy…I'm just checking."

But the thought of Marta struggling in one of the pools of water sends a jolt to my stomach.

"Just stay out of the water…We have more swimming lessons before you're allowed in by yourself," I tack on.

"Yeah, yeah," she waves her hand as she shrugs on the slip she wore yesterday. Our clothing is still piled from where I threw it on the ground last night. "Wasn't planning on taking a dip, anyway." I pull out my data pad and order something small to make me feel better about Marta being without me near the water.

She's slipping through the door and down the stairs before she even stops talking to me. Nubbins bounds in front of her, excited for his swim.

I'm already trying to figure out how to keep the estate staff from seeing her as Marta's world inside my home expands. Jens'i will handle it, we can handle this.

I already feel my grip on my mate slipping, and it terrifies me.

CHAPTER 25
☆TUCKED IN☆

THE CRACKED bathroom door remains ajar, a sliver of light filtering through as steam lingers in the air from my recent shower. It makes little sense for me to close it. What's the point of modesty when the big gray alien in the other room has eaten me out?

I squeeze the water from my hair, the droplets cascading down and beading up on the nonabsorbent fabric. I'm swathed in yet another of Raf'ere's enormous robes. As always, the clothing here tents over me.

Amidst what would normally be silence in the duke's chambers, I catch the hushed whispers of Raf'ere's voice. Curiosity gets the better of me, and I cautiously peer through the crack, the soft blue glow of my alien lava lamp casting an ethereal aura. There, I see the duke on his knees, facing the armchair that Nubbins has taken a liking to. I catch the imposing and scarred alien offering some kind of treat to the small creature.

Nubbins eagerly devours it, his antennas flickering with luminescent delight. Raf'ere reaches behind him, retrieving a nearby throw blanket. Cocooning Nubbins snugly within it, he secures the excess fabric beneath the plumpness of the space puppy's butt. Nubbins, all warm and tucked in, is the cutest little burrito I've ever laid my eyes on.

The heartwarming scene causes a tightness in my chest. To see him be so sweet to the little animal he pretends he's indifferent to makes me swoon a little.

Raf'ere's typically stern tone softens as he whispers what I assume are sweet nothings to the space puppy. He leans in close and tenderly scratches behind Nubbins's ear. The animal nuzzles the scarred side of his face, getting a few licks in.

Overwhelmed by the sweetness of the moment, I instinctively cover my mouth to stifle an audible, "Awww."

My attempts at stealth prove futile as Raf'ere's eyes dart toward me. Surprise briefly flashes across his face before he swiftly rises, smoothing his hands over his suit to compose himself.

"I'm sorry, I didn't mean to interrupt." I stumble over my words, a pang of guilt washing over me.

"Interrupt what?" he responds, attempting to downplay his affection for the little kahne'ah. But I refuse to let him brush it off.

Walking toward Nubbins' armchair, I gesture dramatically to the slumbering space puppy emitting loud snores.

"Oh, that." Raf'ere's expression falters, his mouth is turned down as he avoids my gaze. "It's nothing."

"Suuurrre it is." I roll my eyes and pat Nubbins's soft fur, feeling his warmth against my palm, before sinking into the plush sofa nearby.

"I mean, you literally tucked him into bed—you *love* him, admit it. I mean, how could you not? He's perfect!" I gaze adoringly at the puppy.

"Yes, perfect," he says, his eyes focused intently on me. There's a heat in his gaze, a magnetic pull that threatens to consume us both. But before it can lead to anything, a loud crash in the hallway shatters the tranquility of the moment.

We both turn our heads swiftly toward the chamber doors, where the sound echoes. It sounds like someone has thrown a bunch of plates against the floor.

Raf'ere takes a single step toward the door, his interest piqued. But when a chorus of feminine giggles follows, he moves on quickly. However, I still want to know more.

"What was that?" I tilt my head towards the doors, my curiosity getting the best of me.

"Staff must have dropped something on their way to the kitchen," the duke dismissively explains, his voice tinged with a hint of annoyance.

Exhausted, he flops onto the plush bed, the mattress sinking beneath him. I can faintly hear his fingers tapping on the data pad, creating soft electronic chirps that fill the air. I stand up and make my way toward him, my feet padding on the stone floor. With a seductive smile on my lips, I crawl into bed beside him, feeling the crisp sheets cool against my bare skin.

"Do you think you could introduce me to the staff?" I ask, attempting to sound alluring.

He scoffs, his voice laced with amusement. "Thank goddess you're not in charge of negotiations. Your intentions are as clear as day."

Undeterred, I widen my smile. "What's there to negotiate? You trust me, I trust you. Introduce me to the staff, simple as that." I like Raf'ere, and I'm obsessed with Nubbins, but I refuse to accept they're all that's here for me in this world.

His gaze remains fixed on the data pad as he nonchalantly replies, "We have an appointment tomorrow."

Confused, I frown. "An appointment?"

He smirks. "With a tailor, so you can have clothes of you very own to destroy."

"Do I get to choose what the tailor makes for me?" I ask, excitement clear in my voice. He glances up from his data pad and meets my gaze.

"Within reason," he replies, his tone matter-of-fact.

I can't help but imagine this new person I'll get to meet. A surge of anticipation fills me, and I roll my head back onto the soft pillow, tightly closing my eyes.

Is it strange that I'm eager to go to sleep earlier than usual, hoping to hasten tomorrow? It reminds me of being a child on Christmas Eve, eagerly awaiting the arrival of Santa Claus, or in this case, a tailor.

"What are you doing?" he asks, breaking my reverie.

I open my eyes and meet his gaze, my voice filled with excitement. "Trying to make tomorrow come quicker."

He sighs, his hand reaching over me to pull on the blanket, tucking the excess fabric under my bottom.

"It seems everyone is ready for bed," he remarks before clicking off the lights. As darkness envelops the room, I force myself to sleep.

CHAPTER 26
☆BIONIC & BESPOKE☆

WE WAIT for the fitting appointment, and I anxiously sit on my hands, feeling a surge of nervous energy. Meeting someone new doesn't happen often around here, and the anticipation is making me giddy. It's as if Raf'ere is fulfilling his promise to trust me.

As I wonder if the alien tailor will belong to the same species as Raf'ere, a knock on the chamber doors startles me, and I restrain myself from jumping out of my chair. I wait impatiently for the sound of the doors clicking shut before turning around. I don't want my first impression to be one of panic if I glimpse the ocean over the ballroom.

"Your Grace, the tailor, Hisso, has arrived," Jens'i says in a curt tone, and I swiftly spin my head to face him. The tailor, almost as tall as Raf'ere, is impeccably dressed in a sophisticated blue suit. He exudes a striking handsomeness and is entirely made of gleaming metal. It's shocking to realize that he's a robot.

"Shall we?" Raf'ere stands, acknowledging the shiny metal man with a nod. It annoys me I'm not meeting a real person, but the feeling fades when the robot speaks.

"Indeed," he says in a deep, resonant voice that reverberates through the room, grabbing my attention. I follow them as he approaches Raf'ere's mirror, his movements smooth and deliberate.

At that moment, I can't help but wonder if a robot can be hot. I find myself drawn to his presence. He reminds me of some proper English love interest from a Jane Austen film. His design is undeniably human-like, yet there is a hint of otherworldly grace in his towering stature and elongated features. Maybe he's intentionally crafted to resemble a different species altogether.

"Well, yes actually, Hisso," Raf'ere responds,. "I require some clothing for Marta. The fi'len cuts simply don't suit her."

The android swiftly turns his head toward me, his movement precise and calculated. His gaze is unwavering, unblinking, as he locks eyes with me.

"Something different, indeed, Your Grace," he replies, his voice lacking the natural fluctuations of a human's. Surprisingly, for as bizarre as he is to me, he doesn't trigger a feeling of uncanny valley uneasiness.. For a robot, he emanates a warmth and kindness I didn't expect.

I stand in front of the mirror, the giants behind me, feeling small in their presence. I gaze up at the android in the reflection as he assesses me, his eyes scanning my form with a discerning eye. He delicately twists the tip of his finger, causing a vibrant blue laser light to emanate from it, casting a mesmerizing glow.

"And what, if I may ask, do we require?" he asks, turning his attention back to Raf'ere.

"Everything," Raf'ere says solemnly, his gaze fixed upon me.

"Lift your arms please Marta."

I meet Hisso's eyes in the reflection before I do as he instructs. As I comply, he points his glowing finger towards the crown of my head.

The cool sensation of the blue light washes over me, scanning the contours of my body. I glance upward, glimpsing Hisso's face as he works. His mechanical green eyes have rolled back, and it's a rather unsettling sight. Uncertain of what to do, I remain still, shifting my gaze to Raf'ere.

He stands with crossed arms, his eyes narrowing and his nostrils slightly flaring as he focuses on Hisso's finger. Suddenly, the blue light clicks off, and the android's eyes return to a less disconcerting position.

"Excellent, thank you, Marta," he says, his smile remarkably human. "You can lower your arms now." Hisso winks at me, a gesture I didn't expect from a robot.

"Are you sure you got my measurements already?" I ask, taken aback by the swiftness of the process.

"Well, you tell me," he says, his voice tinged with pride, as he lightly taps the toe of his shoe against the floor. A strange, soft hum fills the air, and I realize it's the sound of a hologram materializing.

The room is suddenly bathed in a warm, pulsating light, and I can't help but marvel at the intricate details that come into view. The hologram paints a dress over my body, its ethereal fabric flowing and shimmering, even adding a layer of skin where my slip dress lies underneath. The gown is an elegant formal number, with its sweeping train and alluring low neckline.

"Wow, so you can make this?" I say, my voice filled with awe as I examine how perfectly the fake dress fits my form.

"I certainly could, but if you'd allow me a few alterations," he says, his fingertips lighting up once again with a soft blue glow. With graceful movements, he draws on the hologram with his lit finger, making subtle changes. His finger traces along the sleeves, he cuts them up to my elbows.

"A shorter sleeve," he murmurs as he slashes away the excess fabric. "And maybe a bit of a deeper neckline—" His finger hovers just above my collarbone.

Before he can finish his sentence, a voice interrupts, cutting through the air with a hint of impatience. "We get the idea, Hisso. I trust your judgment. We'll discuss the specifics of the wardrobe later. Do you have all the measurements you need?" There's a subtle tension in Raf'ere's voice.

Hisso withdraws his hand, the lights on his fingertips abruptly extinguishing. "Yes, Your Grace. I have everything I need from the lovely Marta." A small smile plays on his lips as he catches my gaze in the reflection of the mirrors.

"Thank you, Hisso," I say, turning to face him fully, my hand resting innocently on his arm.

Hisso's piercing gaze fixates on my hand, then his eyes dart to the duke. The room is filled with a tense silence, broken only by the soft hum of machinery I assume is keeping Hisso functioning.

Slowly, he speaks with an air of politeness. "I believe, Marta, it would be wise for you to retract your hand from my arm. I can sense the duke's blood pressure rising to worrisome levels."

I'm taken aback by his request and tilt my head to glare at Ra'fere. "Are you genuinely jealous of a robot?" Disbelief laces my words.

Raf'ere just glowers at me, his hands clenched at his sides.

"My dear, for future reference, I would prefer to be referred to as a synthetic." With a delicate touch, he removes my hand from his arm, placing it neatly at my side.

"Oh, I apologize, Hisso—I didn't know," I stammer, angry that I'm so ignorant of this new world.

Turning to Raf'ere, I can't help but ask again, "Are you really jealous of a synthetic? I don't believe we would be very *compatible*, if that's what you're worried about."

I try to be polite in my wording for Hisso's sake. It's bonkers to me that I'm now concerned about the emotions of a mechanical being.

"Once again, Marta, you misunderstand," Hisso clarifies. "I have no intention of sweeping you off your feet. However, I have no doubt that a pleasure attachment could be procured. It could make us as compatible as you desire."

A sense of embarrassment washes over me, and I can feel the blush spreading up from my neck. Surprises seem to lurk around every corner in space. I notice Raf'ere appears to be biting the inside of his cheek, and I can almost taste the tension.

Sex robots, check.

"On that note, I'm off," Hisso says cooly.

As he nods to Raf'ere, the sound of his footsteps quickens. I stare at the jealous duke as the tailor leaves. Only when the door clicks closed behind him does Raf'ere release a breath.

"Oh calm down." I dismiss his insane jealousy with a casual wave of my hand. "How was I supposed to know that you can fuck robots here?" I plop into one of the lush armchairs, still annoyed.

Raf'ere's eyes darken, reflecting a dangerous glint.

"Raf'ere, honestly..." My voice trails off, leaving a lingering silence between us.

He moves to the nightstand, the sound of the drawer opening breaking the silence. Moments later, he retrieves four silver bangles, their metallic sheen catching the light.

"Are you apologizing with jewelry?" I raise an eyebrow.

"Arms out," he says deviously, his voice mirroring the tone of the synthetic tailor from before. I let out an exasperated sigh, feeling a mix of annoyance and amusement. I extend my wrists towards him.

If a man wants to give you jewelry, let him, and work out the specifics later.

With a gentle touch, he slides two of the bangles over my hands, their size comically large on my wrists.

"I think they're a little small," I say sarcastically, the corners of my lips curling upwards.

"Mmmhmm," Raf'ere hums, unamused.

He retrieves his data pad from the inner pocket of his jewel-encrusted suit jacket, the fabric rustling softly. With a flick of his fingers, he navigates through its operating system, completely disregarding my presence.

The silver bangles encircling my wrists suddenly vibrate, causing a tingling sensation to dance across my skin. They shrink down effortlessly, conforming to the size of my wrists. I bring my hands up, turning them over to examine the now perfectly fitting adornments.

"What the heck?" I'm taken aback, but there's a hint of bemusement in my tone. "I guess you don't need jewelers here, do you?"

"Oh Marta, if I was going to give you jewelry... *you'd know it*," he says, a genuine smile finally gracing his lips, erasing the tension that had lingered since Hisso's arrival.

"So what are these bracelets for, then?" My voice is filled with genuine curiosity.

"They're not bracelets at all," he replies, a mischievous glint in his eyes.

With a flick of his finger on the tablet, my arms are suddenly lifted upward, the metallic cuffs clinking together with a loud snap. My arms pulled upright by a mysterious force, feeling weightless, my wrists dangling in mid air.

"They're hover restraints, and if you're a good girl, maybe I'll let you come," Raf'ere growls, his warm breath brushing against my ear. A shiver runs down my spine, a mixture of anticipation and desire flooding my senses.

I should refuse, assert my independence against this jealous alien. But I can't deny the intoxicating effect he has on me. With each touch, each moment shared, he plays me like a skilled violinist. I revel in the way he makes me feel, his understanding of my body growing with each passing encounter.

"So what'll it be? Are you going to listen to me for once?" he whispers, biting my ear gently. My breath catches in my throat, his nearness overwhelming my senses.

"I'll try... but I've never been a very good active listener."

CHAPTER 27
☆HOVER RESTRAINTS☆

THE SILVER hover restraints hold her arms high above her head. My fated mate is bound and mine for the taking. I kneel in front of her, setting the two remaining cuffs on the ground, slow and deliberate with my actions.

She gazes down at me, heat behind her eyes—her arousal scent filling the room.

My heart already pounds in my chest, my desire for her growing with each passing moment. As I move my face closer, I can smell a note of fear mixing with the aroma of her desire. I worry that I've pushed her too far. But as she settles into the restraints, I can see her body relax. When she bites a her plump lower lip, and the scent of her want overpowers any other, I know I can proceed.

I run my fingers over the skin of her thigh, tracing the soft flesh. She jumps slightly at my touch, but she doesn't resist. She knows what's coming next, and she wants it just as much as I do.

I lean in and kiss her neck, hard and possessive. She moans, her body arching against mine. I feel her heat, her wetness, as I press against her. I want to take her right here, right now, but I know that I have to be patient and wait until she wants me as her mate. Until I can be sure, I can't risk knowing the pleasure of her cunt over my cock.

I kiss my way down her neck, nipping at her delicate flesh as I go. When I reach her neckline, I pull at the fabric, freeing her pert breast. I take one of her bronzed nipples into my mouth.

Marta moans, and I pull back. Grabbing the restraints from the floor, I slip them gingerly onto her ankles.

"I guess those aren't bracelets," she breathes as I activate the auto sizing of the cuffs.

"No, not bracelets at all, but they'll allow me to have you at the angle I want. Which is a good thing, because my back's been killing me, having to bend over to reach you," I tease my short mate, and she narrows her eye at me. I know just the thing to distract her.

I gesture on my data pad, and the cuffs slowly spread her legs wider. She wiggles futility.

"That is, unless you don't want to play." I try and play it cool, but the seething jealousy of the synthetic still courses through my veins. I knew exactly how her measurements would be taken and the close contact it would entail.

To see him there, almost *touching her* was more than enough to get my blood boiling.

Even though I haven't claimed her as my mate, a fi'len woman would know better than to touch another male–synthetic or not.

But she's not fi'len, is she? I remind myself as I push up her dress until her pretty little cunt is on display. She bites her lip as if she's waiting for me to touch her.

"Is that what you want, Marta? To play?" I inch my fingers closer to her sex, refusing to touch her until she grants me permission.

"You know I do," she says, locking eyes with me.

"Then tell me—tell me what you want."

"I want you to touch my pussy," she orders me.

"I will. Soon." My fingers continue to hover a hairsbreadth away from her slit.

"Why are you teasing me?" Her breath quickens as she squirms.

"I'm going to make you earn it."

I lean closer to her pussy and see the wetness gathering between her lips. My cock throbs with need.

"Raf'ere…" her voice falters with each graze of my teeth. I know exactly what Marta needs.

I lick a circle around her clit, thrumming the little bundles of nerves hard with my tongue.

She mewls. "Oh God, you're so good."

I slide my tongue into her, tasting her sweet nectar. I love how she moves under my ministrations. Her body tenses as I bring her closer and closer to orgasm. I can feel her body go rigid, just as she's about to come.

I pause, my hands caressing my sweet little mate's body, savoring the electric tension that permeates the air. With a sly smile, I gently pull away, leaving them breathless and craving more. Marta's eyes meet mine, a mix of anticipation and longing dancing in their gaze. Just a little more torture to sweeten her climax.

"Hey, no! I'm almost there, just keep going," Marta pants, her face in a taut frown as her hips arch towards me.

"What's the point in hover restraints if we can't have some fun? Besides, I'm ready to get off my knees."

I grab my data pad, and spin my four fingers 360 degrees on the screen.

Marta's eyes go wide, her body rising in the air. Once the cuffs determine there's enough clearance to spin her upside down, they do.

"Holy shit!" she yelps as she rotates on her axis.

As she flips her silky dress slides down towards her head, exposing her completely. With a few shakes her head wiggles free of the green garment. The straps catch on her bound wrists, leaving the dress hanging, the hem hitting the floor.

I stand and palm her breast. The apex of her spread legs is just about even with my mouth, a feast laid bare.

"Perfect, I'm going to enjoy this easy access," I say before closing my lips over Marta's clit.

"Oh. Oh. Oh fuck," she chants, arching her hips against my lips. Goddess, I love the taste of her.

"Does my mouth feel sweet on your human cunt?"

"Yes," she moans.

"Should I let you come now?" I ask, already knowing I won't allow her the release just yet.

"You fucking better," she pants.

I have the hover cuffs bring her lower, so that I can work her with my hands.

Reaching around her ass, I slide my finger through her slick lips, before stretching the tight ring of her opening wider.

I push fingers deep inside her, my thumb rubbing circles around her clit. Every thrust in and out of her wetness brings a moan of pleasure from her lips, and I can feel the tension in her body rising quickly. Picking up my pace, I move faster within her core, feeling the pulsing pressure of her orgasm building.

The noises she's making are deliciously obscene as she writhes beneath me, begging for release. I slow down and tease her with gentle strokes before plunging back into her welcome warmth. It catches her off guard, and she shivers as my fingers go deeper. I press against her walls, rubbing the rougher textured flesh.

She gasps, her eyes widening at the sensations I work from her cunt. Determined, I intensify my efforts, driving her closer to the precipice of ecstasy. Finally, when she can take no more, I allow her to reach bliss. I suck on her clit, and relish as her inner thighs tremble.

Her body quakes with her orgasm, and her walls clamp down around me. Her cunt squirts, the droplets of her slick running up her stomach and down my chin. She moans out my name, and I watch with pleasure as she struggles against the restraints, writhing in pure bliss beneath me.

I don't stop until every last bit of pleasure has been worked free, prolonging the waves of ecstasy until she finally goes limp in the restraints. I withdraw, kissing her beautiful cunt.

When I step back to admire my beautiful mate. Her face is red, the blood having pooled there during the inversion. Marta breathes slowly, lolling her head from side to side.

Not wanting my mate to black out, I use my data pad to rotate her right side up, and the hover restraints setting her gently back in the chair. She slumps as they deactivate, her arms falling like dead weight. Marta is completely spent.

"That was amazing," she purrs with a dreamy sigh as she clutches her now freed hands over her still throbbing sex.

I lift her from the chair, kissing her forehead before slipping her into our bed.

Our bed?

I can only dream.

CHAPTER 28
☆ROUTINE, BUT NO ALIEN PEEN☆

☆MARTA

GOD HAS IT BEEN DAYS, weeks, a month? I guess I've never been great at keeping time, but doubly bad at it when there's an alien obsessed with making me come all day long.

I stare at the new clothing Jens'i just brought in. We get dressed up for dinner every night. Raf'ere always looks ridiculous and overdone. A true alien peacock that one is. When I told Raf'ere I hated the clothing he bought for me, for I'm sure all the reasons he loved it, he had this new batch made.

On the rack in front of me is a varying array of slip dresses and tight-sleeved gowns. Raf'ere lavishes attention on the softest parts of my body when he makes me come. So, seeing how every garment will hug my figure now? I'm sure it was very intentional on his part. I can't say I hate that.

I hold up a dark brown gown, its fabric has almost a wet sheen. It's going to make me look like sex on a stick, and I'll need that. I'm going to ask the duke to leave the estate again.

I brought up leaving this place once during however long I've been here…and it didn't go well. Despite being able to travel more freely inside the building, I'm still a captive.

The way he reacted made me feel like I had committed a grave betrayal. It was as though I was begging him to condemn me to my own demise.

I'm not a pet, but I am grateful for Raf'ere when we aren't discussing my captivity.

Granted, I'm a captive who regularly gets her pussy eaten out by a weirdly hot alien duke...but a captive all the same.

I can't blame Stockholm syndrome for the fact that I feel a strange fondness for the duke, despite our circumstances. He's more than generous in the bedroom and never asks or expects reciprocation. I can't help but feel a bit strange about the fact that he has never attempted to put his dick in me—he hasn't even kissed me. On my mouth, that is.

His arsenal of sex toys is astonishing, and he uses them to make me come nearly every night. But on the occasions I have enough energy to even attempt to reach for his cock after he blows my mind, he shoves me off. Distracts me with some new instrument of pleasure.

He must want to, right? I can feel how hard he gets when that monster of his brushes against my thighs. I don't push it, because when I push anything with him, he shuts down.

It could be worse, I remind myself. I've got little Nubbins to keep me occupied during the day. He needs to swim quite a bit, and now that I'm actually learning how to swim, I can play with him down in the chapel.

I'm still not allowed in the water by myself, except when my "alien lifeguard" is present.

He's a good teacher, and our reward system helps, but I feel a bit like Pavlov's dogs. Instead of salivating when the bell rings, as soon as I get into the waters of I'loh, my pussy throbs. She knows her reward is imminent.

For as much as I want to blame him for everything bad that's happened to me, he did save me from the sex trafficking aliens. When I had asked the maid if he was lying about my safety...she said he wasn't entirely wrong.

Maybe I should trust him? Could this be the safest place for me in all of outer space?

Fuck, I want to trust him.

"This one will be perfect, thank you, Jens'i!" I tell the butler. He's still the only staff I've met beyond the alien woman who I got fired. I've been thinking about her a lot lately, especially the palace and the king she mentioned. Her information tells me two things.

There's a king who rules over Raf'ere, and she thinks he should have just sent me to the palace.

Why wouldn't he have done that? I still don't know.

But tonight, at dinner, I'm finally going to ask him.

He thinks I don't see the little treats he sneaks to Nubbins. That I don't notice that he's growing to love "the little beast," as he's come to call him. How I caught him tucking Nubbins in when he thought I wasn't looking.

I know he's happy by how tightly he holds me at night. Despite having my own bed, I haven't slept in it in weeks. His strong arms just feel *right* around me.

When Jens'i closes the door, I pull the dress over my shoulders. The fabric slides easily over my curves. Just as I expected, it fits ridiculously well and hugs every plane of my body. Hisso's work is always perfect. I'm assume the margin of error is slim to none for the synthetic when it comes to sewing. The sleeves of the dress are long, hitting me perfectly at my wrist. The garment's neckline dips low, putting the girls on display.

I feel hot—but just like how I can't quite rectify how fucking good Raf'ere makes me feel with my emotions over this captivity. It tickles some prideful part of my Leo brain to look this good, but what's the point if I can never leave the estate?

We're working on it, I remind myself.

Tonight, I ask him about the palace.

After winding my way through the dimly lit back tunnels to get to the dining room, my eyes need time to adjust. I squint as I sit in my seat to the left of Raf'ere, letting Jens'i pull out my chair.

The room is decked out in emerald green and gold, but the table is made of a semi translucent stone. It reminds me of Raf'ere's iridescent scales peppering his high cheekbones.

"How much longer do you think he'll be?"

"Soon, Marta. I've just received word that his cruiser is docked," the butler says before pouring me a glass of the alien liquor I've grown fond of. It's no vino, but it gets the job done.

I throw back the triangle shaped glass and take a big gulp for courage. It burns as it slides down my throat, but the sting is replaced by that old familiar warmth.

I won't let him shut down tonight—or distract me with some new and amazing alien sex toy. I need to find out about the world outside.

Gulp two goes down just the tiniest bit easier as my body acclimates to the alcohol. It's slightly briny, but sweet, once you get over the initial burn.

The knob of the door to the main ballroom spins, and I turn my head away to avoid catching a glimpse of the ocean ceiling in the room beyond.

"Hello, Marta."

When I hear the door click shut, I turn and smile broadly at him. Jens'i helps to remove his formal coat. He sits in the chair next to me with a heavy sigh.

"Long day?" I ask the alien I've been playing house with.

"You have no idea," he says, and I want to laugh.

I don't have any idea what he does *out there.* I wonder what he did today. We don't talk about his life outside, but to be fair, I haven't asked. Maybe I know I'll be jealous, so why ask and worry about the FOMO?

"Well, it's over now." I place my hand over his much larger one in a reassuring pat. He curls his fingers up around mine and grabs a sip of his freshly made cocktail.

"The dress suits you," he says, letting his eyes linger a bit longer than they should on my chest. I wink at him, and he acts as though he wasn't just ogling my goodies.

He doesn't ask what I did today because he knows. Eighty percent of my day is just tending to Nubbins, and the other twenty is split between waiting for him to return and him getting me off.

I was never good with silence though, and doubly bad when I have something on my mind. I feel the question bubbling up from my belly like some uncontrollable word vomit because I can't stop it.

"So, why didn't you just take me to the palace?" I blurt out nervously. I pull my hand from his and down the rest of the contents of my glass. The cup clinks as I slam it on the table.

He blinks at me several times with his mouth open.

"What—how do you know about the palace?"

"I guess I don't?" I answer after a few silent beats. *No point in lying about it.*

"The same reason I keep you safe here, Marta… Do you even know what's going on there?"

"Well, no, like I said. I don't really know about anything—It's just that the maid had said she was surprised you didn't just take me to the palace, and I was wondering why." This isn't how the conversation went in my head when I imagined it earlier. I was going to destroy him with my feminine wiles, and he would tell me everything I wanted to know!

I'm too impatient to have good plans, I suppose. My inability to lie or sugar coat things has always bitten me in the ass.

"We're not talking about this right now. I spent all day nego-tiating with the Andjin diplomat about how we weren't going to force any of the wo—" He cuts himself off, his eyes widening.

"Any of the what?" Can I keep him talking? This is the first time he's even mentioned what he does outside these walls.

"This discussion is over. You're not ready yet, trust me."

"You know I trust you. We wouldn't be doing what we're

doing if I didn't. But I can't live half a life, and you can't keep me locked up forever." I'm laying the guilt on thick.

"No, you can't, and that's why it's not forever—just not right now."

"Well, for the record, I hate that," I tell him, grabbing the bottle of booze and pouring myself another drink. I don't stop until the glass is nearly spilling from its brim.

Raf'ere frowns at me as I down nearly the whole thing in a single go.

"Don't you think you should slow down a bit?" he asks cautiously. He's learned I don't like being told what to do in our short time together.

Well, outside the bedroom.

"There's lots of things we both should do, wouldn't you agree?" I finish off the rest of my drink.

"Marta, I'm telling you to slow down. You're going to hurt yourself if you keep drinking like that." His voice deepens.

"What, like you're going to stop me?" I grab his own glass out of his hands and put it up to my lips.

I barely get a sip in before his hand snatches the cup from my grip, while his other hand flies to my neck and applies a firm pressure.

"You're not allowed to hurt yourself," he growls.

Fuck.

Suddenly I see the Raf'ere from when I first woke up. Angry, primal, and absolutely in fucking charge.

"Are *you* going to hurt me, then?" I mock, unable to help myself from getting in the last word.

His jaw sets, and he clears the table with the arm not on my throat. Expensive looking alien dishware and cocktail glasses go flying against the wall. They shatter in a symphony of destruction, the pieces clinking against the floor.

Raf'ere moves his hands to my waist and pulls me from my chair, before standing me in front of the door to the ballroom.

"What would happen if I opened these doors?" His voice is gruff as his anger with me is barely contained.

"I…I don't know," I lie.

"You know exactly what would happen. You would see the ocean through the biofilm windows, panic, and completely shut down." He turns me to him, putting my face between his hands. "I'm trying to help you, I'm trying to protect you! Just because you can tread water doesn't mean you're ready for the ocean, Marta." He's talking fast and loud, and I'm not entirely sure he's talking *to me* so much as *at me.* "When you hurt yourself, you hurt me. I don't want to tell you no…I don't like to tell you no! For f'tee's sake, what if they took you from me? What if I am found undeserving?"

His anger shifts, and I can see the deep sadness he tries to keep buried flash through his mask.

"No one's going to take me away, Raf'ere…" I whisper.

"You don't know that. You don't know anything about this world," he says bitterly.

"Because you won't tell me! You can't just keep me in the dark to protect me. That's what my father did and look how it turned out! I got fucking kidnapped by aliens right out of a wine bar, and now I'll never see him again!"

"That's different. I promise this won't be forever." He softens his tone slightly.

"Then why are you bothering teaching me to swim?"

"What? That doesn't have anything to do with this," he sulks.

"Bullshit, it's how you're protecting me from drowning—you're teaching me, you're giving me information I need to *protect myself.* Don't pretend there are no risks with that! You promised you would trust me, Raf'ere! Don't break your promise because you're scared." I grab his hand and put it over my heart.

"Teach me," I beg him.

His eyes go wide before they soften.

"The palace," he grits out, "is the home of my cousin, the

king. He has a…refugee camp nearby. That's why I should have taken you there."

"Okay, that wasn't so bad, was it?" I reassure him, but I don't think he agrees. "Why didn't you take me there? It would have been easier for you, wouldn't it?"

"No, it wouldn't have."

He pulls my face toward his, cupping it with his large hands.

He wants to kiss me, I know he does, but he doesn't. Even as I try to bridge the distance between us, he runs the hands that were on my cheek through my hair as he lets me go.

My stomach drops.

I wanted to kiss him too, despite all his faults and failures.

"Come with me," he says, pulling me by the hand back to the hidden corridor's door.

CHAPTER 29
☆BE MY GUEST☆

"COME WITH ME," I tell Marta as I drag her to the service corridors.

She's trusted me, she's given me her body, she's asking me for help to understand this world.

I can take a step today and prove to her I am worth trusting.

I drag Marta quickly down the service corridor, but my pace is one that she's not able to match.

"Raf'ere, slow down," she huffs, unable to catch her breath. "Why are we running, what's going on?"

My feet feel leaden, making my legs fumble as I drag her behind me. I can't stop and explain because I'll lose my nerve. No longer can I keep her locked away forever. The loud little human has wormed somewhere into my heart when I wasn't paying attention. Some deep care for Marta compels me to hold myself accountable to her. I have to prove myself worthy.

I can do this, together we can do this.

Past the chapel, at the end of the hall, is a set of locked doors. I pull my data pad out, knowing full well what's happening right on the other side of these doors.

I click the button, unlocking the doors, and kick them wide open. Marta's hand is in mine as I step through.

The sea of unblinking blue eyes stares at us as the house staff has been enjoying their evening meal together. A few cooks are lingering in the attached open kitchen, preparing our first course.

"Your Grace?" Even Jens'i looks surprised, his fork hovering on the outside of his mouth.

"This is Marta," I boom through the room. "She is my…my…"

Mate, mate, just say the f'teeing word!

"Raf'ere?" Marta strokes the inside of my arm, as confused as everyone else in this room.

"She is a royal guest, and will be treated as such," I tell them.

I am a coward.

"Yes, Your Grace." The staff, snapped from their daze by my request, responds in unison.

"Hi," Marta says, still clinging to my arm. She raising a hand up for an awkward little wave to the dining fi'len.

The room, still thick with confusion, is at a standstill. I hate how they stare at her. I want to tell them to shut their eyes—that she is mine and mine alone. But she will never love me if I treat her like a captive.

"Is there anything else you need assistance with, Your Grace?" Jens'i asks.

"No, continue your meal," I say before turning heel and dragging Marta with me.

My hearts still beat in a furious rhythm from the fear of opening up Marta's world. A buzzing begins in my ears, and I swear I can feel pain in my scars.

But the small hand in mine squeezes tightly.

"…'fere, Raf'ere?" I hear her sweet voice as my hearing returns to normal. "Raf'ere, are you okay?"

"I'm okay," I say, a bit unsteadily.

"Have they been here this whole time?" Her tone is unsure, and she brings one hand to rub her biceps.

"Yes."

"Okay. So, the house knows about me?" Marta asks.

"Yes, and if they weren't at dinner, they'll know soon enough. Word will travel fast that there's a human at the Lin'-gaan Reefs estate." It's true, I'll be lucky if someone doesn't leak her presence here to the tabloids. The gossip publications eat up anything to do with the Royal family. A secret human mate for the duke of the Lin'gaan reefs? They'd eat up every bit of this story.

If I don't get a call from the king in a few hours, I'll be shocked.

"So, I'm not a secret anymore?" The corner of her mouth lifts into a devious grin.

"No," I say, trying to hide the disappointment that I can't keep her to myself any longer.

Her eyes light up, and a manic smile splits her face.

"Thank you!" She pushes me against the wall with a crushing hug.

I grab her face between my palms, tilting her chin to meet my gaze.

She runs the back of her hand down my cheek and cranes her neck to kiss me.

I almost let her, but I turn my head at the last moment.

"Let me make you feel good?" I whisper into her ear.

I'll make you feel so good you'll never want to leave me. I'll make you come so hard you'll forget the rest of the world exists. I'll be the drug you're dependent on.

Just please don't leave.

Marta stills, her face dropping before she passes me a conflicted look. Her mouth pulls into a taught frown before sliding on a more neutral demeanor.

"Is that what you want?" She pouts.

I know she wants me to kiss her. I don't deserve her.

"It makes me happy to pleasure you. Don't pout—you know I can make you feel all better."

She pulls back her shoulders, sighing, before giving me a sly smile.

"Yeah, I know you can. Lead the way to pleasure town," she says with a wave of her hand.

I cradle her in my arms, drawing her intoxicating scent into my lungs. My cock stiffens, as if it doesn't already know I won't allow myself to find a release with her, and if I kiss her I'm sure I would surely lose control. This small step towards her independence has me scared. If I double down on my efforts to keep her satisfied sexually maybe it'll be enough for her to want to stay. Maybe she could look past my disfigurement.

I hit the wall with my fist, activating the hidden door. It pops open, steam and red lights pouring out from the space.

"I swear you have like a secret tunnel fetish. Who in the hell needs so many hidden doors?" She laughs into my chest.

The only fetish I have is for Marta. "There's only one tunnel I'm interested in right now," I waggle my eyebrows, trying to break some of the tension of our unresolved kiss.

"Wow," Marta says with raised eyebrows before I step into the room. "Ohh, it feels great in here!"

I set her on a long bench in the middle of the room. Marta closes her eyes, and her shoulders relax into the welcoming warmth as she reclines.

I haven't been to the steam room since my mate bond activated, but it used to be one of my favorite spots to *entertain*.

I frown, walking over to the far wall and activating a hidden panel. Maybe Marta's right, maybe I do have one too many secret spaces.

But I like secrets. Secrets are safe.

"I want you straddling me, writhing against my body in pleasure tonight," I say as I trail my hands over the many devices the wall panel holds.

"You know, if I didn't know what you can do, I'd assume a

lot of the stuff you say is just a shitty pickup line." She chortles at her own joke.

"What do you mean?" I'm confused.

"Could you imagine if you told me you wanted me to straddle you and writhe in pleasure if we had just met? I'd have probably smacked you right in the face for being a creep." She turns to her side, lazily bringing up her head to rest on her hand.

"What's wrong with being upfront? Fi'len females appreciate knowing exactly what your intentions are." Humans will never be easy for me to understand.

"Well, number one, I'm not fi'len… and number two, human women like a little warming up before you tell them you're going to fuck us. I mean there are always exceptions to the rule, but you don't want to lead with that without someone's consent." She narrows her eyes at me. "Also, for the record, I don't want to hear about fi'len females."

"Are you jealous?" Some strange happiness wells inside me.

"No!" she balks, flopping onto her back and crossing her arms.

"You are," I say, unable to control the smile that forms on my face.

"Do the fi'len like to hear about each other's sexual partners too? Maybe you'd love to hear about my ex—?"

"You're lucky they're on Earth. The odds are good that if you tell me his name, I'll never be able to kill him—but it's not a guarantee I couldn't find a way."

"Is that a promise? Because I have a few jabronis I wouldn't mind you knocking off…" She trails off, thinking that I'm joking.

I grab my weapons of choice and decide not to tell her how serious I am.

"For the record, I like being upfront, no surprises."

"Well then, don't surprise me now. Tell me, what weird alien sex toys are par for the course tonight?" Marta motions to the hand behind my back.

"Take off your dress."

"You do it," she commands.

Who am I to disappoint my mate?

"My pleasure."

I grab the lowest part of her neckline and rip the dress in two. Marta holds onto the bench with her hands, the force of the dress tearing threatening to pull her to the floor.

"Didn't you just get this made?" she complains, her eyes growing wide.

"I'll order another if you liked it." I speak softly as I run the back of my hand from her neck, down between her breasts. She arches into my touch, wanting more.

I set the devices in my hand on the bench by her feet and remove my jacket and shirt. Marta watches me all the while, her gaze roving over my bare chest with hunger. I want to feel her skin on mine, but our position tonight would be far too tempting without some barrier—so the trousers stay on.

Straddling the bench near her feet, with the toys in front of my crotch, I pull the naked Marta so that her thighs rest over mine. Her back is still reclined on the smooth wood, but her hips are tilted up and I'm able to get a full view of her delicious cunt.

"So, what's on the agenda tonight?" She cranes her chin down, trying to get a better view.

"I thought we'd give the pump a spin." I hold the soft plastic dome up in one hand, and the trigger, connected by tubing, in the other.

"Excuse me?" Her eyebrows knit together. "What are we pumping? I've only ever heard of a penis pump, and that's been as a joke in comedy movies...you know I don't have a penis by now, right?"

A devious smile creeps across my face. I love it when she has no idea what something does. It feels like I'm introducing her to some new realm of pleasure.

"We could start with your breast. I think you'd like that," I say confidently.

"And where might we be finishing?" Her hand finds her way

to her nipple, as though she's imagining what the pump might feel like there.

"I'd love to finish by pumping this irresistible cunt of yours. To draw more sensation to your pretty *pussy*." I use the human word she likes and trail my hands over the soft curls of her sex. I've learned that Marta enjoys being teased, to have the pads of my fingers just barely touch her lips. She likes her pleasure dragged out as long as possible—and so do I.

"Raf'ere…" She moans my name before closing her eyes. Her cunt throbs just as my thumb brushes over her clit.

I take her reactions as my cue to begin.

I lean forward, sucking her hardened brown nipple into my mouth. I lap at the pebbled skin as Marta runs her fingers through my hair, urging me to stay the course.

But I have important work to do, and nothing will make me shirk my duties tonight.

I release her nipple from my mouth with a pop, and her eyes shoot open as she loses her hold on my head. I grab a small bottle of lubricant and squirt a generous amount into my hand. Rubbing my palms together, I warm the slick liquid before spreading it in broad strokes over Marta's chest.

She seems to enjoy the roaming of my fingers, so I make a point of kneading the flesh of her shoulders and neck with one hand. The other plucks at the nipple that wasn't in my mouth, as I certainly don't want her to think I'm playing favorites between the two. When I find a small knot near her collarbone, I work it until it dissolves.

"You know, you're really good at massages…why have you been holding out on me?" She places her hand over mine as I work.

"All you had to do was ask—I'll gladly touch your body whenever you need it."

"Mmmhmmm…"

"Are you ready?" I ask my mate, holding up the pump just over one of her breasts.

"Um, I guess as ready as I'll ever be." Although more relaxed than before, her brows draw together.

"Let me know if the suction is too intense. I don't know what your human body can handle."

"Okay, just start slow?"

"Always." I place the soft plastic dome over her breast. Pushing it down, I try to find the best connection to her skin so that it will be airtight. Because of the lube, it slides easily against her skin.

I take more time sliding the dome than I need to. Marta's mewling lets me know she enjoys the feeling of it gliding over her breast. But eventually I settle on the perfect position.

I click the trigger and watch as her nipple is gently tugged upwards toward the air valve at the apex of the dome.

"Oh!" Marta peeps, her lashes fluttering.

"Is that alright?" I ask quickly, decreasing the pressure with the quick release in case it hurts. The air whizzes out, and the dome collapses.

"It's fine...it's just different than I expected. I thought it would feel like your mouth—but it's much stronger. It feels like it's pulling my whole tit up." She tucks her chin down, getting a better view of her breast. "Do it again."

"My adventurous little human," I growl before setting the pump in the same spot again.

I click the trigger a few more times than before, and I watch as a combination of curiosity and concern crosses her face. With each squeeze of the trigger, her flesh is pulled up and more of her delicate breast fills the dome.

Now that it's securely suctioned against her skin, I move the hand that was holding the pump in place down to her inner thighs.

I avoid her most sensitive spot and dance my fingers up and down the space where her legs meet her cunt. Marta's body calls to mine, and she juts up her hips.

"That feels so good," she moans as she makes eye contact with me. "I want more."

When I move my hand back to the dome, I deliberately trail my finger through the wetness I see collecting between her cunt's lips. Just the faintest of brushes near her clit is enough to make her moan with pleasure.

The combination of the steam room, the lube, our sweat, and the nectar between her legs is making us both a slippery mess. There is no resistance as my hands glide over her body.

How easily I could slide my cock into her slick cunt?

But I know I won't be able to stop myself if I do, that I can't let myself experience the bliss of being inside my mate until I'm sure she'll stay.

But I won't pretend that I don't fantasize about filling her completely. I know her muscles would milk my shaft for every drop of cum I have.

I release the suction, and as the vacuum releases her breast leaves it with wet sounding pop. I rub the red spots from the skin and press the flat of my hand against her engorged breast.

Her breath catches as I play with the pink and puffy flesh.

"How does it feel after being pumped?"

"Sensitive," she breathes.

I set the pump down and put more lube on my hand. I cup her mound with slick fingers.

"Do you want the pump here too?"

Marta bites her lip and nods.

Moving the pump to just over her sex, I slide it back and forth, rolling her lips in and out from under the dome. The bump of Marta's clit is the only resistance. When I hit it, she bucks and grabs her breasts.

I tease her only a few seconds more before I seat the pump over the entirety of her cunt. Marta pushes up onto her elbows, too interested in the visual of the toy on her to shut her eyes. With one click of the trigger, the suction locks the dome into place.

She stills, adjusting to the feeling. The dome fogs with condensation, the outside with moisture from the room, and the inside with her slick.

Her mouth parts when I pump it again. We both watch as her lips and clit pulse up with the suction Marta's honey begins to pool near the base of the dome, a sign that it must feel good for my human.

I lock eyes with her and hit the trigger three more times. Her shallow breaths turn into full-on panting. She bucks, her swollen cunt throbbing.

I click the trigger until the dome is nearly full before quickly releasing the suction. I throw the pump to the floor, pressing my palm against her engorged sex. The temporary effects of the pump have increased the blood flow to her cunt. It's the most beautiful shade of pink I've ever seen.

"I love seeing you so swollen and sensitive. Should I let you come, or draw it out a bit longer?" I slide my middle finger between her plush folds, but don't enter her. Her puffed lips cover my finger, and the ring of her entrance spasms, hungry for something to hold on to.

Her legs snap shut over my hand.

"What do you want, Marta?" I ask sliding my finger up and down against her entrance and clit. I'm sure that she'll ask to come soon.

"I want… I want…" she pants.

"Do you want me to make you come?" I preen, smiling at the mewling mess I've made of her.

She scoots her ass further down, pressing herself against the bulge inside my trousers. I tilt my chin up and lick my lips, watching her hips press against my covered cock with hooded lids.

"I want you to fuck me, Raf'ere," Marta says clearly.

I grab the vibrating egg from under her ass and click it on.

"You didn't hear me," Marta says as she sits up, bringing herself to straddle my throbbing shaft.

She loops one arm around the back of my neck and hits the auto fastener of my waistband. In a split second, she has my pants open and she's gripping me tightly. She tilts her hips, notching the head of my dick at her entrance.

"I want you to fuck me with your cock."

Oh goddess, do I want this. I want nothing more than to sheath myself inside of her trembling and oversensitive cunt—to fuck her into ecstasy.

But I can't do that yet. I can't give myself to someone who might not stay.

I pull her close and position my cock so that it rests between her swollen lips. The feeling of the slick heat that envelops me is bliss, and I pump my hips experimentally.

My cock is stimulated as I slide up and down, and the soft spines of the head of my cock drag against her clit.

I push her head against my chest, and she takes one of my blue nipples into her mouth. My cock jerks at the touch. As if we needed any more slickness, I coat her cunt with precum.

I hold her against me, and our hips find a rhythm. With my free hand, I hold the egg vibrator over the head of my dick.

"Fuck, did you just turn your dick into a vibrator?" she asks into my pec. I don't respond, but I can feel her cunt react to the additional stimulation. The muscle between her entrance and ass bobs.

Moving my hand from her head to her ass, I pull her up, exposing her puffed up clit from under the head of my cock.

I place the vibrator directly onto the sensitive crux and hold on to her hip tightly as she unravels. She snaps her knees shut over me and I swivel her ankles over my right shoulder. Abandoning the vibrator, I lay her back.

Though her thighs are still pressed tightly together, I'm able to move my cock through the folds of her sex. With each stroke, I hit the clit of an already orgasming Marta.

With each stroke, I get closer to my own release.

Eventually Marta's eyes roll back into her head, and I feel her legs start to slacken.

"Stay. With. Me." I breathe through gritted teeth. She places her hand on my forearm as I fuck the folds of her cunt.

When Marta looks at me, with a sleepy, completely spent smile, I know I can come.

My balls draw close and my shaft throbs, and I paint her swollen cunt and inner thighs with my release.

I slump on top of her, letting her legs fall open.

"You are mine," I huff into a barely conscious Marta's ear.

CHAPTER 30
☆JUST A GUEST☆

I DON'T REMEMBER LEAVING the steam room, but I wake in Raf'ere's bed. I'm tucked in tightly under the blanket. My limbs still feel like jelly, and my pussy is pleasantly sore.

The pump was an experience, that's for sure.

But the torture of almost penetration has me second guessing where I stand with Raf'ere. He won't kiss me, and for as hard as I beg, he won't fuck me with his cock.

The more time I spend with him, the more his mask drops. I like the real duke most, not whoever he pretends to be. So why won't he do something that should come naturally?

What's wrong with me?

Maybe it's some alien custom I don't understand. I can't be sure of anything with my limited view of this new planet.

I thought maybe a kiss at least could be the next logical step. When it wasn't I felt a little rejected. Maybe I should have been more forceful in my demands. I knew he could take away the sting, that his skills at pleasing me would make it okay for a while. So I took the easy way out of hurting.

But yesterday, he took a step toward sharing his world with me. He introduced me to a room full of people, *as his guest.*

I suppose that's what I am after all, but the word felt so wrong when he said it.

Would I have minded if he called me his lover? Is that what we are? We both know I'm more than just a guest.

"Who's a good boy?" I hear someone whisper from the other side of the room. Nubbins huffs excitedly as the hidden door to the chapel opens.

I groan as I attempt to wake myself prematurely from the haze of sleep. I sit and see him dressed in a robe with our pet under his arm. He scratches him behind his large ear and smiles, whispering something sweet as he does.

He thinks I can't tell he likes the kahne'ah, but I know he's smitten. He never wants to show it, but he does sweet little things for the both of us.

He'd be a good dad.

What the fuck was that? Woah, we're not seriously thinking of having kids with our kidnapper, are we? Who knows if it's even possible, you know, biologically?

I mean sure, before I left Earth, I always wanted a big family. Losing Mom made me feel like I lost out on that whole experience. That and the fact that my cousins were always afraid they might piss off Pops.

I redirect my thoughts away from the weird family planning blip. Even though it seems out of nowhere to my mind, it doesn't feel that out of place in my heart.

Shit, am I falling for him?

"Raf'ere?" It's like I'm asking myself if it could be true, but he thinks I'm trying to get his attention. He turns to me, his blue eyes finding my own. In one hand he holds a plate. Nubbins sits on the floor, drooling at whatever Raf'ere is holding over Nubbin's head.

The smell of sq'aurks clears my mind slightly.

"Don't you dare give him one of those! You don't know if it'll upset his tummy." I yawn. I've been catching the duke feeding our little alien pug all kinds of things that probably aren't good for him.

"Just one more," he says sweetly, if not a little defiantly, as he drops the puff ball into Nubbins's greedy mouth. "I'll be back soon, Marta. I'm going to take Nubbins out in the reefs for a bit, let him stretch his sea legs. Get some rest, I've got a surprise for you later today." He smiles.

I realize I'll probably never win the battle of overfeeding the kahne'ah. Raf'ere likes to show his love with what he can provide the space puppy, and Nubbins isn't going to argue with that.

"Okay, if you insist." I yawn again and recline back into the pillow.

Big plans? Maybe we're going somewhere new. As exciting as that thought is, I push it to the back of my mind. I stretch, pressing my thighs together. I'm still a little sore, and only half hope the surprise isn't another alien sex toy.

But when my eyes shut, I see his face as he came last night. Maybe it wouldn't be so bad to see him vulnerable like that again.

"You have to be f'teeing kidding me!" a shrill female voice shouts. "It's you?"

I snap my eyes open and pull the covers protectively up to my neck. Hovering over my bed is a tall, elegant alien woman. She's dressed in a stiff, high-necked dress. Its gold foiled texture is extravagant and expensive looking, but the fabric barely moves with her body. Her posture is stiff and rigid.

"Excuse me?" I ask her dubiously. "Who the hell the are you?"

"Me? *Who am I?*" she yelps. "I was a shoo-in for Duchess of the Liin'gan Reefs before you showed up!" There is nothing but rage behind her eyes. If it were possible, it would be easy to see how steam might stream from her ears.

She grabs the blanket and rips it off my body.

"This can't be what the goddess has decided for Raf'ere!" She grits her teeth as she appraises my naked body with her eyes.

I snatch the blanket back from her grip and wrap it tightly around me while jumping off the other side of the bed.

"Don't fucking touch me!" I yell. "Jens'i? Raf'ere?" I call out for help.

"Don't bother you stupid human, noise doesn't carry through the estate. I've screamed my head off in that very bed before and not a person came running." As the implication of her statement sinks in, she cracks a devious sneer.

"What do you want?" I ask, backing toward the closet door. Maybe if I can get inside, I can barricade myself from this lunatic.

"I want what you have. I want what I've been working for. All the hours I've wasted submitting myself to the duke's every whim, hoping it would snap our mating bond into place. I want him, you insufferable little alien!" She screams like a child whose favorite toy was taken away. "I deserve to be the duchess—not you!"

"What? I'm not the duchess, are you fucking high?" I have no idea what she's on about.

"Oh right, like Raf'ere wouldn't wed his fated mate? This isn't f'teeing fair!"

"His fated mate? You've got the wrong girl." I shake my head.

It's not me, it couldn't be me—we're not even the same species. He would have told me, wouldn't he?

"I very much wish I did. In fact, I thought Far'ep had lost her mind when she told me Raf'ere's mate was a human. It made more sense that he was keeping you locked in the estate that way, though. How embarrassed he must be to have you as who the goddess has chosen for him. I knew something was amiss when he hadn't returned my calls. We had something together—something primal. It could have been beautiful. There's no way the goddess would be so cruel as to pair two branches of the royal fi'len house with human trash. As if our human queen wasn't insult enough. Why did you have to take *my Raf'ere?*"

Although I take personal offense to nearly everything this lunatic has said, there's only one part that sticks in my mind.

Our human queen.

"There are no other humans here?" My voice cracks. It can't be true.

A wave of recognition flashes over her face. "You didn't know, did you?" She smiles, although her eyes remain as angry as they ever were.

"No." There's a tightness in my chest. I thought I was alone.

"There are hundreds of your kind at the palace." She crosses her arms. "I can help you escape, and maybe the queen will help you get home." There's something off about her tone. If she's being sincere, she's bad at it. "Isn't that what you told Far'ep you wanted? To escape?"

Hundreds? Why would Raf'ere keep me away from an entire community of humans?

"How can I believe you? I don't even know you!" I take another few steps backward. I feel like the prey being stalked by some big-game predator, like in the nature documentaries I used to watch.

The Earthling cowers from the much larger fi'len as she stakes her claim on her intended mate. I imagine David Attenborough narrating.

She reaches into the purse slung over shoulder and jostles the contents around a bit before she pulls something out. I throw my hands up, expecting it to be a weapon of some kind.

But the woman rolls her eyes and types something on her data pad, flipping the screen to me.

A beautiful blonde *human* woman holds a hand over her

pregnant belly. By her side is a tall and handsome fi'len man in the same green color I see Raf'ere wearing all the time.

Around them are fifty to sixty human women wearing simple tunics. And in front of everyone is a woman sitting in a cryopod, her red hair the only characteristic I can make out, with her face obscured by the tight embrace of another fi'len male.

"There's so many of us here." I raise my finger to the crowd of women—but the fi'len woman snatches her data pad from my touch.

"That's nothing, there are hundreds of you at the palace. Something the humans call the Earth Two dormitories."

"Hundreds?" My heart aches for all those stolen girls but desperately yearns to be with them.

"I can get you there, with your people. Would you like that?" Her grin is too wide, her smile too unnatural.

"I trust Raf'ere," I tell her, even though my heart is breaking at his lie. "He'll take me there."

"He won't...you're his mate. What else is there to understand? He'll keep you locked up in the estate rather than risk anyone finding out about you. You're an embarrassment."

"But...but...he introduced me to the staff last night," I counter.

"The staff? Please, they'll take his secrets to the grave, royal duty or some shit. Don't flatter yourself. Far'ep only told me because she knows I can fix this." The woman points a finger up and down my body, implying that I'm the problem.

She's right. Jens'i made sure I was kept a secret—and he could easily make the rest of the house keep it, too.

Is the duke ashamed of me? Is that why he won't kiss me, why he won't make love to me?

"How would you get me out of the estate?" I ask, my stomach clenching in shame.

"It won't be easy, but I have a plan. Can you swim?" she asks, her eyes lighting up with some sick glee.

"Yes," I say, because the duke taught me. "I'm not a strong swimmer, but I can if I have to."

The woman reaches back into her purse, pulling out a black tube connected to a mouthpiece. She holds it out, and when I raise my hand, she places it in my palm.

"That's an e-breather. It'll get you enough air to get to the shrine at the end of the ceremonial tunnels. I can have a cruiser waiting there to take you to the palace. You can be with your own kind." She places a hand on my shoulder with mock affection.

I can't help it, but tears well in my eyes. As they drop, the alien in front of me sighs.

"You don't care for the duke, do you? It would never work… why else would he keep you locked away?"

I thought I did. I swipe a fresh tear off my cheek. "When would we leave?"

"As soon as possible. I don't think they realize that Far'ep's keycard still works. There's no point in risking losing access with it much longer."

"I have a pet, I can't leave him," I say, realizing Nubbins is out with Raf'ere.

"We don't have time to wait. Every second is of the essence!" She's growing impatient.

Raf'ere loves the kahne'ah. I know he'll take care of him.

"Can you give me five minutes? I need to collect myself."

"Ugh, just hurry. I'm risking a lot to get you out of here, you know?" She grimaces.

Just because she's got ulterior motives doesn't mean we can't work together. If I get out, if I can make it to where the other humans are…she gets what she wants.

I nod and back into the closet. I drop the blanket and quickly throw on the first piece of clothing I was given here, my white uniform. It's simple and won't be too heavy to swim in. I grab the makeshift Italian horn necklace from the tabletop and tuck it under the neckline of the dress.

I won't waste any good luck. I'll need it for what I'm about to do.

The panic that normally fills my chest with dread is replaced by a heavy heart. If I don't leave now, I might break. I'm sure everything this woman is telling me isn't true...but it makes sense he's ashamed of me.

It makes sense I'm his mate, and he's bound to me by some biological response he can't control.

That he would never choose me without the stupid bond—we're too different.

After I dress, I take a deep breath and push all the shitty feelings down, knowing I'll never be able to complete the task at hand if I don't.

I step out of my room with my shoulders pulled back and walk confidently to the writing desk near the curtained sea window.

Grabbing the purple pen, I quickly scrawl a note on the strangely textured paper.

> *You don't have to be ashamed anymore, I won't hold you to something you can't control and don't want.*
>
> *Take care of Nubbins, he loves you.*
> *Marta*

I can set us both free.

"I'm ready," I tell the alien in front of me. "I'm Marta, what's your name?"

Her mouth twists into a grin.

"My name is Tri'ot."

CHAPTER 31
☆A BLAST FROM THE PAST☆

☆RAF'ERE

"NEXT TIME you decide to chase a nar'art, I'm letting it eat you," I grumpily tell the kahne'ah under my arm. I wipe at my chest, in a futile attempt to remove the nar'art's defensive ink. Without a doubt, this cravat is ruined.

He just stares up at me, his antennae pulsing with light—as if I didn't just have to chase him a klick down the reef.

"For being such an awkward little thing, you sure are fast," I say, slightly impressed by Nubbins's agility. He just stares up at me with those big black eyes, not a thought behind them. I can't stay mad. And besides, I'm in too good a mood today to be annoyed. Today is the day I tell Marta the truth. I catch myself with a skip in my step, and quickly right the embarrassing display as I slow my pace. I'm anxious to get back to her, to talk about all the things our futures could hold together.

As hard as it's going to be for me to open up her world, I know now that the risk of losing her is worth the chance of loving her. I want to introduce her to fi'len society with a ball.

I may or may not already have a theme in mind for our

formal attire—which I know she'll hate. That's probably Marta's greatest flaw, she has such boring taste in clothing.

But I want her, flaws and all.

There may also be a grand plan in place about how I'll announce she's my mate—we'll stake our claim on each other for the universe to see.

"Jens'i!" I yell down the hall as I see the fi'len male dart into the kitchen, looking flustered. He stops in his tracks and turns to attend me.

"Your Grace?"

"Did the jeweler deliver the order yet?"

His eyes light up and his fingers fly to his suit pocket. He produces a long black case and places it into my eager hands. Running my fingers over the smooth stone, I gently pull back the lid.

It's even better than I'd imagined it would be. The delicate tre'al stone links of the necklace chain are going to look stunning on the chest of my mate. The pendant, the shape a copy of the bead she says is a human good luck charm, is cut out of emerald. It's not smooth, but the gem holds thousands of tiny facets to give it the appearance of being round. Each facet glitters in the light.

"It's perfect," I breathe.

It's not as ornate as something I would wear myself—but I know she'll appreciate its simplicity.

"I think it will be well received indeed, Your Grace." He gives me a knowing smile.

"Do you think it could work?" I ask the person who, before Marta, was the only one I let see the real me.

"Could what work, Your Grace?" He arches a brow on his weathered face.

"Us, Marta and I…do you think we could work? Do I trust a chemical reaction inside my body to decide my life for me?"

Jens'i chuckles and places a hand on my arm. "The mate bond may start as something biological—but I know from experience that the bond itself is just a spark. If there's nothing to ignite the hearts, the mating bond can fail. I know your hearts burn for her, and I've seen the way she looks at you."

"I worry about the subjects of the Reefs. Marta is going to make the return to aquatic living all the harder," I confess for the first time aloud.

"Oh pok'en spurs!" Jens'i breaks his cool demeanor and slaps his palm onto his thigh. "Get your head out of your f'teeing ass and go claim your mate! If the goddess was wise enough to select her for you, why should they care!" He huffs and clears his throat, regaining his composure. "With all due respect, Your Grace…"

"You like her, don't you, Jens'i?" I let a half smile form on my lips.

"As I said, it shouldn't matter what I think—but yes. I like Marta." He's nonchalant in his response.

I nod and start to head upstairs before he speaks again.

"She'll stay," he says quietly, but I know I'm not strong enough to acknowledge his statement.

I hope she will too.

I bound up the grand staircase with Nubbins under my arms, excited to give Marta my gift, to plan for the future—*to tell her she's my mate.*

I'm careful not to swing the door too wide, not wanting to let the ocean view roof spoil my moment. So, I crack it open and back in, trying to use my body to shield the view that upsets Marta so much.

I'm grinning like an idiot when I turn around—but before I'm able to enjoy the moment, my nostrils flare. An intruding scent fills my lungs, and I nearly gag at the wrongness of it.

When my vision catches up with my other senses, they are just as assaulted.

Tri'ot, the social climbing parasite I used to enjoy bed sport with is lying on her side in the bed Marta and I share. She's wearing a silver lingerie set. The straps cut into her fi'len shape in a way I should find pleasing, her gray skin shining and smooth.

On the nightstand she's arranged a selection of her favorite toys, five or six different devices positioned just so.

"Did you miss me, Duke Daddy?" she purrs. "Because I've missed you so much." She flips to her stomach, her white tresses spinning.

Tri'ot pushes her ass up in the air, as if presenting some gift to me.

"Wanna play?" She winks.

I scan the room, at a loss for words, before I set Nubbins on the ground. He approaches the bed, sniffing the same arousal scent I smell. But Nubbins isn't confused, and as he gets closer, he lets out a low rumbling from his chest.

Nubbins stares up at Tri'ot on the bed and growls.

"Can you put that thing in its cage and pay attention to me?" Her baby voice is saccharine as she pouts.

I ignore her and stomp past the bed. Maybe Marta heard her coming and hid in the closet?

My hand grips the door, and I fling it open a bit too hard. There's buzzing in my ears as I realize the closet is empty.

"Marta?" I yell as I run to the bathroom.

"Raf'ere—" I hear Tri'ot trying to get my attention through my panic.

When my mate isn't in the bathroom, I turn back to Tri'ot. She grins and curls a finger in my direction.

"Forget about that silly little human. Let's have some fun, Raf'ere. It'll be just like the old times!"

Tri'ot knows about Marta.

There's a rage building in the pit of my stomach, crackling and burning like a lit fuse. I can't feel my legs as I walk over to the bed. Tri'ot giggles as I kneel next to her.

The lithe fi'len female lets me roll her onto her back, pressing her tits up toward me as I slide my hand over her throat. Her breath catches when I start to squeeze.

Tri'ot pushes her thighs together and stares up at me with hooded lids.

It's only about two seconds later when her look of pleasure fades to something more terrified. I tighten my grip, cutting off her airflow.

"Where the f'tee is Marta?" I growl, my tone cold.

She sputters, droplets of her spit hitting my face as she does. I release my grip to allow her air, and she gulps it down greedily.

"What the f'tee are you doing?" she yelps, pushing on my hands as she scrambles to get out of my grip.

"Where is she?" I seethe out through gritted teeth.

"Raf'ere, baby, stop you're hurting me." Her eyes are wide and I can scent her fear as it overpowers her arousal.

"Tell me where she is! If you hurt her—"

"I didn't do anything to her. She left you! There's a note on the table, go look!" she yells.

I let go of Tri'ot's neck, and she scrambles to the far side of the bed and wraps her arms around her knees.

I rush to the desk and hold up the notepad. Tri'ot knows the fi'len can't read human script, and I throw the note to the ground in frustration.

"Why in the goddess's name do you care about her? She can't do anything for you or the monarchy! F'tee Raf'ere, she's a liability. *Humans don't belong in the reefs.* Do you remember what you told me after the Deenz ship crashed?" She trips over her words, talking fast and looking at her knees.

"Why are you here, then? And where is Marta?" I ask sternly. I don't believe for a second that Tri'ot had nothing to do with her disappearance.

"I'm here to win you back, although it's proving more difficult than I thought it would be," she says as she rubs her neck. "Can't you see that I'm a better fit for *our lives?* We could rule the Liin'gan Reefs together, with me as the duchess—"

"Even before Marta, you would have never been the duchess, Tri'ot. You were nothing more than a dalliance." I can't help but laugh at her aspiration. "I haven't thought about you at all, not once, since I met Marta."

"What do you mean?" She snarls at my admission. "We've been playing this little game together for years. Raf'ere, darling, there is an unspoken promise between us." Her voice strains.

"How can I promise you anything, unspoken or not, *when I am mated a male?*"

Tri'ot's eyes grow wide and glassy, but her mouth twists into a cruel frown.

"She doesn't count." Each syllable is strained through her clenched jaw. "She's not even fi'len, she doesn't belong here!"

"She is the only one who counts, and you're going to tell me exactly where she is."

The female's face goes blank for a second, before I can actually see her decide which mask to roll out. Tri'ot presents me with a helpless face and crawls toward me.

"Why don't I go get her, and I'll let you keep her locked up with you. You can keep doing whatever you're doing in private, I'll allow it. I'll keep your dirty little secret if you make me the duchess. We both know I deserve it. I would be the perfect female at your side." Tri'ot strokes the back of her palm against my cheek. "No one has to know about your little embarrassment."

She knows where Marta is, and if I don't play her game, she won't tell me.

Even though my stomach roils as I grab her hand and pull it against my lips, I do it.

"You would do that for me?" I soften my voice and try to suppress the urge to vomit.

"Of course, Duke Daddy, anything you want. Just think of how respected we'll be, of the dynasty we'll build together." She clutches the back of my neck. "Think of how proud our people will be."

There's some wild flame behind her eyes as she waxes poetically about *our dynasty.*

"I can't wait." It takes everything in me to keep my mask up, to touch this betrayer.

When she kisses me, it's just that. She kisses *me*, and I stay stock still, not able to muster that level of acting.

Her lips can't leave mine fast enough, but she's so hungry for power that she doesn't realize I'm dead inside when she touches me.

She doesn't realize that Marta is everything, and that it doesn't matter anymore what everyone thinks—and maybe it never did.

Was this all just some convenient excuse to continue believing that I wasn't worthy of love?

"I...I don't want to ruin everything for us, but the mate bond is out of my control. I need her here, secret and safe. Where is she? We can bring her back, and I'll lock her in the closet again." My stomach roils while I try to placate the one person who knows where my mate is.

"I know it hurts, and I know it's for the greater good to let you keep your little human pet... It'll be worth the sacrifice." She's attempting to sound noble. "I gave her an e-breather and showed her the ancestral tunnels."

The tunnels...oh goddess.

"You know they're a labyrinth...she'll never make it out of there on her own." The jig is up, and I can't act anymore.

Marta can barely swim.

Tri'ot thins her lips and crosses her arms in an annoyed fashion.

"Her getting lost in the tunnels was kind of the point," she says, deadpan.

I pull the data pad from my pocket and hit the panic button. "Guards, now!"

Understanding flashes over Tri'ot's face when she realizes she's not getting what she wants—me.

"I hope the goddess curses you! I'll cut you from this world like an infected limb."

"She's probably dead already." She stands quickly, dressing for her imminent arrest, like it's going to matter if she's in lingerie or not when she gets life in prison for attempted murder. "Who knows what kind of charge the e-breather had? I didn't check."

"You're a parasite, beneath me in all ways."

"You're a disappointment." She's as cold as ice, a true psychopath.

As soon as I see the handle to the door of my chambers move, I sprint for the secret stairwell.

"Arrest her!" I order as I pray to the goddess to please let there be enough time, to keep Marta alive long enough for me to save her.

I'd give up anything for her.

I'm sprinting as I enter the chapel. I leap over the smaller pools until I reach the back of the chamber. My beating hearts throb in my ears as I arc my body and dive into the ceremonial tunnel system.

Swimming at breakneck speed, my muscles work on over-time as I snake through the narrow passageway.

I don't see any sign of Marta, and I can't believe she's gotten this far. I can only hope our lessons have made her into a strong enough swimmer to survive this.

I stop dead in my tracks, though, when I come to the first fork in the system. The emerald walls of the tunnel split into two paths.

I know, from a lifetime of navigating these waters, that the tunnel to the right is the quickest way to the shrine and the surface. But what direction would Marta go?

Anxiety wells in my throat as I realize I don't know. When every second counts, one wrong turn could mean Marta's life.

Just as I'm frozen in fear, something brushes my side and barrels at full speed down the left-hand tunnel.

Nubbins rockets ahead of me, howling a sad song as he does.

He knows where his mother is.

I kick off the wall behind me and pursue him as quickly as I can. I follow every twist and turn Nubbins takes as we both swim deeper into the maze.

Without warning, after a hard right turn, I knock hard into something solid. As I shake the impact from my system, I see Marta's hand floating limply in the water. The small metal e-breather floats behind me, caught in the current Nubbins and I have created with our speed.

Marta's eyes are closed, and a bubble floats from her open mouth. I grab her and pull her violently into my embrace. Nubbins peppers her cheeks with mournful kisses.

I press my lips against hers for the first time. They're as soft as I always imagined. Please let this be the first of many kisses, don't let this be the last. I breathe into her mouth, and water rushes out of her nose. I begin to swim back to the chapel caverns. Every few seconds I attempt to replace the briny liquid that's filled her respiratory system.

Marta still hangs limp in my arms as we surface.

Nubbins yelps as I roll my mate onto her side. Her skin is as blue as when she slept in her cryopod.

I reach for the kahne'ah's collar, snapping the silver cylinder off his collar. I've never been more happy for an impulse purchase in my life, that my anxiety over Marta taking Nubbins down to the temple may be the one thing that saves her life.

I slide back the injector's sheath and plunge the medicine into her thigh. A complex cocktail that includes blood oxygenation nanobots, adrenaline, and painkillers begins to course through her system.

"You can't leave me now," I mutter as I thump her on her back, trying to clear her airways. "You don't get to f'teeing leave!" Fat tears well in my eyes as I take a huge breath and blow air into her again.

"You're not allowed to die," I whisper, breaking into a manic fit of sobbing as I refuse to let the goddess have my mate. "I promise I'll let you do whatever you want, I'll let you leave me if that's what it takes. You just can't f'teeing die!" I gather her up in my arms and give her back one last violent thump.

Her chin is on my shoulder when I feel a rush of wetness hit my neck. Marta's body shakes as she rasps and coughs. As she comes back to me, she grips me hard.

"I drowned," she sobs and hiccups. "I drowned!"

I squeeze the little human just hard enough not to crack her ribs. She trembles and shakes, and Nubbins lathes her knee with his tongue.

"I drowned, Raf'ere."

I pull back, clutching her face between my palms. I turn her head gently to either side, looking for any wounds.

"Does it hurt anywhere?" I kiss her forehead. "Take a deep breath."

"I...I drowned." Her eyes are unfocused, and she starts to shake.

"I'm here, Marta. I won't let anything bad happen to you, you're safe," I whisper as I gather her up against me and stand.

She keeps repeating herself, and I stroke her wet hair against her head as we ascend the stairs. Jens'i rushes into the secret corridor just as we hit the top step.

"Raf'ere," he says, completely out of breath.

"The guards." He clutches his chest. "They've detained Tri'ot. I don't know how she was able to gain access to the estate..." His eyes see the shaking Marta in my arms. "Oh goddess..."

"She's alright," I tell him. "Make sure the estate is secure. I've given her medicine, call for a medic."

I push past the butler and sit on the bed. Jens'i runs as fast as his elderly legs can carry him out the door.

I grab the blanket and wrap both our bodies inside it, rubbing my hands down her biceps in an attempt to warm her.

"I drowned—"

"And you didn't die, and you're here in my arms."

"I..."

"Why did you do that?" I can't control the fear in my voice. "Why would you leave me?"

"You...you lied to me, about the other humans." Marta's body still shakes, but her skin starts to warm. "You kept me locked up here because you're ashamed of me," she says hoarsely.

My stomach drops.

"What do you mean?" Now my voice is shaking.

"Tri'ot told me, she told me everything. Just let me go and I'll disappear. Take me to be with my people at the palace, and I won't be your shame to hide." Marta asks me to let her go, but the misting in her eyes betrays her confident tone.

"I..I..." I don't know what to say.

Instead of talking, I pull her lips to mine and try to let my kiss explain everything.

She balks at first, but as I hold her tight, she eases herself deeper into our embrace. Her tongue darts out, and we explore the feeling of each other's mouths.

The warmth between us turns into searing heat. Our hands dance wildly over each other's skin as we search for anything to hold on to and ground us in this moment.

I pull back, and Marta gazes up at me expectantly.

"You can't listen to Tri'ot! She's a social climbing parasite. She'd say anything to obtain me. I'm nothing more than a trophy she can add to her case. She tried to kill you, Marta! She knew that you'd get lost in the tunnels and die!" I kiss her again, hard. I can't control myself anymore.

She pushes back, her hands on my chest—like she wants to stay angry with me, like she can't shake the lies Tri'ot told her.

"I'm sorry," is all I can get out. I press my lips to her again, unable to find the words. "Why did you leave Nubbins?" I ask, knowing she loves that little beast.

"I knew he'd be fine with you–I left you a note!"

"I couldn't read it," I say as I kiss her face all over.

"You're illiterate?" Marta's mouth drops open, and she brings a hand to my cheek. "Why didn't you tell me that? I could have taught you to read!" The sympathy in her voice makes me laugh, even though I know my timing is rough.

"F'tee, Marta, I can read—just not your strange alien language."

"Oh"—her eyebrows shoot up—"of course you can read…"

"You have to promise me you'll never put yourself in that kind of danger again." I brush my thumb over her swollen lips.

"Promise me you'll stop lying." She stares into my soul as she makes her demands.

"I swear it."

This time, Marta leans into me and initiates the kiss. I pull back, unsure if it's safe to continue.

"Marta, you nearly drowned—are you sure this is okay? That I'm not hurting you more?" My voice shakes as I press my hips against hers.

"I feel…weirdly amazing?" She says, peppering kisses along my jawline. I rub my hand on her thigh over the small bump left by the rescue medicine I gave her.

"The shot, I gave you a shot that would make you feel better…it's oxygenating your blood right now…" I didn't think it would be so effective at recovery, but it's proving to be worth every penny.

"I don't care what it's doing. All I know is I need you!"

It's the permission I need to lose any of the control I had before.

She grabs a chunk of my hair, pulling me into a deeper and more passionate kiss. Our lips search for purchase. Aching with need, I pull her dress up over her head.

She reaches for my waist fastener and opens it, letting my hard cock bob against my belly. I stand, kicking my legs free of the trousers. Marta bites my lower lip as she grabs my painfully hard shaft. Her warm palm feels like heaven.

I push her back against the wall, pinning her to it with my hip. Cupping one hand under her succulent ass, I brush a curl out of her eyes and stare in wonder at the flushed beauty before me.

"If we keep going, I won't be able to stop. I need you to tell me you want this as badly as I do." I don't recognize the sound of my own trembling voice as I speak.

Her breath slows and her pupils dilate. Every millisecond she leaves me unanswered feels like a lifetime.

"I need you, Raf'ere. I'll always need you."

With those words, I'm hers.

CHAPTER 32
☆LIKE A BUILT-IN ROSE TOY☆

☆**MARTA**

OUR LIPS CRASH TOGETHER AGAIN, his kiss hungry and searching. He's lifted me up and pinned me against the wall, his hips settling between mine. His cock throbs in my palm.

He came for me, he saved my life.

While cupping my ass for support, his other finds my pussy. He runs a knuckle down its length, teasing my entrance.

"I wanted to take my time, I wanted to make sure you could take me, Marta…I don't want to hurt you." He groans as he grinds our hips together. "But I think I'll die if I don't rut you right now. I want to feel your tight cunt grasping my cock. I need all of you." His breath is coming in pants and sweat beads on his brow.

He's so much bigger than me, and I know it would be smart to work me up to his impressive length. But I need him as much as he needs me right now. I need to feel like one part of something bigger.

"I don't care, I want you inside me now," I beg, using my hand to notch his cock at my entrance. I'm so slick, I can already feel him sliding past the tight ring of nerves.

"Tell me you me want me again," he whispers hoarsely, like he doesn't believe me.

"I want you, Raf'ere. I want your cock. I need you to fuck me," I moan into the crock of his neck.

Nothing has ever felt more urgent to me than that.

"If it hurts, if it's too much…" He stops talking and the tip of his cock stretches my pussy wide.

It is intense, and there's an edge of pain that taints the pleasure as I acclimate to his girth.

When it gets to be too much, I bite into his shoulder. It's as if maybe I can transfer some of my pain to him when my teeth mark his flesh. He stills, feeling me tense.

"Are you okay?" His voice shakes as he tries not to move. Raf'ere reaches down and strokes my clit. It soothes the stretching. He goes so much slower than I want.

As I adjust, I realize he's probably right. His cock is a big one, and no matter how much of the pick-me-up medicine he gave me, I'm still so much smaller than him.

"Don't stop," I tell him, convinced that I can take it. "I want you to fill me up, Raf'ere." I groan as he slides just the tiniest bit further into me. "Fuck, fuck, fuck." I'm lost to sensation.

"You're so beautiful," he breathes. "You're such a good fucking girl for me."

He rubs my clit, pushing further. He fits into every available space inside me, and when I look down at his progress, I can see that he's almost to his hilt. The small cup of flesh at the base of his dick lines up neatly with his thumb on my clit.

He keeps his hand between us, a barrier to feeling his true length. Even though it feels amazing, I want all of him.

I push his hand away and tilt my hips until the root of him is flush against me.

"Fuck," Raf'ere moans as his head rolls back.

We don't move, just relishing every inch of one another. I can feel the blood pumping through his shaft, and I know he can feel the muscles of my pussy desperately clamping around him.

"You feel so good," I whimper against his shoulder.

"Marta, I can't stay still much longer—tell me it's okay to move, tell me I won't hurt you."

"For the love of god, please fuck me. Claim me!"

Raf'ere's eyes go wide as I beg. I grab at his skin because we're both slick with sweat. I try and grip the back of his neck, but my hands can't find their purchase.. He looks down at me, locking our eyes together.

"Your cunt is mine?"

I nod, willing him to move, wanting him to slam his cock into me again and again.

When he slides out, I feel something suck my clit, pulling it before it pops off with an explosion of pleasure.

"Oh, fuck, Raf'ere!"

"Mine," he growls, sliding back in. "This cunt is mine, you are mine!"

I push at his chest, looking down as I watch the cupped flesh grab my clit. It clasps over the *my gem* as he fills me completely. He picks up his pace and withdraws., his hips moving too quickly for me to see what's happening to my clit any longer.

But even if I can't see it, I can feel it. It sucks and releases over and over again. Our bodies slap together, and Raf'ere braces his hand on my tit, massaging it as he relentlessly pounds into me.

It feels so fucking right.

"What the fuck is that?"

"My"—he groans—"sucker!"

Raf'ere's movements start to become erratic, and I know he's close.

Fuck, I'm close too, every muscle of my sex tightening.

"Don't' stop, please don't stop." My words are garbled as he fucks me. "I want to feel you inside me as I come."

Raf'ere doesn't stop, he only picks up the pace and kisses the side of my neck. His tongue licks at the column of my throat before pulling my earlobe between his teeth.

"This cunt is mine, and I want you to come so hard around

me." He slides his hand from where it works my breast to my neck.

I make ungodly noises, and he picks up his pace, his cock nearly completely unsheathing on the downswing. A cord inside me tightens. As his sucker grabs my clit again, as the head of his dick slides past my G-spot, I explode.

My thighs try to snap shut over him, but he won't relent.

He fucks me as I come. I shake as waves of pleasure roll through me, my eyes rolling into the back of my head.

"Too much," I pant.

"Mine. Mine, all mine," Raf'ere repeats over and over.

I swear I'm about to black out when I feel his cock slide against my belly. He leans his body weight against me entirely.

"You are mine, Marta," he says as he pushes our lips together, and I feel his ass contract. He spills a hot wash of semen on my belly as he comes.

"Yours," I agree, breathlessly.

The door to the bedroom opens slightly before hitting Raf'ere's thigh. The meaty leg blocks it from opening any further.

"Your Grace?" Jens'i's panicked voice floods in from around the door. "The medic, he's here."

"A moment, please." Raf'ere doesn't sound much better. He kisses my eyelids and rests his chin on top of my head, completely spent.

"We should have the medic check you over." He pushes the door shut, lifts me off the wall, and cradles me in his arms as he walks us to the bed.

He lays me down gently, tucking me under a sheet, before crawling in right beside me. We're sticky with each other's release as we lie in some postcoital bliss.

He takes one of the blankets and rubs it over my chest before spreading it back over the bed.

"What are you doing?" I demand.

"Some scents I'd much rather be yours is all," he sighs.

"You're so weird." I roll my eyes and turn into his chest.

"It was worth the wait," he whispers to me, throwing his arm around my chest.

The wait?

"What in the fuck were you waiting for?" I'm confused.

"I was waiting…" He pauses like he can't think of the right words. "I was waiting until you wanted me as badly as I wanted you. I wanted to prove to you I was worthy enough to fill you… that I could give you any pleasure you could need."

"Word to the wise, you don't need the toys. That sucker is the only sex toy I'll ever need again." It seems like overkill to have anything when his alien body couldn't be designed better to get me off.

"It's all yours," he says, kissing me again. Our lips are sore from passion, but I don't want to stop. I've waited long enough.

The door creaks open and a frantic Jens'i enters, followed by two strangely uniformed fi'len men.

"I must insist that we look over Marta, Your Grace," he says sternly. As if there was any doubt about what we have just done, I know that as Jens'i's nostrils flare, he's fully aware of our fucking.

"Don't f'teeing look at her," Raf'ere growls, clutching me tightly.

The two men behind him avert their eyes from me, but cautiously walk toward the bed.

"Enough, Raf'ere, don't be a dick. Can you guys give me a minute? I swear I'm alright," I say as I sit up, clutching the sheet to my chest. "Jens'i, can you please grab my robe?"

He brings it to the bedside quickly and holds it out for me to slip into discreetly.

"I think everyone would appreciate it if I showered first." I place a hand subconsciously over my stomach where the plush fabric sticks to my skin. "Have a seat," I say to the strangers in the room.

Raf'ere stands to join me, his cock still *al dente* and flushed.

But he's obviously not embarrassed. He grabs my elbow and leads me to the bathroom. Closing the door behind us, he activates the shower and I drop my robe.

Even though what just happened felt wonderful, it was fast and rough. My chest still burns, and a bruise forms on my back between my shoulder blades.

Reaching my hand gingerly over my shoulder to inspect it, the duke winces.

"I'm sorry, I think that might be my fault. I lost it when you wouldn't wake up...I might have hit you a bit too hard."

I flinch only slightly when my fingers graze the spot. I turn my head and can see the blooming purple and brown mark. The round bruise is slightly raised from where the blood has welled.

"Better bruised than dead," I say with an awkward chuckle, but Raf'ere doesn't find it amusing.

"Don't ever do that to me again," he says distantly, holding his hand in the spray to check the temperature. He motions for me to step into the warm waters.

It feels amazing, and I let my sore muscles relax. Raf'ere steps in behind me and grabs the soap, lathering his hands together.

"I wish I could keep you painted in my cum forever," he breathes, rubbing his hand over the mess he made of me.

"But can't your people smell that kind of thing? I don't want to be known as the human who smells like cum." I groan, wishing the fi'len had somewhat less acute senses.

"That's the whole point. Everyone would know you're *mine.*" His eyes get a dreamy, far-off look.

The emphasis he places on the last word sends a thrill through me. How the duke can make me horny with just his voice is ridiculous.

I can feel his fingers drifting lower, and I know I need to put the kibosh on his intentions quickly.

"Raf'ere, we should get the medics to check me over. The longer we wait, the more anxious you're making poor Jens'i." I try to be the voice of reason in this bathroom. I've never seen the butler in the state he was in just now.

He groans, turning my front to face the jets that rinse me of suds.

"Do you think they can do whatever they need to do without touching you?"

I can't tell if he's asking seriously or not.

"You'll survive," I tell him before bringing his hand up to kiss it.

CHAPTER 33
☆I MISS EVERYTHING☆

☆RAF'ERE

THE MEDICS ARE THANKFULLY BRIEF. They run a field scanner right in my chambers and have their data pads collect the information needed.

Marta is bruised, her lungs and throat will need time to fully recover, but with a few days' rest she should be as good as new. They did make mention of her vitamin D levels being danger-ously low, and provided us with a supplement.

"Yeah Raf'ere, more sunshine less locking in closets," she jibes at me with an eyebrow waggle

I don't see the humor. In my anxiety, my blind fear to keep her safe, I've managed to cause her some level of harm.

I must do better by her, I have to.

When everyone leaves, and we're finally alone again, things grow strangely quiet between us. I'm positioned at my desk, leaned back in the chair, observing my mate.

She sits in the arm chair, wearing one of my oversized shirts. Pulling her knees up against her chest, her head is lolls to the side. She stares out the open bedroom door into the ballroom.

"Marta?"

Oh god, the door is open. Marta is staring right at the biofilm ceiling.

I jump to my feet and rush to slam the door.

"What?" she asks, as if snapping from some daydream when the door crashes against its frame.

"The ocean…" I cock my head. *She didn't notice?*

"Oh, yeah, weird," is all I get from her with some far-off look. Could she still be in shock? She stands slowly, her body obviously achy, and walks toward me.

She puts her hand over my own, which is still on the door-knob, and turns. The door creaks on it's hinges, and I let her look around my arm as it opens.

She frowns and stares up at the expanse of water that floats directly over the ballroom. Unlike previously, she doesn't freeze in fear.

Marta takes a step through the doorway of our bedroom.

She tilts her head up and, with eyes wide, stares into the waters that teem with life.

"It's kind of beautiful now that I'm looking at it…" Her voice trails off, and she leans over the banister to get a better look.

"Since when does this view not terrify you?" I ask, dumbfounded.

"I don't know, maybe since I drowned?" She seems just as confused as I do. "I guess when your worst fear happens, it gets a little less scary?"

She turns back to the room, and I follow.

"Open the curtains," she says cautiously. A finger slips into her mouth, and she bites at her nail.

I click a button on my data pad and reveal the floor-to-ceiling biofilm window for the first time in a long while. It feels out of place after being hidden for so long.

I turn back to my mate, waiting for any sign of panic—but she remains calm as ever.

"Bizarre," she mumbles before plopping back into the chair.

"Do you think..." I trail off, not wanting to admit what's crossing my mind.

"What?"

"Never mind, it's silly," I brush off the thought.

"Raf'ere, tell me." She looks at me intently, deserving of the truth now more than ever.

"Do you think the waters of I'loh might have taken away your fear? Maybe the goddess...I don't know. The water was inside of your lungs, it surrounded you. Could our myths and legends be right?"

"Something happened, I feel...different," she says, letting her eyes follow the undulating light that filters through the seas on display beyond the window.

I watch her, watching the waves, and am struck by her beauty, but also her melancholy.

"Why didn't you tell me about the other humans?" There's a hurt in her eyes that breaks me when she turns.

"Because I knew you would leave me."

Marta jolts, her eyes going wide.

"So you took away my choice? That's not right!" She blinks back tears of anger. "They're my people, they're as close as I'll ever get to Earth again. God, I miss it!"

She's homesick. Of course she's f'teeing homesick. You've kept her locked up in your home for the past month, you monster.

"What do you miss the most?" I ask. Maybe there's something easy I can get smuggled in for her. A favorite food?

"I miss everything."

Oh, not so easy then.

"I miss my family, of course, even my stupid cousin Nick. I miss people watching from the brownstone window. I miss good wine, I miss little Italy, I miss reality tv, and I miss holidays—I would kill to have a Feast of the Seven Fishes." Her face pales. "Oh god, I don't even know what day it is. Did I miss Christmas?" Marta's eyes get even sadder.

I was so busy worrying about if she would fit into my life here, that I didn't bother to think of if I would fit into hers.

We're different species, with different cultures, and I'm nearly as oblivious as I was when she first arrived.

"Marta?"

"Yeah?"

"What does Italian mean?" I ask, finally brave enough to look stupid in front of my mate.

Marta opens her mouth with a look of disbelief.

"You didn't know what Italian meant?"

"Well no, obviously, that's why I'm asking," I tell, her only a little bit miffed at her reaction.

"Um, oh god. Italians are like a type of human, from a specific place, Italy."

"So, it's just a heritage? Italians aren't warriors?"

"I mean, I guess you could say that." She arches an eyebrow at my inference about her people. "We do have a tendency to stick together, especially in America where I live. When Italians immigrated, they weren't very well liked by the established populations. So, we banded together and relied on each other. I think our community is stronger for that today. Granted, my father isn't the best example of an upstanding citizen—I know he tried his best. I hope he's doing okay without me." She drifts deeper into sadness at the mention of her father.

"I'm sorry that the Deenz took you from your planet, I really am—but I'm glad I got to meet you."

She sighs as I speak, forcing a mournful little smile.

Could she ever truly be happy here, without her people or her culture? I don't even know what Christmas is—my data pad only shows me a fat old man in a red suit in some kind of spaceship pulled by flying livestock. We definitely don't have that on Sontafrul 6.

"Raf'ere?"

"What?"

"Do you really think I'm your mate?" she says in a near whisper.

She knows, Tri'ot must have told her.

This isn't how I wanted it to happen, none of this is right. I wanted to tell her about the bond and give her a choice to stay or leave. I wanted to be fair to her, to give her a fighting chance at the life she wanted.

But most of all, I wanted Marta to choose me.

Nubbins, sensing my distress, nudges at my shin. I shoo him away.

"What do you want?" I ask her, not wanting the mate bond to sway her. She can't feel it, so it should be my burden to shoulder alone. I can at least protect her from that.

"I—I don't know Raf'ere. The only thing I wanted when I first got here was to go home, but things are complicated now." She gives me a knowing glance.

I am a complication. I make everything worse.

I'm the monster everyone thinks I am.

"You should be with your kind, you miss them," I say numbly.

I don't want to do it, but I can't keep choosing what's right *for me*...I need to choose what's best *for her*. It's what a good mate would do.

"Raf'ere, answer me. Am I your mate?"

When I don't answer her the silence between us is tangible. I can't let my burden be the reason she stays. Standing, I try my best to regain my composure. I don't know how I'll be able to survive if I lose her, but my survival isn't the most important thing anymore. Her thriving is.

I have to do what's best for Marta.

"Raf'ere! Tell me...what do you want, what am I to you? Am I your mate?" She pleads with me. She wrenches her hands in her lap.

"Am I yours?" I ask her softly.

"I, I don't know…" Marta bites her lip, turning away from me.

There is it, that coldness creeping in from the darkest parts of my soul—it protects me from the crushing sadness I should feel right now.

"I'll take you to the palace in the morning," I manage to say numbly.

"Raf'ere," Marta whispers, reaching her hand out to me as I pass by her. For a split second, I think that maybe she'll beg me to stay. "How long are *we* staying?"

"A night or two, I'll have Jens'i pack a bag for you," I lie, knowing that it's best for me to leave her there with her kind. To let her live a life without someone as damaged as I am.

I know I might never feel joy again, not after knowing my mate and letting her go…but it's the only fair and honest thing I can do now.

I love Marta.

CHAPTER 34
☆EARTH 2, ELECTRIC BOOGALOO☆

☆MARTA

I cradle the suitcase Jens'i provided me with against my chest. I shift a bit uncomfortably in my seat. The pack is bigger than I expected, but who knows what kind of wardrobe you need to at an honest-to-god palace?

Raf'ere sits across from me in the cruiser, staring out the window with a forlorn face. When we came out of hyperspeed the buildings and people seemed to appear out of nowhere. I should be amazed at the city I catch glimpses of through my peripheral vision, but I can't keep my eyes off the duke.

Am I yours? His words from last night haunt me almost as much as my answer.

I know that I love the way the duke makes me feel, that he's saved my life twice over, and that he's trying his best to make sure I'm happy.

So why can't I just say yes?

The cruiser rocks violently and begins to descend. I grip the armrests and finally look out the window. A palace, situated on land and not even that close to the water. It's much grander than the duke's estate, I realize as it looms into view.

Everything here is so different from the Liin'gan Reefs.

There's so much traffic and aliens of all kinds crowd the roadways. The palace sprawls over what seems like could be ten or fifteen city blocks.

"It's alright, just a little turbulence as we get into position for the landing," Raf'ere tells me. Obviously he's much more seasoned in all the forms of space travel than I am.

We move laterally until we're directly over what looks like a courtyard. There's a quick buzz and a purple force field becomes visible all around the building.

"Hmm, that's new." Raf'ere cranes his neck to get a better look at the laser-like lines.

"This is Reefs One, requesting landing access to The Palace, over." the captain's voice buzzes over the intercom.

"Landing permission granted, begin descent at will, over," someone with a very obvious midwestern accent says over the feed. As soon as she clips out, a hole fizzles in the purple rays of light that guard the palace.

"A human?" I ask, getting excited for the first time since we've left.

"Certainly not a fi'len—they're doing their best to get all the women jobs. Air traffic control must be on the list." He smiles at my excitement.

We lower smoothly and quickly into the courtyard. As soon as the cruiser hits the pavement, a flock of women crowd around the vehicle, like they've been waiting for us to arrive.

"There's so many of us here," I whisper, surprised at the sheer number and different types of women I see flooding out from the building.

"And more arriving every day," he says as he looks at me.

"Guess so." I try to keep my voice steady, but even my own ears can hear as it cracks.

I stand as the dust from the boosters settles, clutching my suitcase to my chest. Raf'ere takes my arm, tucking it under his.

"Ready?" He asks me forcing, a smile.

"Ready," I tell him.

Walking over to the bay doors, I hold my breath when they drop open. My eyes squint as the sunlight streams in, my vision acclimating to the soft lighting of the estate and the dim glow of the caverns.

But god, does the sun feel good on my skin.

I put my hand over my brow and try to see everyone who stands at attention for our arrival.

"Who the hell is that?" I hear someone with a valley girl accent ask.

"Shit, that's not the marauders…I was really jonesing for that damn cotton candy vape." A tall brunette looks completely crestfallen.

"Hi," I squeak out over the groans and disappointed stares of the human women around me.

"Hey," someone says dismissively before turning away and walking back to whatever she was doing before.

"A cotton candy vape?" Raf'ere asks, brows arched.

"Just a bad habit lots of humans love." I pat his arm and walk down the steps that have unfolded from the cruiser.

As everyone's attentions shift, there's one woman who goes against the flow of the crowd and waddles closer. She's blonde, gorgeous, and struggling to move with what looks like one of the biggest pregnant bellies I've ever laid my eyes on.

I recognize her, she's the woman from the photo on Tri'ot's data pad.

"Opal," I say before dropping into some strange uncoordinated curtsey.

"Oh stop that right now!" she drawls in with a thick southern accent. "Welcome to Earth 2 darlin'! Raf'ere, it's not like you to bring in refugees yourself." She eyes us both with a bewildered stare, before turning to me with a warm grin. "So, where'd you find this beauty?"

"A cry-cryopod," he stutters slightly, and the queens brows knit.

"Y'alright cousin?" She places a hand on his arm and he nods.

"Yes, Marta was found in a cryopod, I think she was on the crashed Deenz ship." He pulls his shoulders back.

"Oh my god, Jessy is going to freak out! You're our missing crash survivor!" Opal tries her best to wrap her arms around me, but there's simply too much belly and not enough arm.

"Excellent, how is Gra'eth's mate?" Raf'ere asks in a strained small talk kind of way. It doesn't come naturally to him.

"Oh you know, she still hates you," Opal laughs. "In fact, just as they announced your cruiser had landed, I think I heard her stomping down the hall. You might wanna hide." She winks.

Raf'ere scoffs and changes the subject. "I was wondering if you might be able to host Marta with the other women tonight?"

"Just tonight? I kind of figured you'd be staying with us for good. People don't usually come to Earth 2 for sleepovers."

Raf'ere sets his jaw, and looks at me. There's something he's hiding behind those blue eyes of his.

Why the hell won't he answer her?

"Just a few days, right Raf'ere?" I ask.

Opal looks at me, then looks at Raf'ere, and then back at me.

"Is there...some kind of situation I should be aware of between you two?" She seems suspicious.

I look over at Raf'ere, wanting for him to fight for us, to fight for me.

But he just crosses his arms and grits his teeth.

"I guess not," I say with the shittiest of attitudes I can muster.

"Riiiiight," Opal says, grabbing my hand. "Well, let me show you around." She drags me quickly away from the duke.

I can hear his heavy shoes plodding quickly behind us.

"Oh darlin', don't worry, I've got her. Ke'ain should be overseeing the renovations in the council's chambers. Why don't y'all go catch up." Although her voice is dripping with sweetness, I know that it's not a request but an order for Raf'ere to leave us alone.

He sighs and turns the opposite direction without saying another word.

As soon as he's out of earshot the queen turns to me, placing her hands on my biceps and giving me the most serious of faces.

"Did Raf'ere hurt you?" she asks completely serious.

"What? No, he would never…" Is his reputation really that terrible?

"Ugh, thank god, I mean don't get me wrong…I've been itching to get into a fight—you know my hormones are wild right now. I'm glad he's not being a douche." She nods to herself and then keeps dragging me the direction we were going before.

I try to take it all in. The gaggles of women, the odd fi'len guard, the massive palace. It feels bizarre to be somewhere so big after having my world be so hyper focused these past few weeks.

"So, where ya from?" she asks as we walk.

"Brooklyn."

"Oh, jealous. I was saving up to go see New York City right before I got snatched. Is the pizza really that much better there?"

"I don't know. I've lived in the city my whole life so I don't have anything to compare it to." Could pizza ever be bad?

"Well, enjoy those memories. Despite Betty's best efforts there's nothing we've been able to find that's close to the ingredients for pizza here. Betty is our resident human chef. She's gotten pretty close to a lot of human foods…but the fi'len really don't have the palate for cheese, so it doesn't really exist here yet." She frowns.

It's weird what can be the final piece of information that can make you snap—sometimes it has nothing to do with what's actually wrong.

"There's no cheese?" I say, a sob catching in my throat dramatically. But what my mind is actually doing, in addition to breaking down over the lack of cheese in outer space, is realizing that Raf'ere is planning on leaving me here.

That this stupid heavy pack isn't just for one night, it's for forever. That instead of us working through everything together, he's dumping me off with the rest of the humans. My home at the Reefs might be gone forever all because he's scared to fight for me. All that and the fact that I'll never be able to sprinkle parmesan over pastina again.

If my heart wasn't breaking, I'd march right over to him to give him a peace of my mind. But I'm frozen with the realization that I'm being abandoned.

"Oh sweetie." The queen puts an arm around me. "It's going to be alright. Betty's trying to figure out how to get the cheese ball rolling here so to speak." She rubs my back. "You really like cheese, don't you?"

"I'm Italian," I sniffle.

Opal nods knowingly before pushing our way through a set of swinging double doors.

Rows and rows of bunk beds fill the expansive space. The lights are off. I hear a few snores in the distance, but for the most part the beds are empty.

I shiver as the air from the room hits me—it must be at least twenty degrees colder in here than in the courtyard.

Opal pulls a data pad out from the pocket of her gown and flips through a spreadsheet.

"I always kind of feel like I'm in Ikea when I do this," she jokes. "It looks like row nineteen, bunk D is open. Aw, that means Janae moved in with her mate!" She clutches her chest with some fondness over the situation. "Good for her."

She motions for me to follow her down the hall.

"Opal, why is it so dark and cold in here?"

"Oh, yeah, sorry. I didn't go to college and I never rushed a sorority, so I didn't know anything about cold dorms either," she confides. "There's a few women here who stepped up to help us get Earth 2 organized. Unsurprisingly, they were often presidents of their sororities back on Earth. I guess cold dorms are like an old school sleeping arrangement for lots of people to sleep better in a smaller space. The lights in here are always off, we keep it cool, and it's really only for sleeping. We've got all kinds of different halls for day-to-day activities, but this was the best solution for everyone's different sleeping habits. We're big on compromise here."

We finally reach my bunk. "This is mine?"

The twin bed is devoid of any of the comforts back in the estate. The blanket looks sad and hospital grade. There's a small table, but no magic glowing lava lamp. It's entirely lacking in magically cold bedside water as well.

And, most importantly, there's no Raf ere.

I take a deep breath, and Opal gives me a little smile as I set my luggage on the bed.

"Tell you what, I'm gonna give you a bit of time to yourself and let you get your stuff set up. I'll be in the mess hall. You just go right through those doors and ask any of the guards or the women where that is and they'll show you. Sound good?"

"Sure, I'll meet you there," I whisper, staring at my sad new bed.

Opal waddles away quickly, and I snap the closure on my suitcase and fling the lid up.

Inside is something I don't recognize. A long and narrow rectangular box is nestled on top of what looks like the entirety of my wardrobe from the Duke's estate–far too much clothing for an overnight stay, just as I predicted.

I pick it up gingerly and remove the lid. Inside, on a beautiful black chain, is one of the most stunning Italian horns I've ever seen. Even in the darkness of the cold dorm it glitters, its tiny facets catching even the dimmest of light.

I clutch it to my chest and let the fat tears flow down my cheeks.

My shock at what he plans to do quickly turns to anger.

That fucking *stronzo!*[1] Who does he think he is, just leaving me here? He can't just sneak into my luggage one of the most beautiful gifts I've ever received and have me act like it never happened.

I won't accept it.

Wiping my the tears from my cheeks, I slide the necklace over my head, and walk toward the swinging doors. I damn near kick them open, even though I have no idea where I'm going, but Opal said everyone would help me find my way.

Of course the hallway is empty, so I go the direction we came in. Rounding a corner, I see a human woman sitting on a bench.

"Hey you!" I holler.

When the girl tilts her head up to me, her russet brown skin is tear streaked, and she clutches her chest mid sob.

Shit.

"Are you okay?" I ask her, really regretting I've never been able to mind my own business.

"Do I look okay?" she says dramatically, pulling the corners of her mouth back into a grimace.

"Stupid question, my bad," I sit next to her on the bench. I should go find Raf'ere to give him a piece of my mind—but I can't just leave this girl crying alone in the hallway. "Can I help?"

She scoffs and looks toward the ceiling.

"Can you unmate Medic Hi'rey?" she asks, already knowing the answer is obviously no.

"Oh, I'm sorry, was he your boyfriend?"

"Well, no, but that's beside the point. I know we had something together..." Her voice drifts off, and she gets a starry-eyed look.

"And he's got a mate now? That's gotta be hard." I try to sympathize, but the word mate only makes me think of one person. Raf'ere—and I'm pissed at him.

"She doesn't even like him, what's the point?" she asks to the sky, as if the alien goddess is supposed to explain herself.

"I don't think they have any control over it, maybe your medic is just as surprised as you are. He probably can't even help how he feels about her," I tell the girl, but I think I'm really telling myself something I need to hear.

"I know, it's not his fault—he's so sweet. He's the only person I've ever *been with*, you know?" She takes a deep breath. "But now that he's got a mate, he's only going to care about making her happy, regardless of how she feels about him. No one else is ever going to matter to him again, especially not me. Just being apart from your fated mate can cause the fi'len physical pain. How do I compete with that?"

"Oh, it's that intense to find your mate huh?" Is Raf'ere just trying to make me happy here—will he hurt forever if he leaves me here? Does he care about me so much that he could do that?

"Yeah, it fucking sucks."

A knot twists in my stomach, and I put my hand over the necklace on my chest.

"I'm Marta, by the way," I say holding out my other hand.

"Kamari," she says, weakly grasping my palm.

"You know, I'm the kind of person who thinks that the universe gives us exactly what we need at the right time," I say, knowing that our meeting isn't coincidence—that it's luck. "I'm sure the person that's perfect for you is out there, someone who thinks the sun shines out of your ass and would do anything to make you happy. And you deserve to find them. It's okay to grieve what you've lost, though, but I know happiness can find you in the most bizarre circumstances."

"I don't know, I feel like a lot of the fi'len don't really want us here—unless you're someones fated mate. I feel trapped sometimes." She draws her brows together and runs her hand over her gorgeous, cloud-like hair. "Do you really think I can find someone here?"

"I know so." I squeeze her hand reassuringly.

"Thanks."

"Of course, us humans have to stick together right?" We both laugh. "This place is like Little Italy but for our entire species, isn't it?"

"Yeah but the food's way worse," she says as we both grimace.

How can the food be that much worse than the delicious things I ate at the estate? Maybe Raf'ere's palate matches his taste in clothing—extravagant and over the top?

"Can you help me find the council room?" I ask my new friend.

"Sure, it's back through the courtyard, straight through the doors and your first right once you're back inside." She points the direction I was walking.

"Thank you, Kamari," I give her hand one final squeeze before I stand. I know she's probably not done grieving, but I think she'll be okay, and I have to find Raf'ere.

She just nods and wipes her eyes again. "See you around, newbie."

<hr>

There's a throng of people in the courtyard watching another cruiser descend.

I can only hope that girl gets her cotton candy vape, but I don't have time to see who is landing. I've got a mate to claim.

I find the set of doors into the building on the other side of the courtyard. This building seems more polished than the one that houses the cold dorms. The style of the decorations is like a more subdued version of the estate at the Reefs.

The halls are practically empty, and I assume almost everyone is queuing up for smuggled goods. So I'm surprised when I round the first right turn and smash hard into a gorgeous, tall redhead.

"Ouch!" she yelps, clutching her arm after we collide.

"Oh god, sorry!" I say with my hands up, wanting nothing more than to rush past her.

"It's fine. I keep telling Gra'eth we really need blind spot mirrors around these corners. I'm not really coordinated on the best of days." She looks down at my face, and confusion spreads across hers.

"I don't think we've met, are you new? My name's Jessy. I wasn't informed of any new refugees…did you just arrive with the marauders?"

"No, not with the marauders."

"Who then? They really need to tell me. What's the point in being in charge of orientation if we're just setting new girls loose in the palace?" She seems flustered.

"Um, Raf'ere brought me," I say, trying my best to look around her shoulder. I need to find my mate.

"Oh god." Her face drops. "The duke brought you here? You poor thing—if he said anything to upset you, I want you to know that he's an asshole. Not all the fi'len are like that. Don't let him scare you." She reaches for me in comfort.

"Why does everyone think he's terrible? He didn't scare me, he saved my life, you know!" If Raf'ere won't fight for us, I guess I fucking will.

"Raf'ere? No way…he's like a total pervert." Jessy stares at me in disbelief. "Are we talking about the same guy? The duke of the Liin'gan Reefs, dresses like an asshole, hates humans?"

"He doesn't hate humans." I set my jaw. "But he does dress like an asshole, I'll give you that."

"Well, I mean he hates dealing with refugees. He's plenty happy to objectify us." She crosses her arms, matching my energy.

"He says a lot of dumb shit. I'll give you that. But did you ever think that maybe people can change? I can't speak about how he was. I only know how he's treated me. Why do you hate him?" I ask, because the Raf'ere she's talking about doesn't feel like my own.

"He made a very deliberate pass at me."

"Did he touch you?" I ask, my voice stuttering. Please god, let this be some misunderstanding.

"He grabbed my arm, but no, he didn't do anything like that."

"So, what happened? You turned him down, I suppose."

"I gave him a piece of my mind later, but he caught me off guard at first."

"I'm sorry you were uncomfortable…" I tell her, not wanting to downplay her feelings. "But you do know that fi'len women like that kind of approach, right?"

"What do you mean?" she asks dubiously.

"I mean, I've been told fi'len women like it when the men are very explicit in their attempts at getting a woman's attention."

"My mate would never talk like that…" she starts before pausing abruptly. I can see the gears begin to spin in her mind though as her mouth drops into a frown. "I mean, on our first date he told me wanted to lick my pussy in a BDSM restaurant, but…" She looks back up at me, her eyes wide. "Shit, you're right. I mean our king and queen met by jerking off at each other in traffic."

"What the fuck…"

"It's a long story." She brushes off my comment before continuing with some authority. "I still don't have to like him."

"No, you don't. I barely like him—but I do *love him*."

We're both a tiny bit shocked at my admission.

"I do, I love Raf'ere." The epiphany hits me like a ton of bricks. "He's not perfect, but neither am I. He's my mate."

"Wait, what?" Her confusion grows even deeper.

"It's a long story," I say sarcastically.

"I…I…" Whatever words she's trying to convey fail.

"Now, if you'll excuse me, I've got to go claim him before his dumb ass abandons me here." I push past her, leaving her in some kind of daze.

I stomp down the hall with renewed purpose, toward a pair of black doors. Flinging them open, I'm ready to confess my love to Raf'ere. But I'm met with the face of an alien stranger.

"Can I help you?" The man seems annoyed as he rubs a liquid vigorously into his hands.

"Yeah actually, you can! Where's Raf'ere?"

"Just missed him. I think he's heading back to the courtyard with the king. Why do you need him?"

"The courtyard? I just came from the courtyard!" How could I miss him?

"Oh they took the secret passage. Door's still open if you want to catch him that wa—" The alien nods toward a cracked panel, and the white curls on his head bounce as he does.

"What the hell is it with you aliens and all your damn secret tunnels!" I yell as I wrench the panel wide and sprint down the passage. I don't wait for his response, my feet are already running as fast as they'll carry me.

When the door to the courtyard comes into view, I can just make out the shape of Raf'ere's back as he starts to ascend the steps. The crowd of women is still thick, and my short ass has to fight my way through.

I finally wiggle to the front of the throng of people, and even though I'm out of breath, I dig deep to carry my voice across the crowd.

"Did you think I was just going to let my mate leave?" I scream.

A hush falls over the once chatty group of humans. Raf'ere freezes, but doesn't turn around. I realize no one was even paying attention to Raf'ere. The cruiser parked next to his has several strange aliens and what looks like a masked fi'len man leading a group of scared women off the ship.

"Oh, not you guys," I clarify as I watch the big green orc-like alien point to his chest. He seems disappointed when I tell him, this complete stranger, that he's not my mate. "No, my mate is standing right in front of me." I point my finger at the gaudily dressed man I want to spend the rest of my life with.

---

1. Italian: asshole

CHAPTER 35
☆KISS ME☆

☆RAF'ERE

HER MATE?

Surely I've misheard, my brain twisting my wants into some hallucination to stop this pain inside me as I know I'm leaving my mate behind.

"Marta," I say, turning to her.

My tiny human, shorter than most of the other humans, is flushed red and looks angry.

She holds the necklace, my mating gift, up from around her neck.

"Did you really think you could give me this and just sneak away? You've really got some *coglioni*[1] if you think that's the case." She stomps to the bottom of the cruiser's steps.

"Marta, I'm not good for you—you should be happy, you should be free here with the other humans to live the life you want—"

"I want my damn mate, I want you!" she pleads.

"But…"

"No more buts. This is me deciding for myself! *Sure, you kidnapped me…*"

"He did what?" a human woman behind Marta whispers.

"And there are things we both could have done differently. God, and do I hate the way you dress. You don't fucking need this—"

She gets on her tiptoes and rips the cravat from my neck, throwing it to the ground. I clutch at my bare neck, shocked at her display.

"You don't need to hide behind all this frilly bullshit because of your scars. You don't need all the bonkers, totally enjoyable, sex toys either!"

"She said what?" Another woman inclines her head at Marta's display.

"You are the most beautiful thing I've ever seen! *What more do you want from me?* I want you!"

"I just want to make you happy!" I interject.

"*You* make me happy, you big gray ding-dong!" Her voice trembles. "So don't just leave me here, fight for me! Fight for us!"

I look at the audience that's formed around my cruiser, then back at Marta.

All the expectation in the world shines behind those big brown eyes of hers.

Marta wants me. Despite my flaws, despite my scars, she chooses me.

"Kiss her, dammit!" a girl from the crowd yells, and I do exactly that.

I bridge the distance between us, pulling Marta into my arms. When our lips touch, the crowd of humans rushes around us, cheering.

But it's like they aren't even there. I deepen the kiss, tilting my mate back.

Marta is my forever, and I'll never be without her again.

"Oh my god, did he just dip her? This is so fucking cute!" Another voice rings through the buzz of applause.

Our lips break apart, and she looks up at me with loving eyes.

"That wasn't so hard was it?" She smirks.

"Loving you was never hard, Marta." I pull her tightly against me and bring us both back up the steps of the cruiser. The door closes behind us. "Let's go home."

"I'm home when I'm with you," she says as she nuzzles into my chest.

Home is Marta, now and forever.

---

1. Italian: Balls

CHAPTER 36
☆SURPRISE, I BROKE YOUR AC☆

☆KAMARI

OF COURSE she told me to cheer up…she's got everything I want. I stand in the crowd of cheering women and feel nothing but bitterness as the alien duke dips my new friend in his arms and kisses her passionately.

Maybe some of us don't get alien mates…maybe I'm doomed to spend the rest of my life in outer space alone. Or worse yet, a woman-shaped placeholder until a fi'len finds their true love.

I am a human bookmark on the pages of love.

This scene in front of me? A romance. You can tell those two have fought hard for a happy ever after in their future.

My life, right now? A character study at best.

The other girls tell me I'm lucky. I woke up from cryosleep already rescued. I never had to dance in a bubble, and I've never had anyone here at the palace be anything but kind to me.

It feels like they're downplaying the fact that being abducted by aliens alone could be incredibly traumatic.

I was getting my life together on Earth. My bookstore was finally in the green after a year of hustling my ass off. I was financially comfortable and was about to put a down payment on the most beautiful condo I'd ever laid my eyes on in Seattle.

These were no small feats, but they're reduced to nothing but ancient history now. I will never go back to Earth…ever.

So I tried my best to fit in here, and I even fell for the kind Medic Hi'rey. I think we could have had something, if not for that stupid mate bond. How is that fair? How is anything fair here at all?

I look at the marauder's ship as they help the newest human refugees down the ramp.

They're a true ragtag bunch, each member of the crew a vastly different kind of alien. Sure, their ship kind of looks like shit, but I can tell they must have so many amazing adventures. The craft looks "well loved."

The captain, a strangely masked fi'len with dark hair, stares at the happy couple everyone else is paying attention to…and I swear he rolls his eyes.

Maybe, if I can't write my life as a romance novel, I can write it as an adventure?

I push through the cheering women and slide my way over to the beat-up cruiser. One of the refugee liaisons motions for them with her data pad. I know that she's supposed to get all the humans' information before they move on to the decontamination units—So, I've got plenty of time.

I'm sick of letting the world go by here on Sontafrul 6—it's time for a change of scenery.

Just as the alien duke scoops up his mate and everyone goes wild, I sprint at full speed toward the loading dock of their ship.

I'm not in my prime like I was on my college track team, but I'm good enough to get past the crowd and up the steps before anyone realizes what's happening.

In fact, I'm going so fast that I have to use the wall to come to a stop. I smash into the metal panel with a loud clunk.

I don't wait to find out if anyone else is onboard but climb up a ladder right under what looks like some space-age version of

HVAC ductwork. I'm just small enough to squeeze into the tube.

I pray that it's not some kind of incineration system as I wiggle forward. As the sides of the duct press into my shoulders, I get worried that I've made a mistake.

What if I get stuck, and no one finds me until my body starts to stink up the place? Then I'll forever be the stupid human who got stuck in the UFO's AC system.

I guess the upside is that you can't be embarrassed if you're dead. I laugh at my own joke, like I normally do, and it eases a bit of the tension.

"You can't die here, that story would suck," I tell myself, trying my best to manifest the adventure I crave.

Eventually, after much squirming on my part, the duct widens a bit. I've come to some kind of juncture and I'm able to spread my limbs a bit wider. I use the extra space as an excuse to catch my breath.

I'll just hang out here for a bit, and after takeoff I'll come back down and…I actually don't know?

I didn't think that far ahead. I guess begging to join the crew would be the only thing I could do. Worst case scenario, they take me back. I mean, they're always rescuing human women. They wouldn't hurt me.

Would they?

☆FER'OON

"I'm going to miss him," Gashna says quietly as we board the ship.

For being the supposed muscle of the crew, I swear the Aspian is prone to some of the most intense fits of melancholy.

"He'll be back, it won't last—this thing between him and the human Kayla."

I know it won't, because there's no such thing as a fated

mate. It's just something we tell ourselves to feel better, a bedtime story for scared children afraid that they'll die alone.

"I don't know, I think they're lovely together," the green giant mumbles behind me.

"You would, you romantic." I chuckle as I swing around the corner and bump into the ladder that Sanriri left up. "So lovesick he didn't even bother to finish cleaning the air ducts? A likely excuse."

I fold the ladder and jump up to slam the duct access panel shut.

"Computer, chart a course for Fran'iut station," I yell.

"Charting course, preparing for departure. Arrival in five hours." The computer on this old hunk of junk still sounds like Sanriri's favorite erotic actress. She says each word seductively.

It's one of the first upgrades he spent his own credits on for *Star Thief*. It still seems like the waste of money I told him it was, but it'll remind me of him until I see him next, that's for sure.

"Gashna, can you handle this?" I ask my only remaining crewmate. "I'm beat, I'm gonna try and get some shut-eye in before we get back to the station," The ship feels particularly empty after dropping off the rescued humans, and my best friend, at the palace.

"Of course, Captain. You should have no fear that I'll make sure we arrive safely at the port. I promise I won't crash the ship." He pulls his shoulders back and grins.

One thing about the Aspian people is they say anything that comes to mind. Sometimes, like now, it can make them sound like they intend to do the exact opposite of what they mean.

"You know, when you tell me you're not going to crash the ship...it sounds like that's what you actually are going to do." I raise my brows as I explain.

"But I told you I wasn't going to. That doesn't make any sense—"

"Don't worry about it, don't crash the ship. I'm going to get some sleep and everything will be fine." I wave my hands in the air, shooing him as I cut him off.

Gashna nods, still confused, and I head to my quarters.

I hold my palm up to the lock as it scans my biometrics and the silver door slides open. My bed takes up a majority of the room, but it's kind of nice just to fall into something soft from the hallway.

I put my hands above my head, and drop face down into my mattress. The combination of my mask, the blankets, and the heat of the ship switching to life support makes me sweat.

"Computer, turn on the air conditioning unit. Cool by 20%," I say into my bed.

"Cooling activated," the computer moans.

I wait for the vent over my bed to blow cool air on my back… but nothing happens.

With a groan, I stand on my mattress and hit the vent with my fist and still feel nothing.

"Computer, activate previous cooling request."

"Cooling by 20% currently. Do you have a new request?" The computer mewls her question seductively.

"You hunk of junk! It is not." The frustration I feel with this tech is a common occurrence. But losing Sanriri today has amplified my frustrations.

I slam both fists into the ceiling vent. So hard, in fact, that it swings open and something warm and heavy falls right on my face. I crumple with the impact.

"Oh shit!" the object yells.

I blink rapidly, confused by what just happened.

Lying on my chest, her face inches from mine, a human woman cracks a nervous smile.

"Surprise, I think I broke your AC."

☆ THREE MONTHS LATER ☆

☆ MARTA

RAF'ERE'S massive cock is deep inside me as I ride him. My hands grip his pecs as I look out the window and onto the surface of the open water.

"Fuck Marta, I'm so close," he breathes, his hands on my hips, supporting me and pulling me down onto his cock. His sucker pops on and off of my clit in the way that drives me crazy.

"So fill me up," I command. "Fill me with your cum so that no one is confused about who I belong to." I roll my hips, giving his sucker more time to pull deliciously at the nerves of my gem, as he calls it.

"You're perfect," he groans.

I prove it too. I reach my hand back behind my ass and grab his swollen sack. It draws closer to his body. The throbbing of his cock as he picks up his pace lets me know he's close.

I'm close too. Flexing my inner muscles over his girth makes the tingling in my clit feel all the better. I grind against his sucker, the friction in addition to the suction bringing me closer and closer to the edge of my release.

"Where do you want me to come?" he grits through clenched teeth.

"I already told you, fill me up," I moan, grabbing my tits and rolling my nipples between my fingers.

"Are you sure?" His eyes get big with the implications of my request.

"I know what I want." I lean down to kiss him.

The change in angle has him hitting just the right spot, and we both come hard together. Wrapping his arms around my back, he holds me tightly against him. I mange to rock my hips and draw every drop from his throbbing cock. As I do, Raf'ere's eyes roll back in his head.

"Give it all to me," I whisper into his ear, *breed me.*

With one last final push inside me, he goes limp. His breaths are erratic and he's lost in bliss.

I sit up gently, his cock still inside me, my thighs smeared in his cum.

"I-I," he stutters.

"Good boy." I stroke the damp hair from his brow. I lean forward, kissing each deep groove on his beautiful face. Finally, he drifts back to reality and opens his eyes.

"You want my kids?" he asks, placing a hand on my stomach. His eyes grow damp.

"Correction, *our kids*—but of course I do. You're handsome, thoughtful, kind…" I drawl on with his accolades as I slide his cock out from me and roll to snuggle next to him. "This is your first Christmas, but you'll understand it's more fun with kids when you see how cute Prince Con'or is once he opens his gifts. It's just better, I can't explain it." I don't know why he's surprised. I've told him tons about how he'd be the perfect dad and about how much I want kids over the past few months.

Seeing little Con'or after he was born just sealed the deal. He's gotta be the chubbiest, cutest little gray baby I've ever laid my eyes on. Every time I see him, I swear he makes my ovaries want to explode.

I'm surprised I didn't beg Raf'ere to come inside me when we got to the cruiser after our first visit to see the newborn.

"I guess I will have to take your word for it, won't I?" He chuffs. "I still don't really understand the whole tree indoors or home intruders wearing red...but if you say it's magical, I'll believe you."

"Oh it is, and believe me, you're going to love how over the top you can make the holiday. I have no doubt that you'll be a real Mariah Carey about this whole experience."

If anyone is going to be as gaudy as the self-proclaimed Queen of Christmas, it's going to be my mate.

"Since I have no idea who that woman is, I'll take it as a compliment."

I laugh and roll from the bed, making my way over the window.

"Have I told you how much I love this place?" I say as I crack open the real, non bio-jelly, window and feel the breeze on my face. The tower that holds our bedroom is still connected to the rest of the estate under the waves, but Raf'ere wanted to make sure I had somewhere at home above the surface. "It's just nice to be able to bask in the sunshine again."

"I'm glad," he says, joining me. He cranes his neck over my shoulder and looks down. "It's a little unnerving being this high up, but you know I'd do anything to make you happy."

"It's only like twenty feet above sea level—Raf'ere are you afraid of heights?"

"I'm not afraid, it just seems a bit unnatural is all," He backs up and pulls me with him. "And if you're going to be carrying our baby, maybe we stop leaning out of the tower window?"

"Oh Raf'ere, if I wanted to tightrope walk nine months pregnant, I don't think you could stop me." I smile.

"Nine months? Opal was only pregnant for four months, you know, and that's even longer than the normal three..."

My smile drops. "Three months? That's not enough time.

You're telling me I could be as big as Opal in three months?" I'm spiraling.

But he knows just what to do. Raf'ere kisses me sweetly and brings me back from my anxieties.

"Don't stress. Even if you're pregnant for nine months…or if we never have kids at all, it'll be the perfect timing. No coincidences, remember?"

"No coincidences," I agree with a curt nod.

I grab our jewelry from the bedside table, throwing on my stunning emerald cornicello. I pass him the updated version of my old one. He's strung the broken bead on a simple metal chain.

It's almost like we hold a piece of each other around our necks.

"Next time, you should wear your horn. It's for virility as well as luck, you know." I wink.

"I'm plenty virile," he goads. "In fact, let's enjoy round two before the Christmas Eve guests arrive? I'm sure the kitchen would appreciate you not micromanaging the Seven Fishes Feast more than you already have."

I roll my eyes in protest. "The food is important!" I yelp as he throws me over his shoulder and head toward the bed again.

"More important than pleasing my mate?" He dips low next to the bedside table, pulling out a new toy I'm sure I'll love. "I doubt it."

Flopping me down onto the soft blankets, I laugh with my whole body. The sunlight streams onto his gray skin, and I gaze up at him with pure joy.

"You will always be worth the wait."

☆AUTHOR'S NOTE☆

DEAR READER,

Without you, this series wouldn't exist. What started off as something just for my fellow writing friends is now what some people have told me is their comfort series.

Something I wrote is someone's favorite book.

How I absolutely don't believe anyone when they say that and am also am in utter shock is bizarre. But whether you love this series, read it for the kooky titles, or just like to roll your eyes at its entire premise…thank you.

I wouldn't be here today without support for my writing friends. Specifically Emilia, Emily, and Lizzie—you know what you did.

Also, to my editor, Emily. Thank you for turning my illegible mess into something I can be proud of. I promise to actually make my deadline for book #4!

Speaking of book #4 in this series, I can't believe this story is almost at a close. But don't worry, I'll be writing more in the bubble-verse. An upcoming novel, Love on the Korylan Moon, involves a bubble babe and one of the Andjin species we met in this book. If you're a tentacle girly, keep your eyes peeled for that one!

Thank you, your support means the world to me.

XOXO PETRA

☆GLOSSARY☆

☆FI'LEN WORDS

Alien words with no direct human translation
- **F'tee:** An expletive, similar to our English fuck
- **Thr'uik:** Fi'len liquor
- **Sq'aurks:** Pastel puff balls that are eaten alive. They steam and are hot naturally. They taste like peach pie according to Opal. Delicacy.
- **Si'bok:** A large ceremonial water vehicle. Kind of like a yacht. Used only for parades.
- **Grin'oj:** A fi'len child's breakfast food. Served with cinnamon. Opal thinks it tastes like sweetened mashed potatoes.
- **Waters of I'loh:** The glowing and warm waters that flow through underground springs through all of Sontafrul 6. Are said to have healing/magical properties. I'loh is a major goddess of the fi'len faith.
- **Tr'ael:** Black shiny mineral of Sontafrul 6. The old palace is made entirely of a natural outcropping, the rooms being carved in. Also the rock that the bracelet Al'frind gave Opal. Opal often refers to it as ebony.
- **Ckra'rot:** Large feathered bird.

• **Cor'sopol:** Color shifting alien

• **Poke'en:** Tentacled stinging creature that lives in the seas of Sontafrul 6

• **Mals'in Tree:** Tree that's foliage shifts from bright pink to pale orange throughout the year. Similar to a palm tree.

• **Res'ul Crackers:** The closest thing to bread on Sontafrul 6.

• **Rambola Fruit/Flower/Tree:** Tree that flowers beautiful blossoms before producing a citrus-like fruit.

• **Xor'ro:** A wild animal with a whip like tail, similar to a jungle cat. Native to Sontafrul 6.

• **Scal'pin:** Scary but delicious fish monster, blue flesh.

• **Kahne'ah:** A small, semi-aquatic predator, from the lin'gaan reefs on sontafrul 6. They are highly sought after as animal companions by the fi'len because of their loyalty and affection to their owners.

• **Nar'art:** Underwater animal native to Sontafrul 6.

• **Amorphous Robotic Pleasure Tentacle:** A bespoke sex toy from the Diiyom system. Designed to find the pleasure points on any species. Very expensive, but worth the money according to Marta.

☆MISC.

Things that might be helpful to remember.

• **Security Bubble:** Large acrylic oval-shaped bubbles that human woman are placed in for their protection.

• **The Deenz:** Hive-minded aliens, traffickers of human women, cheap slimy assholes.

• **Go-Go Juice/Hormone Shot:** aphrodisiac shot given to human women by the Deenz before performances.

• **Cruiser:** Magnetic vehicle that can only drive on mag lanes.

• **Transport Unit:** Bus-like cruiser that can only drive on mag lanes.

• **Tactical Cruiser:** Jet-propelled vehicle used most by dignitaries and the military. Is not bound by the mag lanes.

- **Protein Ration:** Seafood-based protein bar given to the military as rations.
- **Data pad:** Alien tech that is almost like an iPad and can make calls like a communicator.
- **Communicator:** Alien cell phone.
- **Decon Tech:** Someone who specializes in decontaminating aliens from potential world-killer viruses.
- **Universal Governing Senate:** The governing system for advanced life forms in the universe. Humans are not considered advanced.
- **E-breather:** Electrolysis Breather, used so that non-aquatic lifeforms can breathe underwater. Thin metal mouthpiece attached to small tube.
- **Cryo pod:** Egg-shaped pod that keeps a life form in long-term cryogenic sleep. Often used when transporting bubble babes long distances by the Deenz.
- **Flex Caulk:** The alien equivalent of duct tape. Used the fix hull damage in space crafts. Pink foam out of a spray can.
- **Sanitizer Foam:** This anti-bacterial and anti-viral foam is used to protect against germs and illness. Gra'eth overuses it with his fear of contamination.
- **Laser Ornamentation:** Decorative skin branding, done by computers.
- **Stasis Bag:** Similar to a cryo pod but used to keep a life form stable for short-term emergencies. Most often used by field medics.
- **Neural Stimulation Collar:** A discrete metal collar that when activated by remote can cause your nerves to feel specific reactions. Warmth, chills, and overload are some specific examples.
- **The Korlyan Moon:** The largest moon of Sontafrul 6, home to the Andjin species.
- **The Andjin:** This species is a distant cousin of the fi'len. While also semi-aquatic they live a much less technology advanced lifestyle. Their natural hide is yellow with blue rings,

but is able to shift for camouflage. They possess many head tentacles, include two longer ones they use as a second pair of hands called foretentacles. Once at war with Sontafrul 6, they now have a fragile peace. Reports of bubble babes showing up on the Korlyan Moon have surfaced.

•**The Aspian People:** An orcish alien species. Green skin and tusks, incredibly muscular. They are a very literal people and have trouble with sarcasm.

•**Synthetics:** A mechanical based life form. Often utilized in detail oriented jobs like tailoring or as a pleasure unit.

☆OUR CAST OF CHARACTERS☆

These descriptions are at of the END of this book for the entire series so far. If you read this before you finish reading the book you might spoil it for yourself–be warned! If you read this book as a standalone it might also spoiler other characters stories for you.

• **Opal May Legare:** Kentucky girl abducted from Earth. Both parents are dead, former waitress at the Crafty Crab. At the end of Book 1 becomes the Queen of Sontafrul 6 and is married/mated to Ke'ain.

• **Ke'ain:** King of Sontafrul 6, married/mated to Opal. Really likes sq'aurks, but not as much as Opal's cunt. AKA Sharkboy, AKA Keanu.

• **Jessy Whitley:** Former NASA scientist from Cape Canaveral. Neurodivergent and analytical. Has been gone from Earth for years. Mate to Gra'eth, and now a human science liaison for Sontafrul 6.

• **Gra'eth Volk'aris:** Royal attorney for Sontafrul 6's monarchy. At the end of this book is also Hand of the King. Mated to Jessy. Saves Opal and Jessy from drowning in the bus crash.

Ke'ain's right hand man. Sarcastic and sick of everyone's shit. Germaphobe. AKA Gray Seth.

• **The King and Queen of Sontafrul 6:** Ke'ains parents who died in the events prior to this book. The king was a greedy man and let Sontafrul 6 go to shit with pollution from tourists. Neither of them were particularly great parents to Ke'ain.

• **Al'frind:** Ke'ain's personal royal butler, but more of a father figure to him. Old and wise fi'len man. He dedicated his life to Ke'ain when the prince was born–the day after his mate Jas'ryn's death. Is killed by the Deenz in the events of Book 1.

• **Raf'ere:** Ke'ain's cousin and ruler of the Liin'gan Reefs on Sontafrul 6. Is arrogant and pigheaded with a huge ego. He rescues Opal and Ke'ain from the island the marauders stranded them on. He is one of Ke'ains few living relatives after the death of his parents. Steals his mate, Marta, from the crashed Deenz ship.

• **Tro'kip:** Ke'ain's wetnurse and nanny. Died before the start of Book 1. His true mother figure.

• **Officer Hy'rul:** A member of Raf'ere's cruiser staff.

• **Jes'inth:** One of Opal's lady's maids once she becomes Queen of Sontafrul 6.

• **Medic Hi'rey:** The first person to know that Opal is pregnant. Has to teach the women living in the "Earth 2" sorority house how to use alien condoms. He is the main caretaker of the human women of "Earth 2". At the end of book three is mentioned to have been mated.

• **Captain Fer'oon:** Fi'len marauder, mysterious background. Seems to have biomechanic modifications-his face is half covered by a mask. Has black hair, unlike the other fi'len's white hair. Captain of the Star Thief.

• **Saniri:** A Redesti male. A marauder who hates slavery. Snake-like alien who seems best suited to a desert.

• **Gashna:** A little bit slow on the uptake, this green goon is very bad at following instructions of his captain.

•**Camille:** A human woman, former daycare worker, and official big sister of all the human women at the palace dormitories. Starts the group therapy sessions held at the palace.

•**Katie:** Human woman, alternative and tattooed. Can come across a bit harsh. Really looking for some alien "D" now that she's gotten used to the idea.

•**Sarah:** Human woman, small and quiet. Has a traumatic past on Earth, thinks her abduction is unfair.

•**Betty:** Human woman, cooks human-ish food in the palace cafeteria.

•**Has'ci:** Fi'len female, Gra'eth's secretary at the palace.

•**Signu:** A Redesti male, smuggler. Gets Doritos from Earth for Jessy.

•**Delvet:** Male alien from Quyasar, host at Jessy and Gra'eth's Linn'gan Reef hotel. Eight feet tall with four arms, blue skin.

•**Au'rinn Des'ok:** Fi'len male, officer in the Sontafrul 6 army and friend to Jessy. Has lots of laser ornamentation, included matching butterflies with Jessy.

•**Marta:** Human woman, kidnapped by Duke Raf'ere.

•**Tri'ot & Kir'ron:** Female fi'len socialites, former sexual partner's of Duke Raf'ere.

•**Far'ep:** Housemaid for the Ling'aan Reef's estate, former sexual partner of Raf'ere. Fired after seeing Marta during her captivity.

•**Nick:** Marta's cousin and bodyguard on Earth, present during Marta's abduction.

•**Jens'i:** Duke Raf'ere's private butler, also his closest friend.

•**Bruno:** Marta's pitbull on earth, former bait dog, passed away from cancer

•**Hil'ar:** Jens'i's wife and mate.

•**Yar'oh:** Raf'ere's former fiancé. Called off the wedding after his disfigurement during the war.

•**Nubbins:** A pet Kahne'ah given to Marta by Raf'ere.

•**Hisso:** An synthetic tailor.

•**Kimari:** Abducted human woman from Seattle. Bookstore owner and has had some kind of relationship with Medic Hi'rey. At the end of book three she sneaks onto the Star Thief.

THE BUBBLE-VERSE

My ebooks are exclusive to Amazon, but my physical copies are available at Amazon and your favorite book retailers. If it's not available at your bookstore, request it! The bubble babes series is also available in audiobook form through Tantor Media. Listen anywhere audio books are sold.

All I Wanted Was Sushi But I Got Abducted By Aliens Instead: Bubble Babes #1

2023

All I Wanted Was To Become A Scientist But Now I've Got An Alien Boyfriend: Bubble Babes #2

2023

All I Wanted Was a Glass of Vino but an Alien Duke Kidnapped Me Instead: Bubble Babes #3

2023

COMING SOON

Bubble Babes #4

ESTIMATED PUBLICATION 2024

Love On The Korylan Moon

ESTIMATED PUBLICATION 2024

Soldiers Of Sontafrul 6 #1

ESTIMATED PUBLICATION 2024

☆WANT MORE NOW?

PATREON [https://www.patreon.com/petrapalerno]

I've got some short stories and other bonus content (including very NSFW art of our lovely couples) on my Patreon! There's also a tier on where you can vote on a monthly bonus chapter for your favorite couple!

ETSY [https://www.etsy.com/shop/petrapalerno]

Art, stickers, page overlays, and other fun goodies are available here!